FORBIDDEN LOVE WITH A THUG II

SHVONNE LATRICE

About the Author

<u>Other Works by Me:</u>

Good Girls Love Thugs 1-5
Falling for a Hood King 1-4
Married to a Distinguished Thug 1-3
She's Gotta Have It 1-2
Me & My Dope Boy 1-3
Yazir & Nina 1-3
Forbidden Love with a Thug 1-3
You Needed Me 1-3
Shorty is in Love with a Real One 1-4
I Got Your Back 1-2
My Baby Is a West Coast King 1-4
Our Love Is the Realest 1-3
She Got It Bad for a Heartless Gangsta 1-4
She Got It Bad for a Heartless Gangsta: An AK Christmas
Hood Boyz Fall In Love Too 1-3
Nobody Can Love You Like Them Roughnecks Do 1-4
She Gave Her All to the Hood's Finest 1-5

Visit TheShvonneLatrice.com for paperbacks!

facebook.com/shvonnelatrice

twitter.com/shvonnelatrice

instagram.com/shvonnelatrice

$15.99

ISBN 978-1-966375-12-8

ONE

Jersey Warren

I was lying down when I heard the sound of a door opening and then closing. My eyes flew open, and I saw my dad smiling at me with a lit cigar in his hand. He was dressed nicely, as usual, and his cologne smelled expensive as always. I palmed my belly as I stared at him in disbelief, causing him to ash the cigar and walk closer to me. Once her got near me, I sat up to make sure I wasn't seeing things. After looking around a bit, I realized I was in the study of my old home. This was the room I always tried to avoid because of the bad memories I had in it.

I swallowed hard and then said, "Daddy, I thought—"

"Shhh, it was all a dream, Jersey," my father smiled at me.

"But I could've sworn—"

"No, look at me. I'm right here in front of you, aren't I?"

I nodded my head slowly before a smile crept across my face.

"Daddy, I've missed you so much! Why did you leave us?" I stood to my feet carefully.

I had to ask about his betrayal, although I knew he might get angry like he always did when I questioned him.

"I was confused Jersey, but after some long hard thinking, I've decided I'm gonna come home," he said, surprising the hell out of me.

I wasn't too sure if my mom would take him back, but there was no harm in him trying.

"Really? What about Trixie?"

"She's gonna move on with her life. She understands that I no longer want to be in a relationship with her. She encouraged me coming back to my family, actually," he said as he caressed my face. "Have a seat Jersey, Hannah will bring us some tea." He pointed to the couch and we sat down.

"Daddy, I'm gonna have a baby." I palmed my belly as if that was the only way he'd see it.

"I know Jersey, I see that. I like Kilexis, he's good for you."

"You do?" I bucked my eyes.

I was not expecting my judge father to like someone like Kilexis, but I wasn't gonna complain. The last thing I wanted was for the people I loved to dislike Kilexis.

"Yes, he's good to you. Don't you love him?"

"I do. I love him very much. I've never felt like this before about anyone. Are you and mom gonna be back together?"

"Well—"

POP! POP! POP! POP!

"Ahhhhh!!!" I screamed as bullets flew through the windows of my father's home.

They tore through his body as blood spilled and spewed everywhere. His body gyrated and jerked as bullets by the millions it seemed, ripped through his upper body. I wanted to save him, but I needed to protect my baby, so I went and ducked behind the couch. I patted my jean shorts for my phone so that I could dial 911, and noticed my stomach was now flat.

"What the fuck!" I screeched loudly as I lifted my shirt and pinched my flat stomach roughly. It was almost as if I was trying to pull and form it back into a belly.

Tears immediately began streaming down my cheeks as I cried and screamed. Where the fuck was Hannah? When would these bullets stop? Finally, the bullets stopped bursting through the windows. I stood to my feet, and touched my stomach again, but it was still flat. I walked around the couch to see my dad laid out on the couch, with his right side soaked in dark red blood.

"Daddy! Daddy, wake up!" I tried to pick him up, but my pregnant belly was in the way. *My belly was back.* "Daddy! Daddy, what's happening? Daddy! What's happening? Hannah!" I shouted repeatedly until I saw bright ass lights blinding me from up above.

"Jersey! Jersey, baby, calm down!" I heard Kill say. I shut my eyes tightly, and then reopened them.

I realized a nurse was hovering over me shining a little light into my eyes. It was painful, but I was too confused and out of it to tell her to stop what she was doing. Where was Kill? I heard him call my name, and I needed him to get my father.

"Jersey, sweetie if you can hear me blink twice," the nurse said. I blinked slowly, still scared out of my mind. My dad was shot, and he needed help. *I must've fainted at the scene,* I thought. "Great. Now honey, if you can feel this, blink twice," she said before I felt her palm my belly. I blinked slowly in response. "Great, honey. Now blink if you can feel this," she said and touched my thigh. I blinked slowly again. She kept having me blink twice until she reached my toes. I felt everything, especially the excruciating pain in my head.

My eyes slowly began to adjust, and then Kill came into view. My eyes were in so much pain, but the sight of his alluring mocha skin was just as calming as always. He stared down into my face with his beautiful one. He stroked his beard, and I could see that he was worried sick. I'd never seen him look so distressed ever. What was wrong? Was my father dead? I knew he looked dead on the couch, but I hoped they saved him. I didn't understand anything right now, and I needed some answers.

Kill placed his hand on my face, and then rubbed my cheek for a bit before kissing it. He then pecked my lips, and I felt goose bumps rise on my arms. Pulling away, he just stared at me and smiled. His smooth complexion beamed at the sight of me half smiling. As much pain as I was in, Kill still had the ability to make me smile. I realized that something was lodged in my throat, so I immediately reached up to pull on it lightly.

"No sweetie, don't. We're gonna take that out for you," the nurse said. I could hear her jogging over to me.

She and someone else began slowly removing the uncomfortable things from my throat, and it was a huge relief. Once out, they handed me a plastic cup filled with ice water, and then watched me as I sipped it slowly. The cold water felt so good going down, that it caused me to close my eyes to relish in the moment. After a few more cups, the two hospital employees left the room.

I saw Kill standing a little ways away from me in an all black Nike jogger fit, and he looked just as handsome as he did when he wore his Gucci business get ups. I reached my hand out to him weakly, and he neared me before taking my hand to kiss it gently.

"Kill, my daddy, he got shot. Where is he?" I asked with a scratchy tone.

The pain in my throat was something I'd never felt ever. I gulped down some more of the water, just as the raven-haired nurse reentered with a cup that had smoke flowing out of the top.

"Tea, honey," she said and then traded me for the water I was holding. I slowly sipped it, then took it to the head, not caring how hot the shit was. "This is a pot of it, so you can refill her if she needs it," she looked to Kill and he nodded.

"My daddy, Kill," I whispered once she left.

"Jersey, just relax right now. We can discuss that later."

"No! I wanna know now! We were just talking and he said he was gonna come home and then bullets just flew through—"

"Jersey, that never happened, baby. It was probably a dream. You woke up screaming."

I hated how calmly he was speaking to me. I could tell by his facial expression and tone of voice that he didn't believe me.

"No it was not a dream! Kill, he said the other stuff was a dream!" I yelled as tears spilled some more. My throat throbbed every time I raised my voice, but I didn't care.

"Baby, calm down," he began rubbing my hair back. "Your dad, baby, your dad is gone."

"No, why didn't they save him! He was still alive on the couch!" I complained.

"Jersey, listen to me. Your dad was not shot baby, your mother came through and she stabbed him in the chest a couple times. Well, fifteen times to be exact, and he died before the ambulance and police had even gotten there. She broke in and got him while he was sleeping on the couch. When you saw him in the body bag, you fainted and hit your head on the railing of the stretcher he was on. Thankfully one of the E.M.T.'s caught you before you fell on your stomach, so the baby is fine. You've been in a coma for two weeks straight, shorty," he explained.

As he recounted the events, it all came back to me what had happened that night I saw my mother being arrested. The new worst day of my life was in fact real. It had totally trumped the day my father told us he was kicking us out.

"He's really gone?" I sniffled as my face continued to become soakcd with tcars.

"Yeah ma, he died almost immediately." I began to sob hard but quietly. "I wanna hold you, shorty, but I don't wanna hurt you," he added as he rubbed my stomach. He gripped my small hand into his, and kissed the back of it before squeezing it tightly. "I love you, Jersey," he whispered and kissed my belly, then my wet face.

I couldn't respond as I continued to cry, facing the other way. I kept crying until I had no more tears to produce, and then I fell back asleep, hoping this, too, was just a dream.

TWO

Cheyla Austin

Two Days Later...

I sat next to Jersey as she stared at the TV from her hospital bed. She didn't talk much, she just stared at the screen while sipping water and hot tea. I tried to make conversation with her about thirty minutes ago, but she only gave me one-word answers, even if it didn't make sense to my question. And the only time she initiated conversation with me, was when she wanted me to pour her some more water or hot tea.

"Jersey, would you like more water?" I asked. She shook her head no without looking my way.

I felt so terrible for my friend. In just a matter of days she'd lost both of her parents. Her dad was dead, and her mother was incarcerated, awaiting trial. I couldn't believe Mrs. Warren had killed Mr. Warren, and in such a brutal way. She never appeared to be the violent type at all, so it was crazy that she had gone that far. I only saw shit like this in movies, and usually they were always other races, not black people. I guess what Mr. Warren had done, had taken a bigger toll on Mrs. Warren than we all thought.

I felt bad that he lost his life, but a part of me felt he got what he deserved. The way he left his family behind to chase after some hood rat was disgusting. Then to make matters worse, he kicked them out, forcing them to fend for themselves, knowing they solely depended on him. I mean it's bad enough that you kick the woman who has dedicated so much of her life to you out, but to throw out your children as well was just cold-hearted. Mr. Warren hadn't been my favorite person since.

Every time I saw Jersey struggling to pay for something that her dad could've easily paid for, I hated him more. Mr. Warren was rich as hell, so there was no reason why his children should've had to struggle the way that they did. I do wish that Mrs. Warren had have let it go and moved on with her life, because killing him cost her, her life as well in a way, and now my best friend had no parents in a sense. In my opinion, Mr. and Mrs. Warren cared more about themselves than their children, just like my parents. I guess Jersey and I had more in common than I thought.

"Jersey, I'm gonna go to the grocery store, did you want me to get something for you? I'm gonna stop at CVS first and pick up some things. I can get you some candy. I know you love sour belts," I giggled and rubbed her curly hair.

It was in a bun that was lopsided and messy as hell. She'd been sleeping on it, and Kill was the one who'd put it up for her, so it wasn't too great to start with. She still looked pretty though.

She breathed slowly, and stared at the TV before shaking her head no in response.

"Okay, I will be back tomorrow then, babe," I said and kissed her cheek.

I got no reply, so I sighed dejectedly and then picked up my purse to leave. I hoped that Jersey wasn't gonna be like this for a long time, because I missed her already.

As I was walking out, I saw Kill coming down the hallway with food.

"Is she talking yet?" he asked me and I shook my head no.

"You brought her food?"

"Yeah, I did. It's chicken."

"She's not gonna eat that shit, Kill," I chuckled.

"Yes she is. She's pregnant and she needs to eat. If I have to shove the shit into her mouth like Ike did Tina with that damn cake, then I will," he responded seriously, making me laugh.

"Good luck then."

I continued down the hallway and left so I could stop at CVS. I needed some more toiletries, so I wanted to get them before I went grocery shopping, since I may buy some perishable groceries that I didn't want sitting in the car too long.

As I was walking down the body care aisle of CVS, I felt someone watching me from the other end. I looked out the corner of my eye and tried to make out who it was, but I couldn't tell. I knew it was a skinny guy, but I wondered who it was exactly. Finally, I said fuck it and just turned to him.

"Monty?" I frowned.

Monty was one of my best customers at Starzz, and he'd saved me from getting raped one night, so in my eyes he and I were pretty cool.

"I was hoping you noticed me. You look different," he said.

"I do?"

"Yeah, you look more vibrant and umm, happy I guess." It was probably because I'd stopped popping pills, but I wasn't gonna admit that to him.

"Wow, I guess it's because I don't strip anymore," I chuckled.

"Yeah, I know. I miss you, shorty. Where do you dance now? I'll come down."

"No, I don't dance anymore. But I'm happy to know you would support me like that."

"Of course. You were the best one down there, baby." His eyes roamed my body, making me feel a bit uncomfortable although I was dressed in jeans and a t-shirt.

"Thanks, Monty." I pushed my hair behind my ear.

"No problem, Cheyla."

I snapped my neck to look at him and asked, "How do you know my name?"

"Don't trip. Where do you work now?" he furrowed his brows.

This nigga only knew me as Caramel, so how the hell did he get my name? It was probably from one of them bitches that worked with me. Stupid ass hoes. Luckily, Monty was cool, so I wasn't tripping like that. I guess any nigga that saved me from being violated deserved to know my damn name.

"I haven't found any employment yet. I'm gonna be in school for the upcoming fall semester, though. I'm kind of just focusing on that right now."

"Oh word? Dope. Well if you need anything I'm here, Cheyla, so take down my number."

"Monty, I have a boyfriend."

"So, I'm not asking to be your boyfriend, Cheyla. I'm offering to help you out. I know it can be hard to go to school with no income."

"I don't think my man would appreciate me going to another male for help."

"Well if he ain't got it then how can he be mad? He should be happy another nigga is willing to help out his girl without wanting anything in return."

"It was nice seeing you, Monty," I nodded before placing the Dove body wash into my hand basket.

"Wait, Cheyla, I ain't mean to come off aggressive or nothing. I just care about you and I wanna make sure you're good, ya know? After seeing that guy try to violate you that night, I just wanna make sure that you know I'm always here if you need me, just like that night."

Hearing him say that caused a smile to form on my lips.

"Thank you for that, Monty, again. And I know you have my back which I appreciate, but at the moment you can relax because my man can take it from here."

"Say no more," he smiled and threw his hands up in mock surrender.

"See you around," I smiled and then walked off.

Monty was cool, and I'm sure he meant no harm, but Kantwan

was a no nonsense type of guy. I didn't wanna upset him, because I knew he didn't play with bullshit. Kantwan was not the type of guy who approved of excuses. The last thing I wanted to do was upset my man, because we've already had enough rough patches. We needed nothing but smooth sailing for a while, so Monty would have to find someone else to sponsor.

After finishing up at CVS, I went to the grocery store and spent four hundred damn dollars. I don't even know what the hell I got really, but I think it was because I decided to shop knowing my ass was hungry. To add insult to injury, I assumed Kantwan was home and could help me unload, but his ass was ripping and running, dealing with his own fucking errands, so I had to haul all of this shit inside by myself.

Once everything was packed and loaded into the refrigerator, I decided to make some honey barbecue wings, because it would allow me to go have a hot shower and relax for a bit, since I didn't have to watch it closely. Slipping the seasoned wings into the oven, I closed the oven door, and then rushed out of the large kitchen to head upstairs for a shower.

Freshly showered, I checked the time and saw it was still about twenty more minutes until I had to take the food out, so I decided to call up my brother. Ever since he'd been out of jail, he hadn't been hanging with me like I thought he would. I guess he was too occupied with Marley and their daughter, but I still wanted his time, too. For some reason though, I felt his main focus was on coming up with get rich quick schemes, and *not* his family. Hopefully, he'd prove me wrong when I called him.

"Hello?" he answered his phone.

"Sonny, do you remember me?" I asked sarcastically.

"Don't do that, shorty, I could never forget my baby sister. How have you been?"

"I've been okay, I guess, but I will be much better when my brother makes time for me on that busy schedule of his."

"I promise I will, I've just been occupied with the fam, and trying to get my finances in order."

"I get it. So how is that working out for you? Getting your finances together."

"It's moving slowly, but I'm trying to be patient."

"Well if you're not busy now, you should come over so you can meet my boyfriend and eat some dinner with us."

"Your boyfriend? When the fuck did you get a nigga?" I could tell he was frowning although I couldn't see him.

"See, you haven't been around to realize that I don't even live on Harrison anymore. Neither does Jersey."

"Fuck you live? And who is this nigga? You know you need to run him by me before you start living with his ass."

"Well you weren't around to grill him, so I had to move forward. He's a great guy though, I really like him."

"Again, where do you live? And what's his name, Cheyla?"

"I live on Augustinc Road."

"In Alapocas?" he asked surprised.

"That's right," I nodded even though we were over the phone, and then giggled at how surprised he was.

"That's the good area. You need money to live over there, who is this nigga? Don't make me ask again."

"His name is Kantwan."

"Camren?" he questioned for confirmation, and I was a bit taken aback that he knew Kantwan's last name.

"Yeah, why?"

"Oh, one of them Camren boys. No wonder, how did you meet him?"

"You can find that out when you come over tonight, Sonny."

"I can't right now baby girl, I'm not even in Wilmington."

"Where are you?" I rolled my eyes because I was about 99.9% sure his ass was out of town doing dirt with Portland.

"I'm out in Lynford with Portland. We may hit up this little credit union down here if we can't figure out a hustle."

"Sondre!" I yelled using his birth name.

"Cheyla, don't start, aight? We gon' move smarter shorty, so that I won't end up in jail anytime soon."

"Whatever."

"Well look, I have to go, but umm, maybe I can come by like next week or some shit."

"Yeah, hopefully."

"Aight, love you, Cheyla."

"I love you too, Sonny," I sighed and then we both hung up the phone.

I knew his stupid ass was gonna get out of jail and be right back to his bullshit. I just prayed that he knew what the fuck he was doing this go round, because I did not wanna lose him to the system again. Plus, I was pretty sure that if he went back to jail, he would serve way more time than the little years he just served.

THREE

Ivy Horne

———————

I woke up to Donovan whimpering in his crib, but I didn't recognize my surroundings immediately. After rubbing my eyes, I finally realized I was in the bed with Elijah. I looked to my right to see Donovan standing at the edge of the crib, shaking the gate like a little maniac, while poking his little bottom lip out. Elijah had purchased a crib for us to keep here for him, and had even had a baby room set up as well. Donovan had more toys and baby furniture here than at my home on Chestnut.

I loved the way Elijah cared for my baby, because it was the way Portland should have cared. Of course I would prefer for Portland to love his son just as much as Elijah, but right now I didn't give a rat's ass what Portland cared about. I was starting to think Elijah cared more about Donovan than he cared about me, and you know what, that was perfectly okay.

Portland left the day that I put him out, and hasn't returned since. Even when I texted him about his parents and sister, he never responded to me, and he hasn't been seen around town either. I heard he was at the same chick's house that answered his phone, which was in Lynford. He swore she was nothing more than a jump off, but clearly she held a position much higher in his heart than he let on. Damn, I did not miss the days where I would be in bed crying over him right now. I shook my head at my thoughts, as I slipped from Elijah's comforting embrace to tend to Donovan.

"Hey baby," I cooed and lifted him from the crib.

I didn't understand how Portland could just ignore his baby, one that he hadn't seen since he was only months old. You would think that he would try to make up for the time lost while he was in jail, but then again, Portland was a different breed. And then what about your parents and sister? You don't care to show your face after finding out your mother killed your father, and that your sister was in a coma?

A part of me couldn't believe that I had spent so many years of my life loving a man like him. It was like I was finally starting to see the light, and I was slightly embarrassed. All the nights I spent crying over him, and all the times I let him do me wrong, made me feel so ridiculous right now. Not showing up for the birth of our son and then not caring when I got jumped just a few days out of the hospital? Yet, like a damn fool, I was right back to letting him fuck me and take me out only two weeks later. And the only reason it was two weeks later, was because he hadn't come home for a week and a half. All that shit just made me think back to all the times Jersey, Cheyla, and even Mrs. Warren on occasions, begged me to leave him alone. My only defense was that they didn't understand him, and that I did. Portland was never gonna change for me, and I'm just thankful I came to my senses in time.

I placed Donovan in his high chair, and then began to search for some breakfast. I smiled when I spotted the cereal and kiddie eating utensils that Elijah had purchased for him. I was so grateful that he'd swooped in and opened my eyes to something so much better. It did help that he was sexy as fuck, with dreads, a bunch of tattoos, and a nice ass body. On top of that, he had his shit together, and really made me feel like I meant something to him. I didn't feel like I was dating a dope boy at all, it felt regular, if that makes sense. With Portland, I was always on edge and worried that I would get the call saying he was dead or arrested. The latter came true, and sadly I wasn't too surprised when it happened. As far as Elijah, I knew he had his shit under control, despite us never discussing his occupation in detail.

I made Donovan the bowl of cereal, and then sat down to feed it to him. As I was feeding him, I heard Elijah go into the bathroom to shower. His house was so big and beautiful. Not that his condo wasn't nice, but his new house was breathtaking. It was 5,000 plus square feet, and had four bedrooms with four bathrooms. It was upstairs and downstairs, with laminate flooring, and even central heating and air! I loved when I spent the night over here, but when I went home it made my place feel like a cheap motel.

I finished feeding my baby, and then picked him up and carried him to the bathroom. I bathed him, brushed his teeth, and then placed him into his little playpen down in the den so I could shower myself.

As soon as the warm water ran down my head, I closed my eyes to enjoy it. Even the water felt softer here than at my place. And the shower was so huge that I could literally pace back and forth comfortably if I wanted. I loved the space, because Elijah and I stayed getting it popping in here.

My mind began to wander as I thought about how quickly Portland's and my relationship had drastically changed. I wondered if I would've had the strength to leave him if Elijah hadn't been lurking in the shadows. I would like to think I was strong enough to have done so, but you never know. The heart wants what it wants, and mine foolishly wanted Portland's no good ass.

I finished washing off and then brushed my teeth. I wanted to dress and go home so that I could clean up the place, and clean out the fridge. Because I'd been spending my days and nights here with Elijah in his mini mansion, the food in my fridge was spoiling left and right. In a minute I was gonna just stop buying food and wasting my money, but I didn't want Elijah thinking I was just gradually moving myself into his home, so I was gonna hold off for a little.

I walked into the bedroom I shared with Elijah when I came over, and placed my duffel bag onto the bed to pull out an outfit. As soon as I unzipped it, I felt Elijah's strong arms encase me. His long dreads swept across my shoulders, as he craned his neck around to suck my lips. I could taste the purple mouthwash he'd just used, as his manhood pressed against my ass. He unraveled the towel, and then let it fall to the floor before cupping my breasts. He then trailed his large hands down the front of my body, while sucking and kissing on my neck, causing a moan to burst through my lips. This nigga needed to teach a class on how to touch a woman, because I'd never been felt up in this way until I met him. He knew just where to touch me and when to touch me there, without me having to say a thing.

"Eli," I whispered when I felt his hands reach between my legs.

He began to play with my clit, making me purse my lips and close my eyes. I brought my hand around behind me to play with his dreads as he played with my pussy. He moved his fingers slowly, while sucking on my neck as if he was trying to draw blood. Finally, he bent me over, and then slipped inside me.

"I love how fucking wet you get, Ivy," he grunted as he began working the rest of his big dick into me.

He placed his hand into my hair, and then gripped it tightly before beating it up from the back. I swear this was the best dick that I had ever had. I knew his shit was gonna be good, because his finger game alone was comparable to Portland's dick game almost.

That's another reason I didn't wanna let him fuck me while I was with Portland. I didn't want to be sweating him while I had a man, but damn am I glad he's mine now. Elijah's dick game was so crazy, that I was floored that he didn't have some crazy exes coming at me with stakes. But I believed him when he said the females from his past knew he didn't fuck around with the crazy ex bullshit.

"Uuuh, ahhh, uuuh, baby," I cried out as he slammed into my center. I could feel my inner thighs become covered in my nectar, as he pounded me like a beast.

"Fuck, shit," he grunted.

"Pull out, Eli," I whimpered as I gushed on his rod for the second time. I didn't want him nutting in me, because I was not trying to have a baby just yet.

He didn't respond, and then suddenly he pulled out and came

all over my ass. He panted heavily for a little bit, and then he left out to go get something to clean me with. Upon returning, he immediately began cleaning me off. Once he was finished, I turned over and got off the bed.

"Eli, what's wrong?" I asked because I could see his facial expression. He just shook his head slowly as to say nothing, while he cleaned himself with a separate towel.

"Yes there is."

"Stop fucking ruining shit by asking me to pull out all the fucking time. I know to pull out Ivy, and I don't need you saying the shit," he barked, finally letting me know what was on his mind.

"I know, baby, I was just making sure." I walked up to his tall sexy ass and rubbed his strong arms. He tied his dreads up into a bun, and then slipped into some fresh boxers.

"There ain't no fucking need for you to make sure, especially because you just said that you know I'm aware of the fact that I would need to pull out." I began kissing his chest and then his six pack, before trailing them down. "Move out the way, ma," he nudged me off. I smacked my lips and began pulling on some panties and a bra. "Where are you going?" he asked.

"I'm gonna go home to clean up and empty my refrigerator of any expired food. Then I'm gonna pick up Cheyla so we can visit Jersey, and then go to the nail shop."

"Why don't you come live with me, Ivy? You're always here and you can save your money. You be throwing out food every fucking week shorty."

"No Elijah, I can't."

"Why not?"

"Because Portland and—"

"Did you really just tell me that you can't come live with me, your man, because of your child's father? The nigga who hasn't been around to see his child in weeks?" he frowned.

"No, well when Portland wants to see the baby, he can't come here."

"You damn right he can't, but y'all can meet at his mom's crib.

Well it's just his sister's crib now I guess. Plus, I don't want you alone with him."

"I'm not gonna cheat on you Eli, I have no interest in him."

"Oh, I'm not worried about you cheating on anything. But if you're alone he may try to put his hands on you, and if that happens I'm gonna kill him. So in order to prevent me from putting your child's father in the ground, it's best you two not be alone." This nigga was dead serious, so I knew he would kill Portland in a heartbeat.

"I got it," I nodded.

"Now come live with me. I asked you and you said no, so now I'm telling you. I will have some movers come and grab all of your shit."

"Oh, you think you run shit?" I smirked.

"With the way I make that pussy cum, I do run shit." He neared me as we smiled lustfully at each other. He stepped back out of his boxers, and then placed them on the little couch in his room. "Now show me what you were about to a couple minutes ago."

I got down onto my knees, and then began sucking the tip of his dick, just like he'd asked me to.

FOUR

Kilexis Camren

Two Weeks Later...

My baby was coming home with me, and I was determined to make her little ass shape the fuck up. I knew she was miserable because of her parents' situation, as she should be, but the doctor said it wasn't good for her to be so down while pregnant. I loved my girl, but I also already loved my baby, so I wanted to make sure they were both healthy.

I also wanted to know the sex of our kid, but the doctor told me Jersey declined to find out, so they were keeping it under wraps until she was ready. I felt as the father I deserved to know, but I wasn't gonna push it because I had more important things to tend to than that. When you weren't married, you didn't have many privileges, and that was one of them that I didn't have.

I entered the hospital room with some red roses, and saw Jersey standing there in tights and a t-shirt. Her stomach was protruding more, but it still wasn't too big yet, although she was very far along. Her curly hair was down and disheveled, but she was still beautiful nonetheless.

I was waiting for the day where her beauty wouldn't mesmerize me, but that shit hadn't come yet. Every time I saw her it was like the first time. It was the same when she worked at Starzz, because although I watched her strip every night, each time she revealed her body was like unwrapping a gift on Christmas morning.

"You ready, baby?" I asked and reached the roses out to her. She nodded slowly and then took them from my hands before sniffing them.

I picked up the bag that Cheyla had brought to her, and then took her hand into mine so that we could leave. The whole drive home she said nothing, and nursed the cup of ice water from the hospital. She never looked my way, she just kept her attention on what was going on outside of the car.

"You hungry?" I asked her. She shook her head 'no' as she continued to stare at the cars passing by. "Well I'm gonna stop and get some Boston Market for the both of us," I scoffed.

Just like with that chicken, she was gonna eat this fucking food I was about to get. I hated that I had to fucking bully her damn near, but I would do anything to make sure she and my child stayed alive. And if that included being a little rough with her ass, then so be it.

I made my way to Boston Market, and got enough food so that we could eat now and a little bit later for dinner. From the food spot all the way to our home on Saint Moritz Drive, she said nothing. After making it into the house, she tried to retire up the stairs before eating, but I wasn't having that shit.

"Jersey, come eat!" I barked. She shook her head 'no' as if she had an option. "Jersey, get yo' ass in the kitchen and eat this fucking food. I'm not playing around with you. I understand you're upset, but you're gonna starve the baby. Now bring yo' ass on before I have to shove it down your throat. And you know I will do that shit, so don't tempt me." I walked towards the kitchen, and I smiled when I heard her small footsteps behind me.

I made our plates and then we sat at the bar together to eat. Although I finished my food before her, I sat there and watched her until there were only bones and scraps on the plate. Her ass was eating all somberly at first, but after a while, she was eating like a nigga in jail. I chuckled to myself as she downed the juice I'd poured her, because it was a funny sight, and because I was happy that she was feeding herself.

We left the kitchen without saying a word to one another, and I was slowly but surely getting tired of this shit. I missed her and how we used to talk about everything. Her personality brightened my day, and I hated to see her so down and dull. I needed her to keep the joy in my life, especially with this new position I had recently acquired. When I came home from a long day in the streets, I enjoyed being able to lay up with her and just talk about shit that had nothing to with traps, suppliers, money counts, and keys. Jersey was like my little moonlight in a dark and empty room at times.

When we made it to the bedroom, she instantly began grabbing things for a shower, before going into the bathroom within our room. I plopped down on the bed defeated, until I finally decided to go in there and make her ass talk. I needed something from her, because I hated this disconnection.

I rushed to the bathroom, and walked in without knocking. She was standing there naked already, and tying her hair up into a bun for the shower. I began to slowly undress as I stood a little ways behind her. She glanced at me every now and then through the mirror, until I was fully naked. I turned the lights low, and then walked up behind her. Turning her to face me, I began kissing her neck. Even though she didn't have on any of her favorite perfumes or lotions, her natural scent smelled so good.

"You have to talk to me, Jersey, I miss you," I whispered as I kissed on her neck and rubbed her bare body. "I need something from you."

"Kill, I can't," she began to whimper lowly.

"Then we're gonna connect another way."

I cupped her face and kissed her soft lips. She hadn't let me kiss her in forever. Since she didn't want to connect verbally, we would have to physically.

"Kill, no," she whispered in between kisses.

"Stop it, Jersey," I growled as I made her stay close to me.

She gave in, and our tongues came in contact. I lifted her up, and then brought her down onto my dick, which was rock hard. I began moving in and out of her slowly, and she wrapped one of her arms around my neck, while the other gripped my bicep. This shit felt so good, mentally and physically. I set her down on the sink, and held her body closely as I continued to pump into her wet center.

"You can't shut me out, Jersey," I told her as I sucked on her lips.

She felt so damn bomb, and I missed this pussy. Shit, I had murdered for this shit, and every time I got in it I remembered why.

"Mmm, uuh, uuh," she let out mellow purrs.

I gripped her soft thighs, and began slamming into her, as we both called out loudly. Soon after, I was bursting all inside of her, and she was exploding on my dick. We sat there kissing hungrily for a bit, and then we got into the shower to clean ourselves. That was exactly what the fuck we needed.

"Talk to me," I said as I massaged her feet.

We'd just gotten out of the shower, and she was resting with her back against the headboard, wearing a big t-shirt. Her long curly locks were down, and I admired her beauty like I always did.

"It's hard for me to explain, Kill. My parents are gone," she sniffled. "I don't know if you will get it."

"You don't know if I will get it? Jersey, my mother was killed, not by my father, but she was abruptly taken away from me just like your dad. And my father is in a home, refusing my visits and calls. I understand more than anybody."

"Oh, I guess I forgot about that," she said and pulled her foot from my hands. She crawled to me, and then cupped my face to kiss me gently and longingly. "I'm sorry. And even if your parents were still around, I should've known you would understand me," she whispered and pecked me again. She climbed into my lap, and I rubbed her belly. "What's it like having no parents right there?" she asked.

"It's very hard, but over time you get used to it. Time heals and reveals all."

"I don't know if time will ever heal this."

"I used to say the same thing when my mother died. I'm still not over it, but I've come to accept what has happened."

"My dad wasn't even in my life really before he died. It was probably worse for you losing your mother, since she was right in your life, still caring about you."

"It was bad, yeah, but your father loved you and cared for you for 90% of your life baby, so it's okay for you to feel saddened by his death. For the most part he was a great father to you."

"Yeah, I guess I shouldn't feel stupid for mourning him."

"Not at all." I kissed her cheek.

"I love you, Kilexis."

"I love you, too."

She hugged my neck tightly, and rubbed the back of my head slowly.

"Promise me you will always love me the way that you do?"

"I promise, baby."

FIVE

Kantwan Camren

I gripped Cheyla's waist as she moved her hips back and forth. I licked my lips as her titties slightly bounced, and her sexy ass body wound perfectly on my dick. She was so beautiful, especially when she was making her sex faces. I was deep inside of her and loving every minute of it.

"Shit," I mumbled as she sped up and placed her small hand on my chest for leverage.

"Mmm, uuh," her voice slightly trembled as she moaned.

I gripped her smooth round ass in my hands, and then smacked it hard. She bit down on her bottom lip, and stared me in the eyes as if she was about to cry. I loved seeing what I could do to her with my dick. I didn't care too much for doggy style, because a woman's moans and facial expressions were what got me off.

"Bounce on it slowly," I demanded.

She placed her feet flat on the bed, and then began to glide up and down on my rod. Watching my dick penetrate her, while feeling it at the same time was the muthafuckin' business. I never wanted this shit to end, but too bad my nut was starting to rise.

"You are so damn sexy," I said as I grabbed her round breasts into my hands.

I nibbled on my lip as I watched her continue to go up and down on me slowly. She'd coated it perfectly, and I wanted her to cum once more before I busted; if I could make it.

"Oh my gosh, Kant!" she hollered and frowned.

She began bouncing a little faster, but still nicely and steadily, and my toes began to cramp up. I was holding my nut back and my body couldn't take it anymore.

"Cheyla, fuck, I'm about to nut, ma," I breathed heavily and clamped her nipples between my middle fingers and thumbs.

The harder she bounced, the tighter I grasped her nipples, until we both exploded. She collapsed down onto my chest, and I bent her head back to kiss her full lips roughly. Her caramel complexion was red as hell, and she had sweat on her upper lip, which I found to be a sexy trait of hers.

"You know your pussy is crazy, right," I said in a low tone.

"And your dick got me sprung," she responded shakily. After tonguing her down for what seemed like an eternity, she got up so that I could get my dick out of her. "Where are you going today, Kantwan?" she asked as I walked butt naked to the bathroom.

"I have a meeting to go to, why, what's up?"

"Nothing," she smiled and covered her body with the sheet. "Are you gonna be home late like yesterday?"

"I hope not. We just have this one little meeting and that's it. I should be able to come straight home." I leaned in the doorway of the bathroom.

"Good, I'm not used to you not having time for me."

"Well, I explained to you that shit would change, baby."

"I know, and I'm just trying to get all of the time I can get before you get busy as fuck and leave me at home alone."

"Shorty, I'm not gonna neglect you like that, I'm just gonna be busier than usual. And I won't have a set schedule like when I was working for Costco. I'll be more like a doctor on call," I responded and spread toothpaste onto my toothbrush.

"And you promise not to run into anybody prettier than me?" She climbed out of the bed as I began brushing.

I didn't respond since I couldn't, so I just finished up my teeth.

After spitting out the mouthwash, I walked out of the bathroom to her.

"Now you know it isn't possible for me to run into anyone prettier than you, baby."

"You better lie to me like that for the rest of our lives," she replied making us laugh loudly in unison. I bent down to kiss her, and then went back to the bathroom to shower.

After getting fresh, I threw on some jeans, a t-shirt, and some Jordan 12's in all black. I brushed my waves a bit, and then pulled my cap down onto my head before spraying my cologne.

"Bye, shorty." I kissed Cheyla's lips as she wrapped herself in some sexy ass robe that you could see straight through. "Mm," I tucked my lips in and grabbed a handful of her ass. "You know, just because you don't work for Starzz anymore, doesn't mean you can't strip for me."

"I got you, daddy," she licked her teeth and patted my dick.

▭

I pulled up to Axel's house on Summit Lane, and spotted Elijah's car, as well as Kill's parked up in the driveway. After making it through the gate, I parked near Elijah and shut my engine off. Placing my phone on silent, I exited the car and jogged up to the front door.

I rang the doorbell, and was let in by Axel's housekeeper only a few short moments later. She led me to the back, and then opened this huge wooden door for me. Inside was a huge ass office, and I spotted Kill, Elijah, and Axel sitting at a large wooden table.

"What's good?" I said and greeted them all.

"Axel, you know my little brother Kantwan," Kill said.

"Not yet, but I hope to get to know him better," Axel smiled as we slapped hands. I took a seat at the table with them, and waited to see what we needed to talk about. "So Kill, I know you have plans on how you want to handle everything, so I'm not here to guide you or anything like that. I'm actually here to tell you that you have complete authority, meaning you can fire and keep whomever you want. That includes my plug as well. I've always told him how good of a worker you were, so he is more than happy to be your supplier," Axel started.

"I'd like to meet him first. I have a couple people looking to be my distributor," Kill replied.

"Damn you work fast; just makes me feel even better about my decision," Axel nodded.

"How did Dante and Ahmad feel?" Elijah questioned, referring to Axel's sons.

"I don't know and I don't care. I love my sons with every bone in my body, but I refuse to let something I worked so hard for go down in flames due to nepotism. I decided to instead take the pragmatic approach when picking someone to take over."

"So all of this means that you won't be sticking your nose in anything that we do, right?" I quizzed.

"That's absolutely right. And even if I wanted to, I highly doubt Kill would allow me to do so," he chuckled and glanced at my brother.

"Well just so you know, there are gonna be a lot of changes. I plan to meet with the team you have already, and I'm pretty sure that I will have to clean house a bit. I'm switching up the way things work, and if there are any niggas who don't wanna show respect or are stuck in their ways, they're gonna get released or put in the ground if they don't cooperate," Kill stated sternly.

"Oh, I know. And like I said Kill, this is your shit. I'm sick and I don't have the energy, or the strength to run things the way I used to. Now, the last thing I wanted to tell you guys is that I'm throwing a party for you. All the people there will be people that worked for me and now work for you. There will be a few outsiders there, you know women, but other than that it will be a close-knit guest list. It's kind of a celebration of me passing the torch to you. And I want to celebrate this new opportunity with you now, before I'm too sick to even talk."

I kind of felt bad for Axel, because it was like he knew he was gonna die and he was taking it for what it was. He wasn't gonna cry about it, and that reminded me a lot of my brother. Kill never liked to sit and moan about something you couldn't change. He was all about accepting it and moving on. He would always say "instead of spending time worrying about what has happened to you, take that time to figure out how you're gonna move forward". He always lived that way and I admired him for it, especially when my mother passed, because he was the rock for my father, Ka'Shea, Elijah, and I.

"Well I can't wait, when is it?" Elijah asked.

"Next weekend, and just to let you youngins know, there will be plenty of women ready and willing when you arrive, so bring your significant others at your own risk. We're gonna have women coming in from all over the world just to party, and they're down for whatever. To make matters worse, they're bold as hell." Axel nodded and then chuckled lightly.

"I think we'll be good," Kill nodded and shrugged.

I hoped he was right, because one thing the three of us loved more than money was women. On the contrary, Cheyla was my world, and it would take a little more than a pretty face and willingness to do anything in order for me to cheat on her.

SIX

Elijah Camren

The Next Day...

$\mathcal{I}$ was coming out of my old condo, because I needed to put some clothes there and tidy up a bit. I still kept this place just in case I needed it one day for something. Having two spots was always a good thing, and now that I was about to make way more money than I had been, I could afford that little luxury.

When Axel gave Kill that advance, he gave Kantwan and me a part of it. I didn't want to take the money, but Kill wasn't taking no for an answer. So with that money, I purchased the house that I live in with Ivy and Donovan, as well as a better car. I really felt low as fuck by taking money from my cousin, but he explained to me that it was money for us three to make sure we were protected and had our shit in order. We'd be making plenty of money of our own down the road, and this shit here would be chump change. Looking at it from that perspective made much more sense to me.

Kill let me know he was gonna pay Axel the money back though, and I would be sure to give him the portion he'd given to me as well. I didn't want no nigga holding anything over my head, even if it was Kill. I knew he would never try and come at me like that, but it was just my pride. I'd rather be broke than have another man claiming he supported me.

I finished collecting the mail and cleaning up, so I was ready to head home. It was around 7pm in the evening, and I wanted to spend some time with my girl and her... and my... fuck it, *my* baby. I didn't know what to call Donovan at first, but I took care of him like he was my own, so that was what I was gonna call him. If anybody asked, he was mine, and I hoped it got back to that nigga Portland low-key. I wanted to let Ivy tell him about us like she'd requested, but it was hard not to just hunt his ass down and break the news. However, I cared for my girl enough to respect her wishes and not say shit to his ass.

As I was walking down Franklin towards Third Street to my car, I spotted that dumb ass nigga Portland hit the corner. It's funny that he'd finally returned, but hadn't let Ivy know. And I knew he hadn't because I checked her phone. This nigga really gave no fucks about neither her nor their child. That was cool for me, but I knew it made Ivy feel some type of way. Come to think of it, I kind of felt bad for Donovan, because to think your parent doesn't care for you has to hurt. And Donovan was a cool ass baby, so Portland was missing out.

"Aye!" he called after me. I paused with my back to him, and then turned around to face him. "Aye, I'm looking to cop something from you," he panted out of breath.

"I ain't got shit for you."

"It ain't even gotta be weed man. I'll take anything from you."

If I was a shady ass nigga, I would throw him a bag of pills that would have him in the corner picking his skin, but I didn't wanna do that. I loved Ivy and Donovan, and I didn't wanna do anything to this nigga because of them. That was how I felt now, but as soon as he tried to pull some bullshit, he was out of here and I put that on everything. By saying that, I wasn't going to intentionally fuck him over until he did something dumb. There was no need for it, because I had Ivy and he didn't.

"Nah man, I'm out of everything for the day," I shrugged.

"Where you get your shit from? I'll catch a ride with you there and wait for you to re-up. You don't even have to give me a ride home."

I squinted my eyes at him for a couple moments because I was disgusted. I looked off to my right, and then back at him.

"Nigga, don't you have more important shit to tend to? Asking me to drive you to a damn trap. You sound like a fucking basehead."

"Nah, I ain't no basehead, I'm just stressing like a muthafucka. Some shit don' happened to my family man, and I need to just get away. Anything man, coke, heroin, whatever," he pleaded.

"Fuck out of here." I turned my back to him and stepped down off the curb to go get in my car. He grabbed my shoulder, and I instantly turned around and shoved his ass to the ground. "Don't put yo' fucking hands on me, homie. Get yo' bitch ass out of here and look for someone else to break yo' begging ass off. I told you I ain't got shit now you need to keep it pushing!"

"Man, who the fuck—" I cut him off when I placed my pistol to his dome. "You need to carry the fuck on like I just told you to, bro." I towered over him as he sat on the edge of the curb staring up at me.

It was so hard for me not to just press down on the trigger and splatter his brains. One thing I hated was for a nigga to not take care of home. He had a fucking son who didn't know his ass from Adam because of his careless mistakes, and he had the nerve to be out here on the hunt for something to get him high. This nigga was more ambitious about getting high than he was about getting his shit right for his kid.

I twisted my face up as I thought about Ivy's busted ass nose that day she put his ass out. That along with all the other shit she had told me he'd done to her had me hot as fish grease. *Not right now Elijah*, I told myself.

"My bad man, I'm not myself right now," he breathed heavily.

I continued to stare into his eyes with my gun jammed into his temple. I slowly pulled it away, and he scrambled to his feet. He backed away as we continued to stare at one another, and then he finally turned around and headed towards Third.

"Busted ass nigga," I mumbled to myself as I climbed into my car and placed my gun back into my waist.

I made it to my home on Alders Lane about twenty minutes later, and pulled into the garage to park my whip. When I came into the house, the smell of sweet cornbread hit my nose. Damn how I missed having a shorty to cook me some meals.

I followed the smell to the kitchen just like a dog, and saw Ivy cooking while Donovan sat in his high chair.

"Damn, you earning the fuck out of that wifey title, ma."

"I thought I already had it," she smiled and turned the knob of the oven off. I kissed Donovan's head making him giggle, and then sat down at the island.

"You do."

"I better," she said before nearing me. She slipped her arms around my neck and kissed me. "I love when you pile your dreads up like that."

"Oh, you do?"

"Yes, but I love when you wear them down in bed. You remind me of Mufasa," she giggled.

"From the Lion King?" I frowned and she nodded while laughing. Donovan began to laugh even though he knew nothing of what was going on. "Aye, what you laughing at? Yo' mama ain't funny, man!" I sneered at him playfully, and he threw his head back to laugh harder. Little man was cute as hell, and I couldn't understand how Portland could just diss him like that.

"You're so good with him," Ivy looked at Donovan and then back to me.

"It's not hard to be, he's a cool ass baby," I grinned and so did she. "I still don't appreciate that Lion King comment."

"Oh my gosh, baby, Mufasa was a sexy ass lion. Now Scar was the ugly ass hating one."

"You right, and Mufasa had all the bitches, right?"

"Nigga, no! But if this Mufasa tries to have any bitches, I'm gon' throw yo' ass off a cliff just like Scar did!" She bucked her eyes at me and then pinched my six-pack.

"Don't trip, ma, I'm all about you." I yanked her body closer to mine.

"You better be, Eli." She looked into my eyes seriously.

"I am, Ivy. I wouldn't take you from one situation to do the same shit." She nodded her head saying she understood, as I pulled her into a tight hug. I pulled away and stared into her blue eyes for a bit, then pressed my lips against hers. "Now make me a plate." I squeezed her small round ass, making her jump and smile.

She sauntered away and began piling some food onto my plate to eat. Shit was too good and calm right now, but I knew Portland wasn't going out that easily. Whenever he decided to get buck though, I had a loaded hammer waiting for his ass.

SEVEN

Jersey

Over the past couple of weeks, Kill had been making me feel so much better. I really didn't know what I was thinking by shutting him out the way that I had been. Over a short time, he'd become one of my best friends and also the love of my life. I know it's weird because it seems like we just met, but I didn't feel that way at all. I didn't feel like I was rushing things with him. Everything was moving just perfectly in my opinion.

Although backwards as hell, our relationship had really blossomed into one to be admired. Next to sex, I loved having talks with him. He was so intelligent and always had a solution to things. I was the type to worry a lot, and I loved the fact that he was the opposite, because he could always calm me down. His gorgeous ass looks and phenomenal sex game were just the cherries on top. Kill was just that nigga from the inside out.

I'd never met someone so good looking yet so smart, kind, and caring. Usually, fine niggas are either dumb or assholes, and Kill was neither. If I had to complain about anything, it would be his foul ass mouth. He was so comfortable speaking about sex in detail, and I'd never met someone like that. I enjoyed it in bed though, so I wouldn't exactly change it I guess. He was definitely a Godsend.

I pulled my tennis shoes on, and then grabbed some edge control to slick my edges. I was able to get my wild curly mane into a slick ponytail with no curly bumps in the road. Slick ponytails had always been a damn struggle for me since my hair was so curly, so the fact that I had achieved it had me wanting to click my damn heels.

Kill was out working, and he'd left early in the fucking morning. I remember him saying bye to me and kissing my lips, but a bitch was dead tired from us staying up all night, watching TV and fucking. I don't even know how he was able to get his ass up, because if you put a gun to my head I still wouldn't have crawled out of that comfy ass bed. My pussy was still a little sore too, but guess what? My ass would be right back on that dick tonight. The way Kill made my body feel, was worth all the soreness I endured by morning.

I grabbed my purse and jacket, then the keys to my customized Porsche that Kill bought me. As much as I wanted to deny the gift, I couldn't. I was happy to have a car that actually blew cool air out when I cut the air conditioner on. Shit, the small things were a luxury, I couldn't care less about the built in GPS or leather interior. A bitch was just happy she could press a button to let the windows down, and not have to be driving for fifteen minutes before the air turned cool.

Today, I was going to see my mother in jail. She was locked up in New Castle at Baylor Women's Correctional Facility. I wanted to see her earlier, but I just couldn't look at her at that time. I was still scared to see her and talk to her, but I knew I had to. I wasn't scared because of what she had done; I was scared because I had no idea what to say. I had plenty of questions, but I didn't want her to be uncomfortable upon seeing me for the first time. I wanted her to know that despite committing this heinous act, I still loved her.

I made it to the jail in no time, and after showing them my appointment card and I.D., I was placed at a seat with a telephone on the wall. I was a bit bummed because I wanted to hug her, but clearly that wasn't an option. Kill told me beforehand that it might be this kind of visit though, so I was somewhat prepared. I was still hopeful that it wouldn't be a glass between us still though.

I waited as my palms began to sweat, and my legs bounced. My baby began to move and that made me smile. I began rubbing my belly while looking down, and I was so occupied by what was happening, that I hadn't noticed that my mother was on the other side of the glass.

KNOCK! KNOCK!

She banged on the window, and I looked up to see her with the phone placed to her ear. She looked totally different than I thought she would have. I expected her to look drained and depressed, but she looked refreshed and almost happy. She was beaming in a sense, obviously not remorseful about what she had done. I slowly reached for the phone and put it to my ear.

"Hi ma," I half smiled.

"Hey baby, how are you feeling?"

"I'm doing okay. The baby is in perfect condition despite—"

"Despite what?" she frowned.

"Despite me falling into a coma for a couple weeks."

"Oh honey, was it because of me?" She pointed to her chest.

"Not really, I guess. I fainted at the house that night and hit my head on the stretcher."

"Oh, I'm sorry I upset you that much, Jersey. I love you, baby," she smiled sympathetically. I just stared at her in silence, pondering.

"Ma, why?" I had to ask.

I was gonna refrain from asking until the next couple of visits, but I just couldn't hold back. That question circled my mind from sun up to sun down. I just never got the impression that she was that upset. I mean I knew she was pretty sad about it, but damn, to kill my father in such an intimate way was baffling to say the least.

"Jersey, I couldn't deal with the circumstances anymore. I couldn't live the way that I was, knowing that he was living happily with another woman. I gave him everything, and for him to just move on without a care in the world infuriated me."

"Ma, you took him from all of us," I began to tear up.

"I know baby, and I apologize for that. It was selfish of me to do what I did, but I was fed up. I gave my life to him, and sacrificed a whole fucking lot so that he could become who he was, and he just disregarded it all. And the worse part of it all was the way he threw you guys to the side as well. Cutting me off was one thing, but to put his own children out on the street, physically made me sick. His baby was stripping and he didn't even know because he didn't care," she explained.

I hated to say this but she was right. In a way, my dad brought this on himself. I was mad at my mother, but not mad at her for the right reasons, per se. I was angry that she killed my father and took him away from his children, but I was madder that she took herself away from us. If I'm being completely honest with myself, my dad had left us long ago, and was only hanging around in our lives by a tiny ass string. I'd somewhat mourned the loss of him already, so the fact that he was dead didn't hurt as much as it would have, had he died when we were close. I was more so furious that my mom chose to end her life and relinquish her freedom because of my father. I understand that she was sad and angry, but she should've put us first in front of her feelings. Just like my dad, she put her needs and wants before us, and again, Portland, Raleigh, and I ended up with the short end of the stick. If you would've given me a glimpse into the future five years ago, I would have never believed that this was how things were gonna play out.

"Do you hate me, sweetie?" my mother asked, grabbing me from my thoughts.

"No ma, I don't hate you, I'm just very disappointed. Do you feel bad at all about what you did?"

She looked off for a second as if she was thinking, and then turned back to me.

"Yes and no. I feel bad for leaving you guys, but I don't feel bad at all for stabbing Alvin. I feel free every time I think about what I did. I loved him, but I hated him more."

"I understand."

"You know I would've killed Trixie too, but I got carried away with stabbing your father. And by the time I was satisfied, the police showed up." She chuckled as if it were a sweet and funny memory she was recalling.

We made eye contact, and a half smile appeared on my face. I kind of wish she had have gotten to that bitch.

EIGHT

Cheyla

I stood in the mirror and smoothed down my white dress. It stopped mid thigh, and had thick straps at the top. My hair was freshly done, and so were my nails, all thanks to Kantwan. He'd given me money to shop for and pamper myself, because he said he wanted me to put my best foot forward tonight.

There was a party being held by his brother and cousin's old boss, Axel. He was celebrating passing the torch to Kill, and it was just an event to have fun at. Kantwan said to not be nervous about impressing people or anything, and to just enjoy the night. I was gonna do just that, especially because I had many things to celebrate at this time in my life. I was about to start school, I was clean, and I had a man who loved me and cared about me. Most importantly was the fact that I cared about him as well.

I hadn't cared for a guy, or wanted to be exclusive with a guy since high school, so the fact that Kantwan had my ass certified sprung, was crazy as hell to me. Usually, girls bragged about locking down a nigga who never wanted to be locked down, but in this case it was the other way around. I don't know how Kantwan did it, but he succeeded in turning Cheyla into a girlfriend.

I was obsessed with his fine ass too, and always wanted to be up under him. I found myself even being a little jealous when other women looked at him, admiring his sexiness. My jealousy was healthy though, of course, for now. However, I saw nothing wrong with slicing a bitch up if she got a little too aggressive.

"Shorty, damn. Baby, when I told you to look good for tonight, I didn't want you having niggas wondering how I got you," Kantwan grinned.

He was wearing a black button up, with black slacks, and black Giuseppe Zanotti's. His cologne was very prevalent, but it wasn't too strong, it was just right. I already knew bitches would be salivating like newborn babies when they saw him, making me roll my eyes at the thought.

"Please, when they ask I will just tell them you paid me," I taunted and he yanked me over to him.

"I don't care what you tell them niggas, as long as they know to keep their hands to themselves."

I loved that Kantwan had no problem checking another nigga, but at the same time he wasn't boisterous. He didn't go around threatening niggas for no reason, or beating on his chest like some sort of baboon to prove a point. I loved how calm his gangsta was. My baby could be chill, but still whoop a nigga's ass if he needed to. I think the day I watched him whoop that drug dealer's ass for me, was the day I knew I wanted him all to myself. I was stubborn at the time, but happy that he broke through that shit.

"Aight, you ready? The limo is outside," he said as he looked on his phone.

"Who is that?" I asked and raised my freshly waxed brow.

"It's my brother telling me that the limo is outside," he showed me and chuckled.

"Oh."

"Look at you all jealous and shit," he smiled and leaned down to kiss me lightly.

I pressed my lips together to make sure my lipstick stayed in tact, and then he opened the bedroom door for me so that we could descend the stairs. When we walked outside of the house, I admired my surroundings. No one was outside because it was late. All you saw were other beautiful houses, and people's porch lights on. It was so quiet and peaceful, with no niggas sitting on their porches free styling, shooting dice, fighting, or selling dime bags. It was so different from what I was used to in Browntown, but I enjoyed it.

Kantwan walked to the limo, and the driver jogged around to open the door. When he did, Kantwan gestured for me to climb into the Escalade limo. I grinned widely when I spotted Jersey, Kill, Ivy and Elijah. We'd all come up in the best way, but the one I was most excited about was Elijah and Ivy. Portland was never gonna change, and I was happy she saw that. I remember when you couldn't pay her ass to leave Portland alone, and as of now you couldn't pay her to go on a date with his no good ass.

"Who is keeping Donovan?" I asked as the driver closed the door behind Kantwan.

"Raleigh offered," Ivy replied.

"She didn't want to come?" I frowned.

"No, for some reason her ass wanted to stay home," Jersey replied.

On the way to the club or venue, I wasn't really sure, we poured ourselves some juice and liquor. Poor Jersey had to nurse the juice as the rest of us got lit with the vodka and Patrón. She didn't seem to mind though, as we all jammed to the music in the car. Finally, we arrived at a huge ass mansion. It was probably the biggest house I'd ever seen in person.

"Whose house is this?" I asked.

"One of Axel's," Kill replied just as the driver opened the door. We all climbed out, and the six of us headed up the long walkway.

"I have never experienced anything like this before," I whispered to Jersey.

"I know, a limo? I've never been in one," she replied. It felt good to experience this with her and Ivy.

We finally made it to the door, and a girl was standing there in little to no clothes, holding a tray of champagne.

"Champagne?" she smiled seductively at the men.

I immediately slipped my hand into Kantwan's, and she subtly rolled her eyes. We walked in, and the bouncer guy greeted the boys before letting them by. We walked up the huge ass staircase until we made it to the balcony. This house was almost like a venue inside. Whoever set this shit up knew what the hell they were doing for sure.

The six of us made it to the top, and then sat down on these big square couches. I swear it looked just like a club. A tall, bald headed, light-skinned guy walked up to us, and the guys stood to their feet.

"This is Axel Johnson, ladies," Elijah said. We all greeted and hugged him before he sat down.

"My sons Ahmad and Dante," he introduced them and we shook their hands.

Ahmad looked just like Axel, bearing the same light complexion and clean-shaven head. He had no facial hair, which was a turn off, with thin lips and perfect teeth. Dante was better looking with smooth brown skin, a fade, and a nicely trimmed goatee. Dante was much taller than Ahmad despite them being siblings.

"Congrats," Ahmad lifted his glass to Elijah, Kantwan, and Kill.

They nodded and did the same, before turning their attention back to the party. I noticed when they looked away, Ahmad and Dante gave each other a look. I wondered what it meant exactly, but I could tell it wasn't good. Them niggas were suspicious as fuck.

We all began to dance, drink, and just really let loose. I was having so much fucking fun, and it felt so good to not have any worries. I planned to get pissy drunk tonight, then go home and get some good dick.

Suddenly about four chicks walked into the VIP, and they were thick as hell. They had to be strippers, and if they weren't, they should be because they would dominate the game. They each walked over to Kill, Kantwan, and Elijah, and began to flirt in their own way. The fourth one sat on Dante's lap, leaving poor little Ahmad to himself.

"Nope!" Jersey stated calmly and pushed the brown skinned one away from Kill with the quickness.

The chick stumbled back, sucked her teeth, and then left the area. Jersey did not play at all about Kill, and like me, she would shank a bitch before she let them get too close.

I was about to speak up to the pale hoe that approached Kantwan, but my baby had already taken care of it. Ivy didn't even give the other brown-skinned chick a chance to get close, because she hopped into Elijah's lap quickly as hell, and elbowed the fuck out of old girl's titty. That shit was hilarious.

Once three of the four ladies were gone, Jersey slid into Kill's lap, and he wrapped his arms around her, palming her belly and kissing her neck. I saw him chuckling at how calm Jersey was when pushing that girl off.

"Calm down, shorty," Kill snickered and kissed Jersey's jawline.

"I'm not playing around with these hoes," Jersey responded and giggled herself.

Kill gripped her chin, and turned her to face him so that they could kiss. That was my cue to turn away.

"I'm glad you took care of her before I whooped her ass," I whispered to Kantwan.

"I already knew you were gonna nut the fuck up, so I just did my part," he laughed.

I wrapped my arms around his waist from behind, and kissed his neck. He turned his face to the side, so I craned my neck around to kiss his lips, making my clit tingle. I was tipsy and ready to get fucked, Kantwan Camren style.

Some more girls walked up and I was in disbelief. Was this how this life was? I mean I knew bitches went dumb for niggas with bread but damn. And I could only imagine how bad it was gonna be because not only were Kill, Kantwan, and Elijah about to make major bread, but they were all very attractive. A nigga with money and good looks were like magnets to these hoes. I would cut a bitch like I was in jail if they came near mine though.

"Keep it pushing," Kill called out to the girls, as Axel and his sons laughed.

"Told you," Axel grinned and the boys snickered.

The girls just decided to entertain Axel's sons instead, and I was happy. I was ready to fuck something up in a jiffy, especially with me being a little drunk! I was not feeling Kantwan being so sought after. I liked the fact that he was my fine little secret, and I didn't want all these bitches looking at him. Now that his sexiness was no longer classified, I had a feeling I was gonna be lining bitches up constantly. Fuck.

***

We made it to our home at around 3am, and damn we were drunk as fuck. As I began walking up the stairs, Kantwan grabbed me from behind, and hugged my body tightly while kissing on my neck. As we ascended the stairs, he was pulling my dress up and I could feel his hard ass dick prodding my ass.

"Oooh," I commented and bit down on my lip.

"It's ready for you," he responded as we entered the bedroom.

He shoved me down onto the bed, and then dropped down to his knees. Spreading my legs, I let him kiss my center through my lace panties. He began sucking my pussy through my panties, and that shit felt so damn good. Keeping his mouth latched between my legs, he peeled my shoes off and threw them across the room, before pulling down my panties. He pushed my dress up past my waist, and then pressed my thighs against my stomach to began feasting. I arched my back, and threw my head backward as he sucked on my clit like a maniac.

NINE

Ivy

———

I was walking into work, and dreading each step I took as I got closer to the damn building. I hated my job so damn much, and on top of that I was tired as hell from partying all night with my man and best friends. One thing about last night though, was that it felt good to have a man that behaved himself. I loved that Elijah didn't have his tongue hanging out of his mouth every time a pretty bitch walked by. My baby had discipline, and it just made my feelings become stronger for him.

I walked into the building and prepared to have another horrible ass day. I was so damn tired of dealing with rude ass people who felt they could talk to you any kind of way, just because they were over the damn phone. I wanted so badly to write down their addresses sometimes, and show up to them and fight. This job also showed me how damn dumb people were. People would call for the dumbest shit in the world, then get mad at you because you didn't know how to answer their dumb ass question. On the bright side, Raleigh was here, and also I would be starting school this coming Fall.

I planned to work my ass off at that community college so that I could make something of myself. I was gonna make it to a university with Jersey, get my damn degree, and then get the fuck out of this call center. I wasn't really sure what I wanted to do, but being my own boss was definitely part of the plan.

"Good morning, Ivy," some chick named Shelby smiled. She had the biggest under bite in the entire world. The shit looked painful as fuck too.

I checked my phone and saw I still had fifteen minutes left before I had to clock in, so I sat down in the little hallway in one of the plush chairs. As soon as I did, my phone began to vibrate in my hand. I saw it was Portland and I froze for a second, not knowing what to do. For a moment I thought his whack ass was dead.

"Hello?" I finally answered.

"Baby, hey, how are you?"

"I'm good. How are you? You've been missing in action, and this is not the time for it Portland."

"I know baby, I know."

I felt so uncomfortable with him referring to me as baby, because I was no longer in that place with him. Somehow, even though we spent years together, I felt nothing for him anymore. I cared for him a bit because he was Donovan's father, but as far as me wanting to be with him? Nope!

"So what's up, Portland? Why are you calling me? I'm about to start work." I was anxious to get off the phone with him.

"Oh, I wanna know where you've been sleeping. Every time I drop by no one answers the door, and E-Way said he ain't seen you over by the crib neither."

"Again, what do you want Portland?"

I was not about to disclose my whereabouts to his ass. This nigga hadn't spoken to me since I put him out, and then had the nerve to try and slither his ass back into my life. Where I was living was none of his concern, and he probably only wanted to know so he could fuck. Little did he know, he had no chance of fucking anything over this way.

"Aight look, I wanna see Donovan."

"Okay, well let's look at our schedules and we can figure—"

"Nah I'm gonna be out of town for a couple weeks, and I wanna see him today. What time do you get off?"

I wanted to ask him what he was going out of town for, but I didn't want him to mistake my curiosity for jealousy, or any other kind of emotion that would make him think I was missing him and our relationship.

"I get off at 4:45pm."

"Alright, I'm at the Fairview Inn off of Market Street. Just get him and bring him to me here."

"I'm not leaving him there with you."

"I know, Ivy."

"Okay just making sure."

"See you later baby, I love you."

"Bye Portland," I scoffed before disconnecting.

It annoyed me that he thought I was just blowing smoke when I said we were done. This nigga needed to understand that he and I were no longer. Plus, it's not like he genuinely cared. This is the first time he's attempted to contact me since I put his lying ass out, and frankly I wished he hadn't. If I was a bitch I would have told him he couldn't see my baby, but I didn't wanna deprive Donovan of his father just because I didn't like him.

The time on my iPhone read 7:58am, so I knew I needed to go to my desk and start my shift. As I walked slowly to my area, my phone buzzed and Elijah's name flashed across.

Elijah: *Have a good day baby.*

Me: *I wish, but you know I hate this place.*

Elijah: *Well I already told you that I had you and you could focus on school, but you wanna be stubborn.*

Me: *I don't wanna be taken care of.*

Elijah: *Then deal with the job you dread ma. See you later beautiful.*

I locked my phone and slipped it into my slacks. I really wanted to take him up on his offer sometimes, but my pride just wouldn't allow me to. I needed to continue to get it on my own, and only let him handle a few things for me.

*I*t was finally 4:40pm, and I was logging out of the damn phones. Lord was I happy that Raleigh was able to convince the supervisor to give me an early shift. Raleigh's ass had a 7am shift, so her ass had been gone. We'd emailed one another all throughout the day, and it was the only way I could make it without ripping my hair out.

I said goodbye to my co-workers who were on the nine, ten, eleven, and twelve o'clock shifts, and then dipped. I was so happy I wasn't one of them, especially because I was the only newbie who clocked in at eight. If it wasn't for Raleigh, I'd be on the 12pm to 8:45 like the rest of my training class. One of the supervisors named Norman had a crush on her, and so he did whatever she wanted. He hadn't so much as seen her panties, yet he was obsessed with her.

I made it to my car and immediately peeled off the stuffy ass blazer I was wearing. I cut on some music, and then sped out so I could get Donovan from Elijah at the house. I wasn't sure what excuse I was gonna use, but I needed to be smart about it. That was the only downside to dating a nigga who was beyond clever; you couldn't really fool him or anything.

I pulled into the roundabout driveway, and just stopped there. It was no point in me going into the garage, because I was leaving right out. I walked into the home, and rushed through the foyer and up the stairs to change into some skinny jeans and a t-shirt. As I was brushing my golden locks into a ponytail, Elijah walked in with Donovan on his hip.

"Where are you going?" he frowned.

"I'm going to Raleigh's house."

"Oh, okay," he responded and then began tickling my baby. He didn't even ask me for what, but I wasn't gonna speak on it and make him.

"Come on, Donovan," I tried to take him from Elijah.

"Why are you taking him? We're chilling. And don't you wanna just relax with Raleigh and not have to tend to him?"

"I do, but I missed him so I wanna take him with me."

"Tell her you don't wanna be with her and her home girl. You wanna chill and watch the game, huh?" he spoke to my baby. I liked that he didn't use a baby voice with him.

"Stop it, Eli," I chuckled and pried Donovan from his strong tatted arms.

Once Donovan was on my hip, Elijah plopped down on the ottoman in the room. I walked over to him, palmed his dread bun, and then kissed his lips. My clit started to throb, but I knew there was no time for that. We could do that later.

I grabbed my purse and phone, and then left out of the house. On the way to the hotel, I texted Raleigh so that she'd be up on game in case Elijah went snooping on me. I didn't want her to accidentally blow my cover with Elijah.

I finally made it to the Fairview Inn, and found a park, quickly, before texting Portland. He responded shortly after, and I pulled my baby from the backseat. As I walked through the parking lot, I saw him come out of his first floor room, wearing a huge smile.

Portland was finer than the law allowed, but he was just the worst nigga. I still found him physically attractive, but because I knew how trash his personality was, it took away from the physical. Elijah on the other hand was fine as fuck and had a great personality, which only made him even sexier. There was nothing Portland could do for me, other than be a father to Donovan.

I made it to the doorway, and Portland stepped back to let me in. When I tried to walk in past him, this nigga had the nerve to try and kiss me.

"Move Portland," I pushed his face with my free hand and frowned.

I looked around the room and it was nothing special. It was simply a room. This nigga would never get his shit together.

"You know the least you could do is let me sleep on the couch," he said as he shut the motel room door. *The least I could do, hilarious.*

"No, you should sleep on your new girlfriend's couch."

He just laughed and nodded. "Fair enough." He put his arms out to Donovan, and my baby gripped my shirt with his little hands in fear. I knew he didn't want me to let him go, but he needed to bond with his father. Elijah wasn't his daddy, and I wanted him to understand that.

"It's your daddy, Donovan," I cooed.

I then peeled my shirt from his little clutches, and then put him out to Portland. He immediately began crying and screaming, while Portland bounced him and kissed his cheek.

"Calm down, man, I'm your daddy," Portland smiled but I could tell he was hurt. "Man, take him," he shoved Donovan into me, and he stopped crying immediately.

"He just has to get used to you, Portland. You went to jail when he was only months old, and then now that you're out, you don't see him much for whatever reason."

"Because I've been fucking working!" he barked.

"Working where?"

"See Ivy, that's why I do what I do. You're always in my fucking business, questioning me and shit! All you need to do is chill and let me make this bread for us."

"Us? Nigga, what are you talking about?"

"Fuck it sound like? I'm making this bread so we can move up out of Browntown and live better. I don't want any more kids growing up over there."

"Portland, we are not together. Did you think I was joking?" I stared into his eyes.

He burst into laughter and fell back on the twin bed he was sitting on. I thought about lying Donovan on the one I was sitting on, but I was scared that it was filled with germs.

"Ivy, quit with that shit before I really take you seriously."

"I want you to take it seriously. I don't wanna be with you anymore."

"Okay. I guess you need more time to come to your senses."

"No, you need to come to yours. Look, I didn't come here to talk about our relationship that's no longer. And you clearly aren't really interested in our baby, so I'm gonna go." I stood up.

Shit, I could be at home laid up with my man. These days it was rare that Elijah was off, so the fact that he had some free time was a blessing right now. I would much rather be chilling with my nigga and playing with my baby in the comfort of that huge mansion, than sitting up in some dingy motel, arguing with this nigga who couldn't take a hint.

"Ivy, when I see you again, you better be on some different shit. If not, I'm gon' be for real off you next time."

"I wish you wouldn't wait until next time," I fake smiled as I opened the door and left.

Portland really thought this was like all the other times. He was in for a rude ass awakening if he kept being a delusional fuck.

TEN

Portland Warren

A Couple Days Later...

"Oh fuck, baby!" Breesha yelled out as she bounced on my dick. I gripped her hips tightly, and then began slamming her down before filling her up with my seeds. "Shit," she panted heavily as she fell to the side of me and wiped the sweat off of her face.

I'd been spending way more time with Breesha these days, since Ivy was on that bullshit. I didn't know what had gotten into her, but I was sure she would be blowing up my phone for another chance like always. She'd gotten strong in the past, and as soon as a nigga didn't come home for more than three days, her ass was all in my inbox, crying and shit. I will admit that she's never been strong for this long, so it was slightly alarming.

KNOCK! KNOCK!

"Who is it?" I called out as I snatched my boxer briefs from the floor. Breesha brought the sheets up to cover her body, and then lit the blunt that was resting in the ashtray.

"E-Way!"

"What's good?" I asked from behind the door.

I was staying with my boy E-Way, because Breesha lived too fucking far from Wilmington. Wilmington was where I had work, so I couldn't be staying all the way in fucking Lynford, especially with no wheels. I wished Ivy got her shit together so I could sleep wherever she was, because recently when I went by our old spot, I saw it was back up for rent. That shit had me hot as hell.

"Sonny is here my nigga," E-Way replied.

"Aight." I stood up and then grabbed my jeans off the chair in the room.

"Where are you going now, Portland?" Breesha rolled her eyes up into her head.

Her ass had been getting way too entitled these days. She needed to remember her position, and the fact that it didn't give her the privilege of questioning my whereabouts. All she needed to do was fuck me, cook for me, and make me happy. All this other shit was not part of the plan. Shit, if I wanted to be interrogated every time I got up to get dressed, I could've stuck with Ivy only.

"You heard him, Sonny is here and we have to handle some business. You know I'm starving out here, ma."

"I know, but I thought you were gonna get in with that guy who sold to you a couple of times. You said it'd be easy as pie."

"I am, but I need to figure out how to have a sit down with him. Or even better, find out who is boss is."

"I think his name is Kill," she said and took a pull on the blunt.

"How the fuck do you know?"

"I know people in Wilmington, Portland. They told me this nigga named Kill is that nigga, and he has the blocks on lock. I'm sure that's old boy's boss."

"Yeah, you're probably right."

"They also tell me about how you're checking for your blue eyed baby mama still, when you told me you wasn't fucking with her anymore."

I was so tired of hearing Breesha complain about Ivy, to the point where it made my stomach hurt. It's almost like she was obsessed with Ivy. How the fuck could she be so damn jealous when I was laid up under her ass day in and day out? I couldn't be doing too damn much. Man, as soon as I found me another shorty, or when Ivy came to her fucking senses, I was off Breesha's ass.

"Shorty, you knew I had to get up with her so I could see my son."

"And you didn't fuck her?" she raised her brow. *Oh my fucking gosh, yo!*

Breesha was sexy as fuck, with a fat ass and big titties to match. Her waist was small, her stomach was flat, and her skin was the sexiest shade of caramel that I'd ever seen. Baby girl really shouldn't be sweating any other bitch, but because she knew I loved Ivy, she was always hating.

"No, I didn't fuck her, Breesha, she wouldn't let me," I chuckled and brushed my fade.

"So if she would have let you, then you would have fucked her?"

You damn right! I missed Ivy's pussy like a muthafucka, and sometimes fucking Breesha wasn't enough. My dick craved Ivy and only Ivy some nights, so no other woman could satisfy me. She needed to get some act right ASAP, because I was tired of beating my dick using memories of us!

"I don't know! Probably, because with the way you've been acting I don't even wanna fuck with you like that no more!" I spat.

She stared up into my eyes as if she was about to cry, and then climbed out of the bed after ashing the blunt she was smoking. She sauntered over to me completely naked, and I licked my lips at the sight.

"You sure you wanna let this go?"

"I don't wanna let it go, but I need you to chill. I told you that you be pushing a nigga away when you get to grilling me and acting all jealous and shit. You be acting just like Ivy's ass."

"I know, but sometimes I just can't help how I feel."

"Well you need to start or I'm gone. Now get dressed and go home because I don't want you here alone with E-Way."

"You'll call when you get home for the night?"

"Yeah ma, I'll hit your line so you can come back through," I sighed and she grinned widely. "Go," I ordered and squeezed her ass.

Once she and I were both presentable, we exited E-Way's crib together. I kissed her soft lips and then slid into Sonny's whip, dapping him up before securing my seatbelt.

"What's good with you?" Sonny asked as he peeled down Chestnut Street.

"Man, just trying to figure out how to get this bread consistently," I replied as I rolled down the window of his whip.

"Same. Aye, guess what though?" He glanced over at me and then back at the road.

"What?"

"Cheyla is fucking with one of them Camrens; them niggas we've been hearing a little bit about, and I think Jersey's ass is too."

"Nigga, you fucking lying."

"I swear to God. My little sister told me out of her own mouth that she was fucking with a Camren. She gotta be telling the truth because she's staying over in Alapocas."

"Damn, for real? Shit. I don't know though man, how would she even have met the nigga?"

"Hell if I know, I ain't been able to get up with her little ass since our phone conversation. Dealing with Marley and R—" he stopped mid-sentence.

"Marley and who?" I asked.

"Marley and this new little jawn I'm smashing named Re-Renee."

"Man, ain't nobody got time to be dealing with these hoes right now. I'm thinking about letting Breesha go, because she's clouding my fucking mind and interfering with a whole bunch of shit. All she does is complain about Ivy and what I'm doing with her."

"Ivy don't even fuck with you."

"Exactly, but she refuses to believe it. She must know that Ivy and I will be back together soon."

"You think so?"

"I know so, nigga. Now on to more important matters. Breesha told me that the nigga to see about eating is Kill."

"That nigga sounds like he's vicious as fuck," Sonny joked and we laughed in unison.

"Don't he? But I ain't tripping off that. I just want him to put me on so I can get this bread. I remember hearing about some cat named Kill Cam before we got locked up, but that Kill was just a pusher for that nigga Axel."

"I ain't heard shit about Axel lately, maybe that Kill nigga took over his shit."

"Nah, Axel ain't passing his shit off, and if he did, it would go to his kids. But shit, that would explain why Kill is the nigga to talk to now; if it's the same one."

I was slightly confused as fuck. The Kill I'd heard about was just a pusher for Axel, but now everyone was talkin' about Camren this and Camren that, so I knew he was more connected than a pusher would be. But for Axel to give his shit to someone other than his sons, was strange.

"True. Well shit, maybe I can have Cheyla set up something with her nigga. Shit, if he knows I'm her brother, we should have a shoe in."

"Bro, Cheyla is not dating no nigga from that Camren crew."

"I think she said her nigga's name was Kill. Nah, she said Kantwan."

"She said neither. But yeah, I'm gon' hit up that nigga that's been getting me smoke and see who he's working with. I recently saw his ass pushing a Lamborghini."

"That day he placed a chopper to your dome?" Sonny laughed.

"Nigga, fuck you. I don't know what his problem is, but I'm willing to forget that shit in order to make this bread."

"I feel."

ELEVEN

Kilexis

———————

$\mathcal{I}$ was excited as hell about today, because Jersey finally agreed to find out the sex of the baby. I'd been wondering what we were having because I wanted to get in the idea of it already. I also wanted to start having the walls painted, and the room prepared for when our son or daughter came home.

"You ready?" I asked Jersey as I stood at the bottom of the stairs.

"Yes, Kill," she playfully rolled her eyes.

"Fuck you rolling your eyes for?" I grinned.

"Because you're too fucking excited!" She smacked her lips.

Once she made it to the last stair step, I pulled her little ass close and kissed her lips. She was wearing some little dress that clung to her body just right. Her golden skin had that pregnancy glow, and she just looked so bad.

"I need to be more careful with you," I whispered as our tongues made contact. After tonguing it up for a cool minute, we pulled away.

"What do you mean more careful?"

"I mean after you have the baby. I've gotten used to us doing it freely. And you know I'm gon' be fucking the shit out of that pussy once the baby is out."

"Kill, watch your mouth! And I'll get some birth control so that things won't change."

"Sounds good to me," I nodded and opened the front door for her. "And your pussy is fire, baby," I added to fuck with her since she hated my foul mouth.

"Kill!" she squealed.

We made it to the doctor about fifteen minutes later, and boy was I anxious as hell. I wanted to rush back there and have them do it right away. I wasn't sure what I wanted either. A boy would be good, and so would a little girl. I didn't mind either way, I just wanted him or her to be healthy.

After Jersey signed in, we sat down to wait.

"For some reason, you being pregnant makes me hornier than usual."

"I can tell, Kill. You've been wearing me out. In the shower, the bed, the kitchen, the living room, and anywhere else you can get me," she chuckled and so did I.

"I know I can't help it. I love making you cum," I said in a low tone in her ear, and saw her bite down on her full bottom lip.

"Stop talking like that in here, Kill."

"Talking like what?"

"All nasty and stuff," she responded making us both laugh in unison.

"I was like that when you met me ma, you should be used to it by now."

"I know and I'm getting there. I'm just not used to someone who is so blunt with things that people are usually scared to talk about."

"You gon' sit on my face when we get home?"

"Kill!" She bucked her eyes as I cracked up.

"Okay, I'll stop until we leave."

"Thank you."

I craned my neck around, lifted her chin, and then planted a few kisses on her lips. She caressed my cheek for a bit as we indulged in one another. The world always seemed to stop when our lips met. Man, Jersey had me sounding like I was in a Shakespeare play, but I didn't even care.

"Warren!" the nurse called us after twenty long ass minutes in that freezing cold ass waiting room.

After they weighed Jersey, we were finally taken to a room to wait. I got excited just looking at the equipment that I assumed would be used to tell us what we were having.

"Have you thought of a name?" I asked Jersey.

"No state or city names, please," she shook her head.

"You don't like your name?"

"Not really. I'm used to it now, but when I was little I used to beg my mom to change it for me. She would always say that it hurt her feelings for me to ask for a name change."

"I think your name is dope."

"You think everything about is me dope, Kill."

"What's wrong with that?"

"Nothing at all," she blushed. "I think everything about you is dope as fuck too. It's good that the feeling is mutual."

"I still make you nervous?" I asked and she nodded. "Why?"

"I don't know. Just your demeanor, and then how fine you are," she responded making me cheese widely. "Oh my gosh! I shouldn't have even told your ass that!"

I stood up and towered over her on the examination table, then began to kiss her some more. She placed her soft palm against my cheek as we sucked face. I loved when she held my face with her small hands like that, whenever we kissed. I don't know why, but that small gesture just made it all the better.

"Don't be nervous around me."

"I'm comfortable around you too. It's a good nervous. I'm in love with you but I still have a crush on you."

"I like that."

"Me too," she whispered before we started kissing again.

"Well, I see the baby wasn't conceived through artificial insemination, but through the old fashioned method," the doctor joked as she walked in.

"Oh my gosh," Jersey nudged me back and then I shook the doctor's hand while laughing.

"Good morning, how is everyone feeling?"

Jersey's doctor was this super chipper black lady who was always smiling. She smelled like peonies or some shit, and had super white ass teeth. She seemed like the type of mom who cooked baked chicken instead of fried.

"I'm doing great. My baby daddy wants to know the sex though," Jersey pointed to me and I nodded.

"And you don't?" she asked while drying her hands.

"I do, but I don't have the same urgency that he does."

"I see… well let's get the show on the road," Dr. Carl nodded.

Once she'd gotten that clear shit on Jersey's belly, she began moving this defibrillator looking thing on it.

"Oh, we have a beautiful little girl here," she beamed and continued moving the thing around. Jersey looked at me smiling, and I smiled back.

Damn, I was gonna have a daughter. I was gonna need all kinds of guns to raise her. I would be known as the dad who would kill a nigga. I already had the perfect nickname to match the description. As soon as my baby girl told niggas her daddy's name was Kill, they'd keep it pushing.

We finished the appointment, and then decided to go home so we could order some pizza. I didn't want her to have to cook, I just wanted us to relax, eat, and enjoy some time together since I worked so much.

"Did you want a daughter?" Jersey asked as she placed her hand on top of mine, which was on the gearshift.

I moved it from under hers, and then took her small hand into mine before kissing it.

"I didn't care what it was. Anything we make is good."

"Anything we make?"

"Anything."

"You trying to get your dick sucked when we get home, huh?"

"I'm always trying to get my dick sucked by you, but I'm just telling the truth. I didn't care what it was, I'm just happy it's you having my baby." I saw tears start to stroll down her cheeks as I pulled into the garage. "What's wrong, ma?" I asked as I unbuckled my seatbelt to turn and face her.

"What you just said, Kill," she sniffled.

"About you having my baby?" I quizzed and she nodded. I leaned over into her seat and kissed her full lips a couple times. "I'm for real, I can't think of any other woman that I would rather have my baby." I thumbed her tears away, and then slipped my tongue into her mouth.

I was thinking about getting married, but if I said that right now she might cry her eyes out, so I'd save it for another day.

TWELVE

Kantwan

"**S**o I think it's best that the three of us have our main area of focus, but assist one another in them all. I've already sat down and figured out who would be best doing what," Kill explained as we sat in the den of his home.

Although not sure at the beginning about this whole thing, I was ready to work. For some reason this shit had my adrenaline on high, and I wasn't as worried as I was before. I was ready to make this money. I prayed for a way out of Costco, and here it was.

"Alright, so, I think it's best that I focus on balancing the accounts, books, and shipment schedule. I will be keeping my eye on how much is being sold, and making sure that everything is being accounted for. If I find that any niggas are stealing or trying to bull-shit me, I will take care of them as well. As far as you, Kant, I think you should focus on the deliveries. Now, the supplier that Axel had, has some really good shit, so we're gonna stick with his ass. I asked for him to have the product brought over in a food delivery truck, driven by two women named Rachel and Tanya. Here is the phone that they will contact you on whenever they've arrived, so that you can go meet them. You'll be responsible for making sure all of the product gets to the warehouse. Then Elijah, that's where you come in. You will be in charge of making sure everything is divided up and delivered properly to the traps. I want us all to keep in mind that if there are any discrepancies in any of these areas, all of us will be responsible, but naturally whoever is in charge will be in the most trouble. When it comes to the money count that will be my area as well, but something we all take part in. Do you guys have any questions or anything?"

"It's pretty much self explanatory. Just one thing, the chicks are already stored in here? Or will they be calling from unknown numbers or what?" I asked and lifted the phone up.

"Nah, they're stored in there so that you'll know who's calling," Kill replied.

"I don't have any questions, I pretty much got the shit handled," Elijah chimed in.

"Cool, so just so we can make sure. I will handle how much product is delivered, making sure it's en route, the books, and accounts, as well as the day's earnings count. Elijah, you will be taking care of getting the product to the traps, making sure it's being divided up properly, and also collecting money. As far as that goes, we don't want the houses holding too much, so I will let you figure out a cap. And Kantwan, you will be making sure the product gets in safely and makes it to Eli," Kill explained once more.

"Sounds good," Elijah smiled.

"Alright, cool. So the first delivery is in two days Kant, so make sure that phone is charged and all that good stuff. We need everything running like a well oiled machine around here."

"I got you," I nodded.

"Well, meeting time is over," Kill smiled and then set a bottle of Bourbon on the table. He then grabbed some glasses from his liquor shelf, and set them down onto the table before pouring some liquor into them. "I'm in the process of getting Shea out."

"Word? How long you think it's gonna take?" I quizzed happily. I missed my brother.

"Shouldn't be too long. I don't have an exact date or anything, but the bro should be home soon."

"Does he know?" Elijah questioned.

"Nah, I wanna get a sense of when he's gonna be out before I tell him. I don't wanna mention it this early and some shit goes wrong, letting him down."

"I almost killed Portland's ass the other day," Elijah sighed, changing the subject.

"What the fuck? Why?" Kill chuckled.

"Because he was up in my face trying to score some drugs, and when I told him I didn't have shit, he grabbed on me like a fucking fool."

"What stopped you?" I inquired.

"The fact that he's Donovan's father, Ivy would be mad at me for being reckless, and the fact that his sister is Kill's girl. But I had my hammer to his head, I only needed to press down on the trigger."

"That nigga is lucky you have a conscience."

"Yeah, because if it had been Shea's ass, ole boy would have been dead," I said as we all laughed in unison.

"Don't I know it."

"You think he's gonna be a problem? Like a for real one?" I asked.

"Not if he knows what's good for him," Kill raised a brow before sipping his drink, as Elijah and I nodded in agreement. I hoped not, because damn would that cause a lot of problems on the home front.

We discussed a few more things, continued to chill, and then Kill let us know when the meeting with the whole team would be before we went our separate ways.

Two Days Later...

It was around 5am, and the sound of a phone ringing woke me up. I sat up to look at the three damn phones I now carried, to see the name Tanya on the screen. I immediately knew it was game time, and that I couldn't mess this shit up. I knew I wouldn't, but there was still some nervousness there.

"Hello?" I answered.

"Hey, Kant right?" she asked to be sure.

"That's right."

"Okay, we will be at the location by 6:30am."

"Aight, cool."

We disconnected and then I went to the bathroom to start getting ready. I didn't wanna lay back down and oversleep, so I just decided to get up now. There was no room for me to fuck up, especially not for the first damn day on the job basically.

Once I was showered, I brushed my teeth, and then came out of the bathroom to get dressed. I saw Cheyla was awake, and I knew her crazy ass would be when she heard me talking on the phone. Her sneaky ass always tried to pretend like she wasn't paying attention to my phone conversations when she really was. I would sometimes just leave and go talk in my office, because I'd recently had it soundproofed.

"Who was that, Kant?" Cheyla asked calmly.

"Work."

"Work is named Tanya?"

"Yep."

I looked over my shoulder after pulling some boxers from the drawer, and her little ass was pouting and shaking her head. I began laughing as I put some deodorant on, because she was so ridiculous. She knew she had nothing to worry about, but she was still paranoid for some reason.

"What the fuck is so funny? I'm not about to sit up here and play stupid, nigga. I don't know what type of bitches you're used to, but I'm not the one," she spat.

"Play stupid? How are you playing stupid, Cheyla?"

"You expect me to believe you're fucking working with Tanya? Okay nigga. If I had somewhere else to go right now, I would. But don't trip, I'll figure some shit out," she said as she sat up. She pulled out her little Jessica Simpson suitcase as I continued laughing. This was for real the funniest shit ever.

"I'm not even gonna dignify that with a response, Cheyla. You know deep down I'm not fucking around on you, so you can kill the theatrics. I'm not feeding into that bullshit. If you want a nigga to have problems with, you need to be with someone else," I stated calmly as I began to get dressed.

"Just tell me who she is," she whined.

"She is someone who I do business with! I just told yo' nosey, annoying ass that!"

"Fine," she plopped down on the bed.

"When I get back your face better be fixed, Cheyla. The only thing I wanna do when I step foot in here is eat and fuck, so you better be in the mood to provide both." And with that said, I left her psycho ass sitting there, looking pretty and dumb.

Once I left the house, I drove to the warehouse to pick up the Nissan NV Passenger whip that Kill advised me to drive. I parked my own vehicle under the warehouse like he'd instructed, and then drove out in the van.

I pulled up to the meeting spot and saw two girls who appeared to be from the islands. Tanya kind of had an accent on the phone, but I couldn't really tell too much. It's not like it was some iPhone we were talking on.

I grabbed my skullcap and pulled it down onto my head, because I could feel how cold it was even from inside of the car. As I climbed out, I saw them fold their arms simultaneously, as they waited for me to near them. The truck they drove read, *Sweet Bellini Bakery*.

"Rachel," one stuck her hand out and she sounded almost identical to Rihanna, confirming she was from the Caribbean.

"Kantwan," I said and then reached to shake her hand then Tanya's.

"Okay, so let's start putting this stuff up," Rachel smiled and turned on her heels.

I couldn't help but watch her ass the whole way. Her figure was perfect, but I still preferred Cheyla's small shapely frame.

Tanya unlatched the back door of the truck, causing it to slowly rise up, exposing the contents. There were brown boxes everywhere, labeled to look just like bakery items. I saw some were bagels, brownies, fritters, doughnuts, and all kinds of other shit. We each began loading boxes onto a dolly, and then taking them over to the van I drove. After about thirty minutes we were all done, and I took the fake work order just in case I was pulled over.

"Okay, each box has a layer on top and on the bottom with the actual food listed, just as Kill requested," Tanya explained.

"So the bagel boxes have actual bagels on top and on the bottom?" I asked to be clear and they both nodded. "Fasho. Once everything is double checked, Kill will get up with Darrow to pay."

Darrow Santana was our supplier, and the only way Kill agreed to work with him was after we verified the first shipment was legit. Once we could trust him, we would begin exchanging money and product at the same time. So today, I would only be taking the product, and once it passed Kill's inspection, he would handle paying Darrow for this specific shipment.

"Exactly, nice meeting you Kantwan," Rachel grinned, licked her full lips, and then ran her hand down her long ponytail.

"Likewise. So see you guys in two days," I responded.

"Yep, bye," Tanya said and they both waved before rushing back to the bakery truck.

I climbed into the van, and then sped off towards the warehouse to pack all the shit away, so Elijah could bring the team and begin dividing and delivering. Once I was finished with that, I put the van back into the garage, removed the New York license plate, and then climbed into my Mustang to head home to pissy ass Cheyla.

I entered my home and checked my phone to see it was now 10am. I walked to the den since I heard music coming from it, and just as I'd suspected, I saw Cheyla watching TV on the couch, with her sexy legs spread out.

"Is your attitude gone?" I peeked into the den.

"Yes," she nodded and smiled at me.

"Good, let's go get in the Jacuzzi." I stuck my hand out, and she cut the music off before slipping her hand into mine.

We left out of the den together, and then walked up to the bedroom.

"I'm sorry about earlier, you know I'm just obsessed with you," she said as we began to peel our clothes off in the bedroom, and grab some pool towels.

"I know, and I feel the same. But you have to understand that I'm not that type of nigga. If another woman has my attention to the point where I wanna fuck, I'm gonna break it off before I cheat. That won't even happen though shorty, I fuck with you and you should know that by now."

"I do."

THIRTEEN

Elijah

"I'm about to cum, fuck," Ivy whimpered as I pounded between her legs.

Her pussy had a nigga's head gone, and sometimes I didn't know if I'd be able to pull out in time. However, I knew if I fucked up and nutted in her pretty ass, she would go the fuck off and start making me strap up. I didn't want either of those happening, so I was gonna continue to follow the rules.

"Me too ma, shit," I grunted. I gave three more hard long pumps, and even though her pussy was gripping my dick like a muthafucka, and begging me to stay, I pulled out and came on the towel she was lying on. "Damn baby," I panted as I looked down at her.

A sweet smile covered her face, and then she rolled over. That smile alone let me know she knew how lethal her shit was. She could make me do anything because of the power she held between her legs. A part of me didn't like that, but wasn't shit I could do it about it now.

I picked the towel up, nicely folded it so that nothing would spill, and then I rushed it to the laundry room. I returned to the bedroom shortly after, and then climbed into the bed with my shorty. Just thinking about how low-key sprung I was getting, had me wanting to talk to her ass about a few things. I had no plans on letting anybody else get up in that. Ivy wasn't going nowhere unless she planned to snap that pussy off and leave it on the dresser.

"Has your baby's daddy called you?" I asked as she snuggled up to me.

"Yeah, he wanted to see the baby."

"And what did you say?"

"I told him I would let him see him when I had some time," she sighed.

"Oh, so then why did you meet him at the motel that day?" I questioned and I could feel her body tense up.

I knew her ass was lying that day she claimed she was going to Raleigh's. I could see all in her face how worried she was when I asked where she was going. She wouldn't have been that nervous if she was just going to Raleigh's house, and my mind immediately knew whatever she was doing involved Portland.

So what did the crazy side of me do? I followed her ass. And because she was speeding and in such a rush, I didn't even have to be as discreet as one would think. She paid no attention to the fact that someone was following her. That was bad for more than one reason.

Upon hearing my question, she quickly sat up and looked down at me with a worried expression. I pursed my lips and bucked my eyes, waiting on her excuse as to why she'd lied.

"Eli, I'm sorry. I just knew you would be upset if I told you."

"Why would I be upset?" I furrowed my brows.

If she let this nigga fuck, I was murdering him on sight, putting her ass out my crib, and keeping Donovan. I laughed at myself on the inside.

"Because you said you didn't want him seeing Donovan, right?"

"No, I said I didn't want *you* seeing him with Donovan alone. So why the fuck would you do that? It's disrespectful for you to be meeting with this nigga behind my back, knowing I just said I wouldn't like it. I'm your man and when I say not to meet with another nigga alone, the shit shouldn't happen Ivy."

"Eli, he's Donovan's dad, I should be able to meet him with the baby whenever I feel like it."

"Yeah and you can, just when there is a third party like Jersey, Cheyla, or Raleigh. And that nigga ain't his fucking dad, he's a fucking sperm donor. If he really cared about Donovan, that visit would've lasted longer than the five minutes you were in there."

"I know. I'm sorry, baby. I promise the next time he wants to see Donovan it will be at Raleigh's house, since she's right down the street from where I used to live."

"Good."

"You forgive me?" she smiled and straddled me.

"I don't even know yet. You need to understand that you're my woman and I'm trying to protect you. If you don't want that nigga found dead somewhere, do what I ask. He's reckless Ivy, and if he lays a hand on you or Donovan, I'm killing his ass and there won't be anything you can say to stop me from doing so," I responded. I stared up into her face to let her know I wasn't playing any games, and she nodded while massaging my dick. "I know what you doing ma, mmm, and it ain't gon' work."

"It's not?" she cocked her head as she continued to make my erection grow. Once it was nice and hard, she slid her sopping wet pussy down on it.

"Fuck," I threw my head back just a little as she began to bounce slowly.

Every time she hit the base of my dick, she whimpered and scrunched up her face. The sight alone was enough to make me nut. Her blue eyes became glazed over as she continued to bounce on me, looking like she was about to cry.

"Oh, I'm gonna cum so hard Eli, shit," she cried out.

She started moving faster, taking me high as hell. I gripped her ass roughly, and then we both screamed out as we came. We panted heavily, and then I realized she hadn't hopped off. She hadn't realized it yet, and I didn't wanna ruin the mood by mentioning it.

"I'm serious about what I said, Ivy."

"I know, and I promise it won't happen again," she exhaled heavily as she continued to lay on my chest with my dick resting inside of her.

I hoped she was telling the truth, because I was itching for a reason to pump some lead into Portland.

FOURTEEN

Jersey

I was sitting on the couch in the den, just stuffing my face and watching movies. I had pickles, chips, doughnuts, cookies, candy, juice, and everything else that I loved these days, thanks to Kill. I enjoyed pigging out and not having to answer to anyone about it. Funny enough, I was all belly and had only gained a little weight that I didn't mind being there. Kill couldn't keep his hands off me, so it was all working out. I smiled as I bit into my turkey sandwich that was piled with chips in it.

My phone rang and I looked down to see it was from my old home that I used to share with my parents. I frowned because this was the last place I expected anyone to be calling from. My father was dead, so who the fuck would be calling me from that line? Shoot, he didn't even call when he was alive.

"Hello?" I picked up.

"Hi Jersey, are you busy?" Trixie asked. I rolled my eyes as soon as her high ass Minnie Mouse voice came through.

"No I'm not busy, what's up?" I sat up and stuffed the rest of a half eaten doughnut into my mouth.

"Great, can you come by the house?"

"When?"

"I was hoping right now."

"Okay, sure."

Now usually I would've told that bitch to go suck a fat one, but I was interested in finding out why the hell she wanted to see me, so I took the high road. Hopefully she didn't piss me off, because lately all I'd been wanting to do was eat, fuck, and fight. I couldn't do the latter, so the depravity was killing me.

I quickly hung up and then began grabbing my snacks so I that could put them away. I was really trying to figure out what Trixie wanted to talk to me about before I even got over there. It couldn't be about the funeral, because she wasn't part of handling that in any way. My sister Raleigh and I were setting up the funeral since Kill offered to pay for it. I really didn't want him to, but if he didn't we would have to wait and see how much my dad's life policy was, in order to use that. That would take way too fucking long since they were bullshitting us, so I was forced to take Kill up on his offer.

The insurance company was taking their sweet time because of the circumstances of my father's death. They were trying not to give us the payout because he was murdered by one of the beneficiaries, and didn't die from health issues or natural causes. My dad's lawyer was trying to help us out, by explaining to them that his kids should still get their portion, just not my mother since she was the killer. Right now they were in the process of reviewing everything, so we just had to sit and fucking wait.

Once I finished putting up my snacks, I went and put on some maternity True Religion jeans, a simple t-shirt, and some sneakers. Hopping into my Porsche, I pulled out of the driveway and headed to my father's home. We lived in the same neighborhood now, so I got there in no time.

After parking my car in the large roundabout driveway, I climbed out and knocked on the door. I was expecting Hannah to answer, but it was Trixie instead. Her hair was in that same bob that she always wore, and instead of her usual shorts and tube top get up, she wore a skin tight dress.

"Welcome, Jersey," she grinned.

"Hey, where is Hannah?"

"Oh, she quit after the incident, it was just too much for her to handle, you know."

"I bet," I sighed as I followed her to the dining room. When I walked in, a white man in a suit was sitting down with some papers in front of him.

"Good morning Ms. Warren, I'm Jacob Laden, Trixie's lawyer." He stood up and greeted me.

"Hi," I responded a little confused as to what was happening.

"Have a seat, please, Ms. Warren." He pointed to the chair, so I pulled it out and sat down.

"I'm sorry, what is going on?" I finally asked.

"Well Jersey, I'm gonna let my lawyer explain it to you. I'm not that great with words," Trixie giggled.

She was being super nice and friendly for some reason. She was never rude to me or anything, but she was never this warm while my dad was alive. I could tell she just tolerated me while he was living.

"Ms. Warren, although the hearing for the will hasn't taken place yet, we do know some details of it. One of the main details that concerns Ms. Royce here is the home."

I had no idea what Trixie's last name was, but at least I knew now.

"What about the home?"

"Sweetie, your father hadn't gotten around to changing his will, because frankly he had no idea he would go so soon. But due to that unfortunate event, he died way before any of us expected him to go, and therefore wasn't able to update it as he intended," Trixie smiled, finally interjecting.

"Okay?" I frowned. Get to the fucking point, damn.

"So he left the house to you, because you were his baby. He felt that when he died, you may need the house before your older siblings," Trixie explained.

"Alright, what's the problem? I need you guys to get to the point. I'm hungry and I wanna relax, so if you could please stop beating around the damn bush, I would appreciate that."

"Well see, I live here, and I can't live here if the house is yours. I mean unless you're okay with me staying here," she reached across the table and touched my hand, clearly having lost her mind.

I slowly moved it from her touch.

"I'm definitely not okay with you living here in this house. I wasn't okay with it before my father died, so I'm damn sure not okay with it now. It was disrespectful to my mother then, and it still is now."

"Ms. Warren, are you honestly taking up for your mother? I mean she murdered your father for Christ's sake," the lawyer Jacob decided to chime in with his thin lipped ass.

"If you can sit here and defend some home wrecking hoe without any shame, then you're damn right I can defend my mother for murdering a man who didn't give two shits about his family for the past couple of years!" I barked.

"Jersey, he did love you, and I'm not a home wrecker! Your father was unhappy long before I came into the picture!" Trixie yelled.

"And how the hell can you be so sure? All I know is that if this house is in fact mine due to the will, you will not be able to live here! I would rather bring my dad back to life and murder his ass all over again, before I allow you to live in the house that my mother sacrificed her dreams for!" I banged on the table angrily, making them both jump. If it wasn't for my daughter, I would've been across this damn table already.

"Jersey, you don't wanna play this game with me, honey."

"You're right, I don't. I'm not playing any games with you. As soon as that will is read and we confirm that this place is mine, I'm giving you one week to clear the fuck out or you'll regret it!" I hissed.

"Ms. Warren—"

"I'm done here. Fuck the both of you!" I stormed out.

"Ms. Warren, have a heart! Ms. Royce has nowhere to go if she can't be here!" her lawyer called after me.

"Just like my mother, siblings, and I had nowhere to go when she moved in. She didn't say one word to my father to convince him to at least allow his children to stay! So please save that sob story for someone else. Good luck on your life, Trixie; the strip club I just left is hiring."

I quickly left out of the house and got into my car. I was dead fucking serious. If that will read that this house was mine, Trixie was out on her ass. Shit, if the house was given to Portland or Raleigh, she was still out on her ass.

Did she really expect me to have any sort of sympathy for her when she had ruined my family? I wanted to slap the shit out of her for inviting me over here and asking me to do such a thing for her. She was part of the reason my family was ruined, so she could kiss my ass. I struggled for three damn years along with my family, so hearing that she was gonna be homeless didn't faze me one bit! If I had a pocket full of fucks to give, and she needed one, I still wouldn't give it to her! You know why? Because I didn't give a fuck!

FIFTEEN

Cheyla

I was walking out of the hair salon feeling like a new woman. I really enjoyed being able to get my hair done on the regular now. Pressing it myself was never fun, and it never looked as good as when the professionals did it. My favorite part was getting that good old shampoo and scalp massage though.

"Cheyla!"

I turned around to see Monty walking with some light-skinned chick and two niggas. I stood there and waited until he got closer to me, then I gave a faint smile. I really wasn't in the mood to make conversation with him and his friends, but I felt obligated to give him some of my time since he did save me that night.

"How are you doing, ma?" he smiled.

"I'm doing good, how are you?"

"I'm great. Oh Cheyla, this is my girlfriend Tahvi, and my brothers Kevin and Isaiah," Monty introduced me.

The girl rolled her eyes, and the guys shook my hand. I laughed at the fact Tahvi rolled her eyes, because she had absolutely nothing to worry about. Monty and I were just cool, and not even as cool as she was probably thinking. If she saw my nigga, she would understand that Monty wasn't even on my radar.

"Well nice seeing you Monty, and nice meeting you three," I smiled before turning on my heels to walk away.

"Hey, we're having a party next weekend, you should come!" Monty called after me.

"Umm, I will think about it."

"The pay is good," his brother Kevin added.

"The pay?" I raised a brow.

"Yeah, the pay for you to perform. A lot of hustlers and shit are gonna be there with fat ass pockets, Cheyla. So not only will you get the $1200 just to come, but you'll also get all the tips," Monty bit his lip and smiled, as his girlfriend adjusted her grip on his arm. She smirked at me as if she felt like she was better than me because I was a stripper.

"Monty, I don't dance anymore, I told you—"

"Just take my card and call that number if you change your mind," Kevin spoke for Monty as his eyes wandered all over my body.

I took the card, stuffed it into my jean pocket, and then walked to my car. When I got in I sat there for a minute, wondering about the offer. I was done stripping, but I had no job at the moment, which I didn't like. I'd become accustomed to having my own income, so this felt weird to me. The only money I had was Kantwan's money, and I hated going to him with my hand out. I knew he didn't mind, but I did. I'd tried getting a job, but just like last time, no one wanted to hire me, which is how I ended up at the strip club in the first place. And as much as Ivy complained about the call center, I definitely wasn't going there. She said you'd be fired if you hung up, so it was no point in me even wasting my time applying. As soon as someone got foul with me, they'd hear that dial tone.

The amount of money that Monty was offering sounded good as hell. I couldn't do it though, I just couldn't. I'd come too far to go back to that lifestyle, and I knew it would bring me nothing but trouble. I didn't wanna come in contact with anything that would have me ready to pop pills again.

I cranked my car and sped to my home with Kantwan. Since the shop took forever to finish my hair, it was already 9pm at night. I was her second to last client that got out, and the only reason I didn't say shit was because it slipped my mind when I saw how laid my damn hair was. That was the only downside to visiting the shop; you got left under the dryer for ample amounts of time, because the stylist overbooked and spent too much time gossiping and eating. Chante was trifling, but she knew what the fuck she was doing.

When I got inside my home, I immediately went to the kitchen and pulled the pork chops from the fridge, since I'd placed them there before I left, to thaw. I washed my hands and then began seasoning them, before placing them into the oven. I wanted to have that started before I went and undressed and shit. I heard the sound of video games, letting me know Kantwan was in the den, so I headed over.

"Hey baby," I smiled once I entered and walked closer to him.

"Mmm, you smell like perfume and seasoning," he smiled making me laugh.

"Shut up!" I nudged him. He paused the game and then sat me down into his lap. I played with his chain hairs for a little bit, while admiring his sexy ass features. "What would you think if I went back to Starzz?"

"What? Why would you go back there?"

"I just wanna make some money, that's why."

"Get a regular job, but one that won't interfere with school."

"What if I did private parties?"

"Cheyla, hell no. I'd rather you go back to Starzz than do private parties, the fuck?" he twisted his face up, and I couldn't tell if he was irritated or disgusted. Maybe it was a combination of both.

"Well I was just asking because private parties pay a lot, and they wouldn't be as frequent, giving me time for school."

"No shorty, I've seen *The Players Club*; I know what happens at private parties," he shook his head and shoved a chip into his mouth.

"It's not like that, Kant," I chuckled. "I would only go to the ones held by people that I know, I promise."

"Cheyla, no. I don't want you doing private parties. Just do school and I got you."

"What if we break up? I won't have anything and I will be assed out, Kantwan!"

"We're not gonna fucking break up."

"How do you know?"

"Because we're not. I can feel it, you're gonna be mine forever." My heart melted a little, but I still needed to play tough, that was just who I was.

"You can't be so sure."

"Well I'm sure baby, so chill out. I don't want niggas looking at your body, especially in a damn hotel room with no security."

"You met me in the club, Kant."

"Exactly, so they saw your body enough. Now it's for my eyes and no one else's. The only time you need to be popping that pussy is for me. And I can throw some cash at you every now and then," he grinned.

"You know I got you for free." I grabbed his face and then pecked his full lips slowly, so that I could bask in the moment.

I exhaled heavily because I was really interested in getting that money. But I loved my man more, so I wasn't going to defy him. If there was only some way for me to make that easy bread and keep my man...

SIXTEEN

Ivy

———

Saturday Morning...

*T*oday I was giving Portland's ass another chance to see Donovan. The only difference was that we were meeting at Raleigh's house. I knew Elijah was serious about me lying to him and about me meeting with Portland alone, so I didn't wanna fuck with him. The nigga had found me out once, and I'm sure he would easily catch my ass again. I refused to lose my nigga over Portland's *only wanna be a daddy sometimes* ass.

I parked across the street from the home that Raleigh and Mrs. Warren used to share, then got out to get my baby from his car seat.

"Mom..." Donovan said and then continued talking in gibberish.

He only knew how to say Mom and a couple other things. He knew how to ask me stuff without words, which I thought was the cutest thing. He would just hold whatever the item was in the air, and wait for me to nod or shake my head no. It was little things like that, that Portland's ass didn't even know.

As I made my way across the street, I ignored the hoots and hollers from the porch sitting niggas. What in the entire fuck would make them think I wanted a nigga that believed sitting on the porch from sun up to sun down was equivalent to a nine to five? I wasn't surprised though, because men were just stupid like that. Knocking on the door, I waited for Raleigh to open it while kissing my baby's plump cheeks.

"You are so cute, Don," I smiled at him as he smiled at me. He then grabbed my face and kissed my cheek in response, before speaking in gibberish.

"Hey babe," Raleigh answered the door and hugged me. She kissed Donovan's forehead, and then backed away to let me in.

I spotted Portland sitting on the couch, and when he saw me his face lit up. It felt good that he was happy to see his son, because lately it seemed like he didn't even care about him. I still felt like he only hit me to see Donovan, because he really wanted to see me. I wasn't gonna jump to conclusions though.

"Raleigh, can you give us some privacy," Portland told his sister.

"Okay, I will, but don't get to acting stupid, Portland. I will call the cops on your ass," Raleigh spat.

"Calm yo' ass down, ain't nobody getting buck, aight?" he smacked his lips. I sat on the La-Z-Boy across from him, with my baby still in my lap. "Come sit over here, Ivy," he patted the couch.

"I'm good right here, Portland."

"Just come over here, because you know he gon' act a fool if I come and take him." I rolled my eyes and then stood up to go sit next to him.

I placed Donovan on the middle couch cushion, hoping he would allow his father to touch him. Portland scooped him up and kissed his cheeks, and thank God he didn't scream and cry. He did push his face away, which made me chuckle lightly.

"So are you ever gonna tell me where you've been staying?" he asked as he fixed Donovan's shirt. Donovan squirmed and kicked until Portland let him down so he could walk around Raleigh's living room.

"Why does it matter?"

"Because my son is staying there, and I wanna make sure he's safe."

"You don't care about him any other time, Portland, so there is no need for me to tell you where we've been. All you need to know is that he's safe and happy."

"Well I also wanted to come stay with you guys. I miss my family, Ivy. I promise I'm getting my shit together."

"Getting your shit together? You should have your shit together, nigga!"

"See, look at you always judging! That's why I was always sliding up in other bitches, because you could never just appreciate what the fuck I was doing! The same bitch that was shaking her ass for coins while her nigga was locked up!" he seethed.

"You're exactly right! I was shaking my ass for coins, because my wanna be gangsta ass nigga didn't know how to hustle right and got caught!"

Portland stared into my eyes angrily, and then nodded his head slowly.

"Whatever, I'm gon' let that go. The point is Ivy, I miss you and I wanna be together again. I know you miss me too, so why keep playing this game? I told you I'm not fucking with no other females or anything, so just come back home."

"Come back home? What home? Didn't you just ask to come stay wherever Donovan and I are sleeping?"

"Yeah, that would just be for a little while until I got on my feet. I got some plans in the works and shit, and I'm gonna be making some good money."

"What are those plans?"

"Ivy, you don't need to—"

"No, I wanna know what plans you have?"

I didn't give a fuck what plans he had, really; I just wanted to catch him in his lies. This nigga never had a solid plan to get money that didn't involve robbing small banks, liquor stores, or corner boys. His ass would be locked up soon; I could already feel it.

"What else do niggas with my resume do, huh? You know I'm gonna be in the streets, but I'm gonna be working with some cats who know what they're doing. Shit is gonna be safer, ma."

"Portland, if you ever wanna be able to keep Donovan without me breathing down your neck, you're gonna have to get it together. My son will not be caught in the crossfire when you don't cover your tracks well. You ever heard of street smarts? You need to get some before you step foot back into the game."

"Fuck you talking like you know?"

"I do know. I've been in the company of people who know what they were doing, and it just showed me how much you had no idea about what you were doing before you got locked up."

"Ivy, get out of here with that bullshit, aight? I don't need my woman telling me how I need to run my shit! I know what the fuck I'm doing!" he screamed almost, making Donovan look at him with furrowed brows. I thought it was hilarious that even Donovan found Portland to be doing the most, and he was just a baby.

"I'm not your woman anymore, Portland."

Donovan walked over to me and climbed into my lap on his own. He turned his attention towards Portland, I guess trying to protect me from his father.

"Why are you talking like this whole separation is about to be permanent?" he frowned.

"Because it is, Portland! We are done, boo! I don't know how many times, ways, or languages I have to say it in. We are no longer gonna be together." He bounced his leg angrily as I adjusted Donovan in my lap.

"So you gon' keep this shit up for how long, Ivy? Huh? Because every time you wanted to be strong in the past, you always ended up crying in my voicemail about how you made a mistake and you want me to come home."

I was so embarrassed when he mentioned that. I was such a sad ass case back then, but you couldn't pay me to go back to the old Ivy. At that time, I felt like Portland was my life, and without him I would be miserable. Now I couldn't understand my thought process for anything. The sight of him and the sound of his voice always made me feel like I was sucking on a lemon. I loved my baby, but damn did I wish I was more careful about who I had a child and laid down with.

"Well that won't happen this time, Portland."

"So you wanna for real break up?" he smiled as if he just knew I was gonna be groveling soon. "That means when I'm out smashing other bitches, you can't say shit."

"That is totally fine, Portland. I couldn't care less who you smash, buddy."

He burst into laughter and nodded.

"Alright, Ivy. I'm gonna give yo' ass what you want, but when you get depressed because a nigga ain't fucking with you anymore on some real shit, you better keep your tears and voice messages to yourself."

SEVENTEEN

Kilexis

______

"*D*oes anyone have any questions about how things will be running from now on?" I asked the room that was filled with my team.

I'd purchased that building from that mannish ass realtor, and it was definitely coming in handy. Kantwan, Elijah, and I all had offices in it, there was a break room of sorts, beautiful bathrooms, and heavy security as well.

Just like I assumed, I was always needing to have a meeting, and unlike Axel, all these niggas weren't about to be up in my crib with my shorty and kid. Axel had gotten robbed plenty of times, but because they only took small things like small jewelry, microwaves, and VCRs, he never sweated it. Me on the other hand, I didn't give a fuck if all you took was a bottle of my Axe body wash, yo' ass was gettin' murked. It was about the principle, not what you took.

Everyone in the room shook their heads 'no' in response to my question, so I let everyone go. I wanted to get home because I had to do some bookkeeping, and because I wanted to talk to my girl about a job I had for her. I needed her help with something, and I knew she would be excited to get paid for doing something that she loved.

As everyone was clearing out, I saw Ahmad and Dante enter the room, escorted by my goon Stone. They let everyone pass them, and then sat down at my conference table as if they were scheduled to meet with me. Stone knew better, and I made a mental note to get in his ass about just allowing niggas to come up here and see me. This was exactly why I had hired two new back up guys, because Stone was dumb as fuck and I couldn't afford his mistakes anymore. I gave Stone a look as he backed out of the conference room, and I could smell the fear coming from him.

"Is there something I can help you guys with?" I asked as I continued to pack my shit up.

"We just wanted to chop it up with you for a little bit about some stuff," Ahmad replied.

"I have about ten minutes to spare," I said before sitting back down at the head of the table. I checked my watch to mentally document the time, because exactly ten minutes from now, they were gettin' the fuck out.

"We wanna get down with you. So how can we help? Where do you need us?" Dante quizzed.

"Well right now there aren't any positions really open. The traps are doing great, and I'm pretty sure you guys aren't into being corner boys, so I'm sorry I don't have anything for you at this time."

These niggas weren't even working for their father when he was the boss, so what did they expect from me? If yo' own dad didn't put you on, what the fuck would make you think that I would? They knew damn well Kill Camren wasn't no damn fool, so I was confused as to why they tried to slide up in here and get some sort of favoritism.

"Well you're right about being a corner boy, that's not an option when it's our father's empire," Ahmad said and tried to chuckle lightly. I didn't crack a smile.

"It used to be his. It's mine now and I've switched up a lot of things."

"He passed it down to you so—"

"Let's not get shit twisted. I was bringing your father the most money. My cousin and I were pushing the most into the streets, so let's not really get into the specifics. There is a reason your father gave his empire to me and not you, right? So let's not pretend like there was some sort of raffle style choosing here. You asked if I had a job for you and I told you I didn't. I don't know what to tell you, other than that if something opens up I may hit your line. But with the way you're trying to come at me like I didn't work in this field half of my life, and like I got shit easy, I may not look out for you at all."

"My father—"

BAM!

I slammed my fist into the thick wooden table, cutting Ahmad's half pint ass off.

"Your father has nothing to do with this operation, and therefore anything going on with it is under my fucking control! I run everything, and unfortunately for you niggas, that includes who gets put on."

They both stared at me, I guess surprised by my behavior. I was a calm ass nigga, but when you came at me foul I let the beast out.

"Aye man, we're not here to argue with you or disrespect you in anyway. We just wanna be of some assistance to you. I know you got the smarts to run this shit that's why my dad chose you to take over, but we wanna be a part of it," Dante explained.

"I understand that, and like I said, if something opens up, I will let you know. Stone, please escort them out of the building," I told my goon. Stone waved them over and then walked them out of the building. "Come in and close the door," I spoke to Stone once he returned.

"Wh-what's up boss?" he stammered and rubbed his hands together.

"Since when the fuck do you just let anybody come up in my building without letting me know?"

"I don't, but I thought since they're Axel's sons—"

"Stone, there are only two people that you're allowed to let up here without my permission, and they're Jesus Christ himself and Jersey. If it's not one of them, don't let them by."

"Even if it's—"

"What did I just say?" I asked after whipping my pistol out and pressing it under his chin, forcing his head to tilt back.

"O-only Jersey or Je-Jesus himself."

I pressed the gun deeper into his skin, causing him to shut his eyes tightly and momentarily, to ease the pain.

"I don't know if you get it, Stone."

"No, no, I get it!"

"Nah, now that I've had to pull a gun on you, you hate me don't you?" I questioned with the gun still pressed under his chin.

"No Kill, I swear I don't hate you, man. You're just doing your job and I get it!" he pleaded as his eyes became glazed over.

"I can't afford to have niggas in my circle that despise me Stone, you know that."

"Kill, I don't—"

POP!

The top of his head burst open, and he fell backwards towards the floor. I messaged to have my new men Rogue and Race come up to clean out my office and get rid of his ass. I hated to get rid of Stone, but once niggas started hating, they also started plotting. I might as well get rid of him now, instead of waiting until after he caused me some harm.

After getting all my shit together, and making sure Rogue and Race finished, I headed home. I found Jersey laid out in the den, asleep, with snacks everywhere like always. She had on a little pajama set, and her belly was protruding even more. Her wild curly hair was in a bun, and hanging off to the side like always. In the worst times, I still found her appealing.

"Jersey," I shook her lightly. Her eyes fluttered, and when she saw it was me she smiled.

"Baby, I missed you." She sat up and fixed her pajamas.

"I've only been gone for two hours."

"I know, but you know how attached I am to you."

"I do have that effect on people, huh?" I smiled and she nodded. I rubbed her belly and then sat next to her before pulling her into my lap. "Shorty, I want you to get some art for my building."

"You're trying to hire me?"

"Yeah, that's the field you're studying, and my building needs some sprucing up. The walls are bland, so I want you to pick out some pieces for me. I've created a business account so that's the money you will use, and I had my lawyer draw up a contract for the job."

"Oh my gosh Kill, I would love to do that. I need the experience. Umm, how much are you paying me?"

"Well, I ate your pussy last night until you cried, so I thought that was enough."

"Kill!" she chuckled.

"I'm serious ma, in the contract it says that the payment will be in head."

"You are so nasty! When did you get such a potty mouth?" she grinned and stroked my beard.

"I don't know. I've always been that way I guess. My mom hated it too, but I couldn't help it."

I just didn't see the harm in saying pussy over vagina, or ass instead of butt. And sex was natural, so why be afraid or embarrassed to talk about it?

"That's so funny. But I don't mind you paying me in head. You have a gift." Jersey stroked my beard.

"I know I do. And right now I want that gift between your legs," I bit my lip and humped upward so she could feel how hard my dick was. "I've been thinking about going ham in that pussy all day."

"Are you ever romantic about it?" she blushed.

"Nope! And you don't like that romantic shit either. You like when I tell you how I wanna beat that pussy up while I'm pulling your hair," I said in a low tone as I yanked her bun back lightly, and sucked on her neck. She placed her small hands on my chest, and moaned softly.

"I do, baby," she finally responded.

She began grinding her hips and pressing her pussy against my erection. She reached down to pull my dick from my sweats, and then I moved her panties and shorts to the side. Slowly sliding down on my dick, she placed her hands on my shoulders for leverage.

"You're already wet as fuck. This pussy be strangling my shit, ma," I panted heavily. Jersey always had the perfect combo—tight and wet.

"Mmmm," she cooed as she began to bounce slowly on it.

"Fuck," I grumbled.

Her pussy was so good that I didn't even need her to be naked right now. Usually a nigga liked to see some titties or ass bouncing, but Jersey's shit was good enough for her to be fully clothed.

"Cum on it, Jersey," I whispered before sucking her lips.

"I am, shit, Kill, I'm gonna cum," she whimpered and began grinding harder on my dick. I felt her release, and it made me shiver a little. I gripped her little waist and then began slamming her down onto my dick, causing us both to cry out like we were being murdered.

"Aaahh, uuuh, aaahh!" we both screamed in unison.

I swear when we had sex I felt like we were exchanging something. It was almost like she gave me some sort of energy and drive, and I gave her strength. This shit was deeper than me digging her out. We both released, and then hugged one another as we kissed passionately.

"Kill, I swear you make me love you more everyday. Every time I think I can't be more in love with you, I somehow fall deeper."

"I feel it too."

"You think it's a good thing?" she panted as I ran my tongue across her neck.

"How can it not be?"

Jersey was my fucking soul mate, and the more time we spent together, the more it made sense as to why we fell so quickly for one another. We were like some fucking magnets, and we made one another stronger. This was my baby, and I would take more than a couple bullets and jail sentences for her ass. As long as I had air in my lungs, Jersey would have no fucking worries. I'd kill the whole city for my shorty.

EIGHTEEN

Ka'Shea Camren

I really don't know what the fuck my brother did, or whom he spoke to, but today was the last day I would spend in jail. I'm not sure why Axel never got me out, but I wasn't gon' sweat the shit. I knew he'd gotten Kill out, and I was worried that it was to kill him, but clearly that wasn't the case. I couldn't wait to get out there and see what the fuck was going on in the free world.

Everything was processed and I was walking out wearing a big ass smile. I had one more year and some change left, but Kill had gotten me out early some kind of way. I didn't wanna ask any questions because honestly, I didn't care. I was free and that was all that fucking mattered.

As soon as I walked out I saw a fresh ass whip, which appeared to be a luxury car. When Kill slipped out of it wearing a smile on his face, I knew shit had somehow changed for the better. I lightly jogged towards my little brother, and we embraced for a couple moments.

"Aight, let me go," he nudged me off as we laughed in unison. We both got into the car and I admired the interior and how nice the shit was.

"When you get this, bro?" I asked.

"About a month ago. Here." He handed me a cell phone, making a grin appear on my face. I didn't even know what kind of phone it was, but I was cool with it.

"What is this?"

"An iPhone, nigga. I forgot how long yo' ass has been put away."

"Nigga, I know what the fuck an iPhone is, I just don't remember them being this big." I inspected the phone as he dipped through the streets.

"They switched that shit up. Anyway, where are you staying? You know you can stay at the house with me."

"Yeah, I could do that. Let me shower at your crib, and then I wanna go see what's up with Mercedes."

"Ugh nigga, why?" Kill frowned making me laugh.

"Since you asked, because I want some pussy."

"I thought you had a little something waiting for you that wasn't Mercedes' ass. Nigga I'd rather you pay for pussy than slide up in her."

"I ain't never paid for pussy, and I'm not about to start now. And the shorty I had waiting for me is a classy lady, she ain't about to give up them panties to me right now." We chuckled together.

"You sure?"

"Yeah, I'm sure, nigga. Plus, I wanna take her on a date first and shit. Not every nigga runs across a real ass female who will give it up on the first night." I shook my head, and he chuckled almost to himself. "What's so funny?"

"Nah, nothing."

<hr>

"**C**ome on so you can clean yourself up and meet my shorty." He waved me over, and then we got out of his car.

"Damn nigga, this is all you?" I asked referring to his big ass house.

He for real needed to put me on game about what he was doing, because the nice houses and cars had me wondering like a muthafucka.

"Yeah it's all me, and it's about to be you too. We need to have a sit down."

"I'm ready. As soon as I bust my nut up in Mercedes, I'll be back to catch up," I smirked and he shook his head.

We walked into the house, and the smell of chocolate cake immediately invaded my nostrils. We headed towards the kitchen, and as the smell became stronger and stronger, my stomach began to grumble. Once we entered, I saw Kill's shorty wearing a dark blue dress. She was pretty as hell with golden skin, wild curly hair, full lips, and a cute little body despite her being pretty pregnant.

"Jersey, this is my brother I told you about, Ka'Shea," Kill introduced us.

"Nice to meet you Ka'Shea, I made food for the occasion."

The three of us began setting dishes out, and my stomach growled loudly at just the smell and sight of it. There was macaroni and cheese, yams, fried chicken, greens, stuffing, and then of course a sexy ass chocolate cake.

"Damn shorty, what is it, Thanksgiving?" I smiled.

"I guess so. Kill told me you loved Thanksgiving, so that's what I made."

"Damn, do you have a sister?" I quizzed and the three of us laughed.

"I do, actually; maybe you can meet her pretty soon."

After we finished carrying the dishes to the dining area, Jersey went and fetched some passion fruit lemonade that she'd whipped up, and then we began digging in. Shorty was a catch for real. Based off what Kill told me, she was a real one, and now that I'd tasted her cooking, I really did wonder if she had a sister. I may need her as back up if the shorty I had waiting for me fell through. I hoped not though because she had my nose wide open.

"So what did you do to my brother, Jersey?" I inquired as I placed a forkful of the moist ass chocolate cake into my mouth.

"What do you mean?" She cocked her head and smiled, as Kill shook his head at me. We were both alike in the sense that we always spoke freely.

"I mean you got him to be in a relationship, which I never thought he would be."

"He's had a girlfriend before, the Margo girl."

"Man, that bitch wasn't no fucking girlfriend. She wasn't nothing but a hoe trying to play a girlfriend. I mean you're having his baby, and he got you living here. You did something," I nodded as she laughed.

"I guess I just have charm, right baby?" she looked at Kill.

"That's right, shorty. Don't listen to this nigga right here."

"Anyway, do you know how to braid hair?" I asked, hoping she could get me right before I stepped out.

"Umm, sure, just two like the ones you have now?"

"Exactly."

"Sure, I got you, but you should definitely wash it first," she responded making Kill snicker and me suck my teeth.

She didn't seem like the type to hold her tongue either, so I knew we'd get along.

I finished my cake, and then Jersey provided me some towels and soap so I could shower. Once I was done, I walked out into the guest room to see Kill had someone purchase me some clothes, shoes, and undergarments. I quickly chose my fit, and then went to look for Jersey so I could get my hair fixed. She braided my shit up pretty quickly, and then I took Kill's Denali to go and see Mercedes. I wanted to fuck with that Lamborghini I saw, but Mercedes lived in the hood and I was not about to get my brother's shit robbed my first day back.

I parked in front of Mercedes' crib on Warner Street, and saw all kinds of niggas hanging around outside like always. Shit hadn't changed since I fucking left, and it was good to know I didn't miss too much. I wouldn't know how to feel if everything was different.

"Shea?" the homie Blow called out to me.

Blow was one of my closest homies outside of my brothers and cousin Elijah. He was the only nigga I trusted around here that wasn't family. We grew up together and from day one, he'd had a nigga's back and likewise.

"What's good with you?" I threw my hands out and we dapped one another up.

"Nigga, I thought you had a year or some shit left! Fuck you doing out here, dressed in the latest shit?" he laughed.

"Aye, all that don't matter, just be happy a nigga is free again."

"I am, and make sure yo' ass don't go back! You here to see Cedes?" he questioned and I nodded.

"Yeah man, what she been up to?"

"She ain't been on no snake shit as far as I know. She got you all over her Instagram page and shit, acting like y'all the new age Bonnie and Clyde."

"Fuck outta here man," I said as we laughed in unison.

"I'm dead serious shorty, she out here reppin' Ka'Shea Camren to the fullest. I know her ass is a fraud though, but I ain't put her on blast. I wanted to though, and let her know you had another jawn waiting at home for you."

"I'm glad you didn't because a nigga is hella backed up and I need that. So I'm thankful you kept that shit a secret."

That female prison guard and I fell out, so for the last two months I hadn't had any pussy. She got mad because she wanted me to be her nigga once I got released and I told her ass no. At that time, I still thought I had a year left, but regardless, I wasn't making no promises I knew I wouldn't keep. A nigga was miserable though when she closed her legs to me, and I almost apologized to her ass, even though I hadn't done shit.

"Of course. Well, I'll let you go handle your handle, and let me know when you wanna let loose."

"I got you, B." I dapped him up and then jogged closer to Mercedes' house. I hopped over her little banister, and then knocked on the little screen door.

I looked to my left, and before I knew it, her sexy ass burst through the door and jumped in my arms, wrapping her legs around my waist. I carried her inside, and went straight to the bedroom after locking the door.

"Damn Shea, you don't wanna catch up first?" she grinned as I pulled her little dress over her head. I just shook my head no, and threw it to the floor. She never wore a bra or panties, and right now it was perfect.

She dropped to her knees and began unbuckling my pants, as I pulled off my shirt. Yanking my pants down, she anxiously stared at my hard dick as I removed my jeans and sneakers.

"I missed you," she whispered before taking my head into her mouth.

I palmed the back of her head, and then threw mine backwards as she began to suck me off. I missed her ass too, but for totally different reasons. Once I felt my nut rising, I pushed her off, and then reached for my jeans to get the condom I bought from the liquor store.

"Lay on your back and spread your legs for me," I instructed her as she climbed onto the bed. She did as I asked, and I licked my lips at the sight before diving in.

I pinned her hands down to the bed, and as soon as I slipped inside her sopping wet walls, I began stroking her ass slowly. I wanted to enjoy the shit a little before I started beating it up.

"Fuck Shea," she whimpered.

Mercedes always had some good pussy, but she was shady as fuck. I knew she was out here getting fucked, but I didn't care too much to find out by whom. I had my eyes set on something else.

Once I had enough of the slow smooth strokes, I lifted myself up into the push up position, and began slamming into her. She was yelling out, and then exploded on my dick, making me go even harder.

"Shit," I growled lowly, and then finally filled the condom up. I took a few deep breaths, and then slid out of her and laid down.

"Baby, I've missed that so much."

"Oh yeah?"

"Yeah." It was quiet for a little bit, and then she asked, "Are we official now? I'm ready for kids and stuff, Shea."

"Damn Cedes, I just got out today! Can I enjoy my freedom before you try and take that shit away?"

"I'm not saying today Shea, but soon. I love you and I'm tired of just being someone you smash on occasions."

"Mercedes, just chill shorty, please. I fuck with you and that's all I'm trying to do right now."

I could've easily burst her bubble about fucking with other niggas, but for what? I didn't give a fuck, and it wasn't because of the shorty I had waiting either, I just didn't care. Mercedes was cool and that was it. I've never seen her as someone I was gonna be with forever. She had good pussy, knew how to roll a blunt, and could suck a mean dick. She was cool sometimes too, which is why she was still getting some of my attention, but other than a few dick downs here and there, Mercedes wasn't getting shit out of me but some nut.

After chilling with her ass for a little longer and smoking some backwoods, I got dressed and headed back to Kill's crib. I wanted to catch up and see about some work. I needed to have my shit in order, not only for myself, but baby girl that I was checking for.

NINETEEN

Kantwan

———————

The Next Day...

I was excited as hell about my brother being out of jail. Unlike Axel, Kill got him out early and with the quickness. I never understood why Axel hadn't pardoned Ka'Shea like he'd done Kill, but whatever, I was just happy my big brother was out. Now shit felt complete, because we would all be rocking together like the old days.

Today we were going to a meeting, but Kill wanted me to pick Ka'Shea up so he could fill him in on what his position was within the operation. He'd told him a little bit about it last night, but he wanted us all to be up on game together.

Ka'Shea called me from his shorty Mercedes' crib, so I knew his ass was over there. If I had been in the car when Kill picked him up from the pen, I wouldn't have let his ass go stay with that bitch. Kill said he tried to convince him not to go visit her, but he refused. I just hated that she tried to pretend like she'd been holding him down when she knew her ass hadn't been. I hadn't heard about her fucking with too many niggas, but Mercedes was a sneaky ass bitch so I'm sure she'd hid it well.

I pulled up to her crib on Warner Street in Browntown. She had a nice little crib, and I wondered who paid the bill for it while Ka'Shea was locked up. He wanted us to drop money off to her ass every now and then, but Kill, Elijah, and I refused. That bitch didn't have any kids by him, so why the fuck did she need bread? I'll be damned if I give her some of my hard earned cash just for her to get her hair and nails done for another nigga. If that bitch wanted money, she knew how the fuck to get it... obviously judging by the upkeep of her home.

Pulling my iPhone out of my pocket, I went into my recent calls and tapped the last call. I waited as the phone rang, and finally Mercedes answered.

"Aye, tell Shea I'm outside," was all I said before I pulled my phone from my ear and hit that end button. I didn't even wanna hear her voice, because it would ruin my mood.

I waited for Ka'Shea to come out, while nodding my head up to a couple people I recognized every now and then. Tommy lived around the corner from here, so even though I was a Hilltop boy, they knew me well. They also knew my car. I'd contemplated purchasing a new one, as Kill had urged me to, but I was used to pushing my fresh ass Mustang. Plus, I'd worked many overtime shifts to have it looking as dope as it did, and I refused to lock it up and waste my hard work.

BAM! BAM!

I looked over to see Ka'Shea's ass knocking on my fucking window. I smacked my lips and hit the unlock button for his ass to slide into my whip.

"Fuck you touching on my fucking windows for, Shea? I just got them muthafuckas cleaned," I hissed as I sped down the street towards Oak.

"Nigga, I'm fresh out the fucking pen and that's all you have to say to me?" he replied and then pulled a blunt from behind his ear.

"Welcome home man, when did you get them braids redone? That guard shorty hooked you up before you left? Thank God because ain't nobody trying to have that wild ass hair in their face, I grinned as I pulled onto the freeway.

I could feel him glaring at me, which only made it funnier. But truthfully, his two French braids were looking freshly braided, and I was happy because I hated for it to be down. Ka'Shea had long ass curly hair since we were kids, and my mom used to let him wear that shit out. That was until he was in fifth grade and someone mistook him for being a little girl. That nigga was hot as hell, and from that day on he wore two long ass French braids most of the time. He occasionally wore that shit out, looking like Scar from the Lion King, but it was rare.

I cracked my window as he smoked his blunt, and then turned the music up a little bit.

"Man, it feels so good to be able to sit and smoke," he commented as he nodded his head to the music.

"I bet you're cherishing the little things."

"I am."

"So you still fucking with Mercedes, man?" I turned my lip up in disgust. His ass was gon' catch something fucking with her.

"I'm *fucking* Mercedes but I ain't fucking *with* her. I was supposed to sleep at Kill's last night, but I ain't had pussy in a while so I came back over."

"Didn't you say you had another shorty waiting for you? Did she turn out to be a nigga like we said?" I laughed and he sucked his teeth.

"Man, fuck you. Hell nah she ain't no nigga. I'm gon' get up with her ass soon. I wanna have my shit together first. I ain't trying to get in her grill while I'm sleeping next to Mercedes or at Kill's crib."

"So you gon' leave Mercedes alone once you get on your feet?"

"I don't know; hopefully, because I'm really trying to see what old girl is about. But umm, Mercedes got that good good, bro," he said and we both burst into laughter. "But Kill tells me that you're dating his little baby mama's best friend, and that Eli is with the other one."

"Yeah, it's true."

"What's your shorty's name? You ain't mentioned her to me, really." He took a pull on the blunt and then handed it to me.

"Cheyla, she's crazy as fuck but for some reason she's perfect to me."

"Listen at this nigga," he chuckled. "Her pussy must be fire. That's the only way a bitch will have a Camren man talking like he in love and shit."

"The pussy is on some other shit. It'll have me killing niggas," I said and he guffawed.

"That's good though. I'm happy yo' picky ass don' finally found someone you can be with. Don't be like me though, stick to one woman. Multiples are too damn stressful."

"Oh shorty, you ain't got to tell me shit," I said as I pulled into the parking lot of the building Kill had purchased.

"Yo, this is the bro's building?" Ka'Shea bucked his eyes, and glanced at the ashtray for a second to ash the blunt, before diverting his attention back to the damn skyscraper.

"Sure is, it's where we hold meetings and shit," I nodded. "I got an office up in here too."

We got out of the car, and then got processed so we could walk into the building. After taking the elevator up, we stepped off and walked through the huge wooden door. Elijah and Kill were already at the table, and when they saw us we all greeted one another.

"Shea, how you feeling man? You ready to get this bread?" Elijah grinned.

"Nigga, when have I not been? I'm just ready to take my orders from the boss," Ka'Shea tapped Kill's arm and they both smiled.

"I've already given Eli and Kant their areas, and since I knew I was getting you out, I put something aside for you. I need you to pick up the evening earnings from the traps, and watch over the trap that serves the more distinguished individuals."

"What do you mean the more distinguished individuals?" Ka'Shea cocked his head.

"Like the doctors, policemen, etc. that get high. I will have a crib set up in Alapocas, which will be a trap on the inside but just a regular home on the outside. I need you to run that shit using a very watchful eye. Make sure them niggas are being discreet and doing what the fuck they're supposed to do. You will drop the product to this house and pick up the earnings from this house, and feel free to dead a nigga if you think they're trying to play us," Kill explained.

"Damn, so you gon' do what you tried to get Axel to do?" I asked.

"Yep, for some reason he only keeps drugs in the bad areas. Rich muthafuckas snort coke and shoot up too. They just do it before they go to work in the morning."

"Well shit, I'm with that." Ka'Shea nodded.

"Everything is being fixed up right now, so until it's ready in about a week, I need you to just help out with the money count every night at the warehouse. All of us do that," Kill said.

"Cool, I'm just ready to get this bread."

The meeting was over and I was just ready to go home to eat and chill. The count was later on around 1am, and then I had to be right back out to meet Rachel and Tanya at 6:30am. As I was walking to my car, my work phone buzzed, which was odd. The only time that happened was when it was time to get the shit from Rachel and Tanya. I opened the phone and went inside it to see a text. My eyebrows almost touched my hairline when I saw it was a picture of Rachel's ass in a thong.

Rachel: *Since I saw you looking during the shipment exchange yesterday.*
She sent right after.

"Aye nigga, open the fuckin' door!" Ka'Shea shouted and hit my passenger door.

"Shut yo' impatient ass up!" I barked and slipped my phone into my pocket before hitting the unlock button on my key.

Rachel was on some bullshit; some sexy ass bullshit.

TWENTY

Elijah

____

"Stay baby, this is my off day," Ivy pouted as she laid across the bed naked.

"I'm just gonna do a quick errand, and I will be back shortly, ma."

"You always say that, but then you take hours," she bit her lip and then stood on her knees, showing her naked body. I admired every crevice for a second, and then when I noticed my dick getting hard as hell, I grabbed my hoodie and slipped it over my head. "So you're gonna leave?"

"Yes, Ivy. Baby, I have to work so I can make money. I promise I will be back in like three hours. Once I get back, I will be all yours."

"Are you gonna turn your phone off when you get back?" she raised a brow.

"See you in a bit, shorty," I smiled and kissed her neck. She nudged me off and I started laughing as I left the room.

I loved how attached she had become to me, because now everything didn't seem so unbalanced. I felt like I was doing the most and she wasn't really tripping off me, but I'm glad to know I was wrong. Plus, my aunt Laurie said a man should always care more for his woman than she does for him, and it will even out. That's true, but I think Ivy cares just as much as me, and shit, that's cool too.

I sped out of my driveway and down Alders Lane. I needed to drop by a couple traps and pick up the money. I'd set the cap at $15,000 dollars per house, so once I felt that was there, I would drop by and pick it up. Once I felt like they'd earned another fifteen, I would pick that up too, and keep doing that until Ka'Shea took over. I was gonna set the cap higher, but I didn't wanna risk waiting too long and getting robbed of our day's earnings.

I stopped off at the warehouse to switch cars, and then peeled out towards the first trap. I pulled in front of the one on Broom, and threw my car into park. Jogging down the sidewalk, I finally made it to the front yard of the house.

"What's good, Eli!" this worker named Timon nodded his head up.

"What's good with you? Y'all should've hit the cap by now," I said and looked at the other two niggas sitting there.

"We have, follow me," Timon waved me inside the house.

I made sure my heat was secured, because you could never be too sure. The most unsuspecting times, were when you had to pull your hammer out on these niggas. I was too seasoned to be caught slipping.

I trailed Timon to the back until we made it to the bedroom, and then I hit the wall portion that held the small duffel bags. I pulled the short but thick ass bag from the wall, and unzipped it to look inside.

"Did y'all band it off?" I asked.

"We did; each band is a grand," he nodded.

"Cool."

I took the money out, and checked my surroundings before placing it into my trunk. Kill said he believed that Tommy followed him when he got locked up, so I wanted to take note of all the cars out here, so that I would recognize it if it was following me. Unlike Axel though, Kill wanted us to use 'company cars' as he called them, and not our own damn whip. We had three black SUV's, three vans, and one blue sedan, with license plates from Colorado, Wyoming,

Iowa, New York, New Jersey, Pennsylvania, and here in Delaware. We had plenty back at the warehouse from other states too, but those were the ones currently on there. It was safer that way, and harder for someone to catch us if they were to drop a dime.

Honestly, I was ecstatic when Axel handed this shit down to Kill. Kill thought I only felt that way because he was my best friend and cousin, but that wasn't even half of the reason it made me happy. Kill was smarter than Axel, and I've always believed he was more fit to be in charge. I felt safer working under Kill, than I did when I worked under Axel. Axel didn't protect anyone but himself, and that's why our team was getting locked the fuck up left and right. Kill made sure that everything we did covered the tracks of everyone who worked under him. I fucked with that shit the long way. My cousin had never been the selfish type, so I expected for this to be the way he ran his shit.

I hopped back into the black Nissan Armada, and then sped off to handle the other traps who I knew had hit their cap. Driving all around was tiring, but I'm glad that Kill had split the pick-ups between Ka'Shea and I. I didn't mind working hard, but some shit was just unnecessary, and I'm glad Kill saw that.

Once I'd gotten all the capped houses, I took it back to the warehouse so I could count it. When I was done with that, I packed it all up and stashed it so we could all double check it later tonight. I parked the Armada in the warehouse, and then hopped back into my Lambo before leaving. That was another thing; we were to never park the company cars at our home.

I decided to drop by my old condo, because I just wanted to check on the crib and make sure nothing was going awry. After I finished cleaning up a bit, and throwing out the trash and perished food, it was around 5pm. I'd been gone for hours, but now I could lay up with my shorty until the count later tonight. She'd be sleep by then though, so it all worked out.

As I was locking up, I saw that nigga Portland standing by my little porch steps. What the fuck was up with his ass? And why the hell was he always in my fucking face? He was asking for me to pop him.

"Aye man, I've been waiting for you to drop by here again. I need to talk to you."

"Why the fuck are you always here when I am?" I asked.

"I'm staying across the street right now, that's why. But umm, I wanted to see about getting down with who you work for. I see you got that nice Lamborghini."

"Oh, you wanna get down with who I work for, huh?"

I chuckled a bit at the fact that he had no idea his little sister's baby's father was who I worked for. If he spent more time caring about his family versus himself, he would know that.

"Yeah, y'all getting bread like no other."

"Well I don't know you and I don't feel comfortable divulging that information. Excuse me," I said and stepped around him to walk to my car.

"Come on man, I need the money!" he called after me.

I ignored him and just got into my car. I wasn't about to help this nigga get shit. I didn't fuck with him and I didn't care about what he needed.

I made it home about ten minutes later, and Ivy rushed me once she came down the stairs. I picked her ass up, and as I carried her up the stairs, she kissed all over my face.

"Damn shorty, you missed me that much?" I grinned and she nodded as we entered the bedroom. "Where is Donovan?"

"He's taking a little nap." She raised her brow.

"I guess we'd better get to it then."

I bit my lip before slipping my tongue into her mouth. I was about to hit it harder than usual, just because her bitch ass baby daddy felt the need to approach me. It's almost as if he was asking for me to kill his ass. And if it weren't for Donovan, I would have already.

TWENTY-ONE

Jersey

Revelation Day...

$\mathcal{M}$y father's funeral was over, and Portland was nowhere to be found. The number we had on him, he never even answered, so there was really no way to get in contact with him. Ivy tried to help out by giving us the number he'd been calling her from, but when we tried it, some bitch answered and blew up on Raleigh, claiming she wasn't fucking with Portland anymore.

I loved my brother but damn was he a fuck up! He just would never get his shit in tact. And after this little disappearing act, I was done with his ass. This was a time where we needed each other most, but as usual, he didn't give a fuck about anyone but himself. He was definitely my father's child.

I walked towards the exit of the church, ready to just go home and get this shit off of my mind. Seeing that casket made me feel much sadder than I had been. My dad was really gone, and watching the old home videos just a minute ago, really had me bawling. I really missed the good times that we'd had together as a family. Thank God I had my sister, Cheyla, Ivy, and Kill here to comfort me, otherwise I may have gone into labor or fainted.

My grandmother refused to come, because she was too broken up. I think she couldn't look at us because of my mother. It hurt, but I guess I understood her angle. She was on my mom's team until this happened, and I can't really blame her since my father was her only child; well her child period.

"Today was the memorial service of the well respected and prestigious judge, Alvin Warren. If you'll remember, Warren was brutally murdered by his estranged wife Sabrina Warren. Warren and his wife split up three years ago..." the reporter outside of the church spoke as she looked into the camera.

Every day I saw my mother and father on the news, and had to listen to people bash them both. They hated my mother because she murdered my dad, and they hated my dad because he left his family to chase some young girl. My father was a very celebrated judge, so this event was juicy to people. I hated seeing my parents be plastered on every magazine and news show as if they weren't real people. My life and their life was not for entertainment, but of course people didn't care. They just wanted in on such a juicy story, not caring how hard it was for their kids to hear the shit over and over again.

"Jersey, Raleigh, can you guys come to the back for the reading of the will?" my dad's lawyer, Victor, asked my sister and me.

"Can my boyfriend come with me?" I quizzed and grabbed Kill's hand.

"Umm—"

"Yeah, I will come, baby. Lead us to the room please," Kill cut the lawyer off.

Victor was a short Mexican man, and wanted no problems with Kill's tall, muscular, chocolate ass. My baby looked like he killed people for a living, and then it didn't help that we'd been calling him Kill and not Kilexis in front of him. Victor just nodded in agreement, and then headed to the back room of the church. I hugged Cheyla, Kantwan, Ivy, and Elijah, before following him back there.

We were all seated, and then through the side door, in came

Trixie and her lawyer Jacob. I rolled my eyes, and Raleigh sucked her teeth. I'd told her all about how they'd came at me trying to get me to let Trixie live in the house. I had to convince Raleigh not to go over there and whoop both of their asses once I was done spilling that information. I laughed to myself at the thought.

Once everyone was sitting down, we all looked to Victor. I spotted Trixie damn near salivating over Kill, and I was two seconds from popping her ass in the mouth. Kill was my nigga, and I had no problem letting anyone know.

"Alright, good afternoon everyone. I know this is hard for you all, but it's something that has to be done, right?" Victor half smiled and everyone nodded and mumbled. "Firstly, does anyone have any contact on, or know where Mr. Portland Warren is?" he frowned.

"We've been trying to get in touch with my brother, but he's wandering all over Delaware right now," Raleigh responded.

"I see, well here is my card. I guess I will skip over what he's due, and then talk privately with him when he gets a chance. Until then, what he's earned will sit in limbo." Victor nodded and then shuffled some papers, before powering on his computer. "Okay, so Raleigh Warren, your father left you six million dollars, which he said you could have all at once or in payments. We can discuss that in detail after the reading if you'd like."

"Yes, that's fine," Raleigh exhaled.

I knew she was happy that she would no longer be struggling, but I'm sure she wished it were under different circumstances. That reminded me to ask her how she'd been covering the bills without mom all this time. Raleigh didn't have a man, and she was still working at the call center, so I wasn't sure how she was able to still live there and cover everything. Kill had offered to help her, but she said she had it. I just hoped she wasn't into anything illegal or that would get her killed.

"Jersey Warren, your dad left you six million as well, his home, and all the possessions inside it," Victor said and I nodded.

Kill kissed my face and palmed my belly, making me smile. I looked right over at Trixie, and if it were a cartoon, she would have smoke coming out of her ears. I cheesed widely and winked, making her smack her lips.

Victor scrolled a little bit and kept reading, then stopped again. "Ms. Trixie Royce, I don't see you in here. The only other people mentioned are Sabrina and Portland Warren."

"Well, that was because he hadn't gotten around to changing it, Victor! That will was created five years ago! You know he would've added me in there!" Trixie barked.

"I'm sorry, Ms. Royce, we have to go by the most current will, and unfortunately this one is the most current," Victor shrugged.

"There has to be something you can do. Mr. Warren had plans to cut all of his children out of his will. I mean come on now, do you think he would want his money going to Sabrina Warren? His own killer?" Jacob, Trixie's lawyer frowned.

"Mr. Laden, I am Mr. Warren's lawyer, and he never mentioned removing his kids. As a matter of fact, he never mentioned this will again after it was created five years ago. And even if he had, the will needs to be in writing. I cannot go off of what he told you verbally. And please, don't tell me what my client wanted and said," Victor fake smiled at Jacob, making him suck his teeth and grimace.

Raleigh squeezed my thigh, and when I looked at the side of her face, I could see she was smirking.

"Now, Sabrina Warren, whom I've spoken to earlier in person, said that she wanted her money to be split amongst you three. So it's eight million, and Jersey gets three, Raleigh gets three, and Portland the remaining two," Victor looked in his phone, I guess reading my mothers orders. Damn, I'd gotten nine million dollars that quickly.

Victor continued to discuss the will, and Trixie sat there horrified because she wasn't mentioned in it. My dad didn't know her five years ago, so of course she wasn't listed to receive anything. I don't know if my dad planned to remove us or not, but I was definitely glad he didn't get a chance to change anything, because Trixie deserved nothing.

Raleigh, Kill, and I stayed behind once Trixie and Jacob stormed out. Raleigh and I both chose to get payments of our money; ten thousand a month. I felt like I would go crazy if I had it all, so I wanted to do payments to keep myself disciplined. The first thing I planned to do was pay up my school fees for my next Fall semester, since Kill had paid for the upcoming year.

I told Victor I didn't wanna sell the house, and then after promising to get Portland to call, we left. As Kill and I walked out of the church hand in hand, Trixie cut off our path.

"You need to make this right!" she hissed, towering over me.

"I'm not making anything right, it is *right* already," I shrugged.

"Aye, back up out of her face," Kill grimaced.

"What?" She looked Kill up and down like he had shit all over him.

"I said back the fuck up out of her face before I make you!" Kill got into her face.

"Kilexis," I tugged on his arm.

Kill never took me as the type to hit a woman, or threaten one, so I was perplexed by him right now. I didn't like it at all. I'd noticed he'd been furrowing his brows in confusion at her the whole time during the will reading, and I just thought it was because he knew she hated me. Even then, I didn't want him hitting her or any other woman.

"Get out of my face!" Trixie put her hand up in Kill's face, and he shoved her back so hard that she fell onto the ground.

"Kill, what the hell is wrong with you!" I shouted and pushed him with all my might. He didn't budge because he was way stronger than me. "You're not supposed to put your hands on women!" I hollered at him.

I was so disappointed I didn't know what to do. I loved this man, and he was showing me a side I hated. Besides his nasty mouth, I loved everything about him, but I guess it was time I saw things I didn't like. I didn't need him acting out right now; I needed him to be the guy that I thought he was all this time, and that was not a nigga who put his hands on women.

"That ain't no fucking woman, Jersey!" he growled.

"What?" I frowned and looked at Trixie as she dusted herself off.

"He's right! And if you don't fix this shit, I'm gonna tell the whole world who your daddy really is!" Trixie smiled. I blinked repeatedly as I stared at her. She couldn't be saying what I thought she was saying. "Real name is Tabari Royce. Get me the house, or I'll go public with the fact that your daddy plays for the other team," Trixie winked and then switched off.

Tears fell out of my eyes as I watched her get into her lawyer's car. I looked up at Kill, and he pulled me close. I took a deep ass breath, inhaling his cologne along the way.

"What is she talking about Kill?" I cried into his chest.

"Relax Jersey, let's go get some food so you can calm down." He rubbed my back gently.

Like always, his touch soothed me even in the worst of times. I couldn't believe what this bitch Trixie had just dropped on me. My mind couldn't even process the shit. And how the hell did Kill notice before me or my siblings? Fuck my life!

━━

I'd just awakened from a nap, and I could barely sleep from thinking about what had happened earlier at the funeral. For some reason it was hard for me to believe that my dad was with a transgender person. It was like living his betrayal all over again.

I looked over at Kill, who was sitting next to me typing on his laptop. He had on some glasses, and he looked so smart and sexy. See, every time I looked at him, he made me forget about what was bothering me.

"How did you know?" I asked him.

"It's obvious, isn't it?" He glanced at me and then back at the computer.

"Obviously not," I chuckled.

"Well for one, the Adam's apple isn't shaved well, her hands were 'bout big as mine, and them heels she had on were a cool size fourteen."

"Some girls have big feet."

"Not that big, shorty. That shit was like an eyesore."

"So my dad knew, huh?"

"I'm pretty sure, especially if they engaged in sexual activity." It was quiet for a few moments and then he asked, "Would you like me to get rid of her?"

"No, no, I wanna try and figure something out. I mean if she goes to the press she's gonna embarrass the whole family and probably give my grandmother a heart attack."

"Well if you change your mind just say the word. I got you shorty."

I half smiled and then peeled the covers off of myself. I got on my hands and knees, and then pecked the corner of his mouth. Lifting my hand, I caressed the side of his face and began sucking his lips into my mouth. He moved the computer onto the nightstand, and then rolled me onto my back to get in between my legs. I needed him right now, because he always took me away from the real world, just for a little while.

TWENTY-TWO

Cheyla

Saturday Night...

I know you're gonna be shaking your head at me, but oh well. I had to do what I had to do. I wasn't used to depending on anybody, and quite frankly I didn't want to. Sabrina Warren was the exact reason I needed to have my own. All the promises Kantwan made to me, I'm sure Mr. Warren had made to her. I couldn't go out the way she did, and I wouldn't. I would figure a career out soon, but right now I had to get in where I fucking fit in. And the only way I knew how to make money was to shake my ass, so that's exactly what I was gonna do.

Kantwan had left a little bit ago to go handle some business with Kill and Ka'Shea. His brother had just gotten out of jail, thanks to Kill pulling some strings, and ever since that happened, they'd been hard at fucking work. Usually I would complain, but tonight it was perfect. I needed him to stay out as long as possible, so I could slide through, make my bread, and then get back home and pretend I'd been there all along.

I slipped into my tennis shoes, and then grabbed my duffel bag off of the bed before leaving. I made it to the Westin Hotel on Shipyard Drive, and smiled at how nice it was. Since this was where the event was, I knew I was about to make big money tonight. Only niggas who had money got rooms here, and that's just the kind of customers I needed.

I parked my car and then checked the time before getting out. I texted Monty to let him know I was here, and he promptly replied, giving me the room number. Rushing inside the hotel, I got onto the elevator and took deep breaths as it took me up to the floor I wanted. I was about to do my first private party, and this shit was crazy. I hoped that it didn't turn out like *The Players Club*, but then again Monty was cool and would never do me like that. Hell the nigga *saved* me from getting raped before, so why would he let it happen now?

After making myself feel better, I sashayed down the hall until I reached the right room. Hitting my knuckles against the door, I bobbed my head to the music that was playing from inside. Suddenly the door opened, and Monty was standing there smiling with his perfect ass teeth. He had a blunt hanging between his fingers, and his eyes were low as hell. He was rocking a basketball jersey, cargo pants, and chucks.

"Come in, ma," he stepped back.

I walked into the room and I swear it was about one hundred niggas chilling and drinking. There were two other girls, but only one appeared to be a stripper. I didn't mind because the fewer dancers there were, the more money I was able to make.

"I need my $1200 before I change, Monty," I whispered to him, even though the music was loud enough for me to talk regularly.

"I got you." He reached into his pocket and pulled out a band of money.

I took it from him and then asked, "Where is the bathroom?" He started walking so I followed him until we reached the bathroom door. "Thanks," I smiled.

I closed the door behind him, locked it, and then counted the money. There were twenty-four fifties, which made me smile. I changed into a skimpy fit that probably took about two seconds to make since it didn't cover much. It was like a monokini that only covered my nipples and pussy. I combed down my fresh press, put on some lipstick, and then sprayed my body mist all over myself. I made sure my heels were fastened around my ankles, and then walked out to the party. I stuffed my bag with my clothes and money into the little closet by the door, and then turned around to start working.

I became nervous all of a sudden as I watched the rowdy niggas from afar. I was used to having bodyguards at Starzz, but here it was nothing of the sort. The only protection I really had was Monty, and his skinny ass could only do so much. If only Kantwan supported this, I always felt safe with him.

"You good?" Monty appeared out of nowhere it seemed.

"Y-yeah I-I'm good."

"I got a pill if you need it," he smiled and held up a baggie full of my favorite thing.

I looked at the pills and contemplated taking one down to calm me. I then remembered how hard I worked to get clean, and knew I didn't wanna throw all of that away just to get through one night. Also, Kantwan would kick my ass to the curb if he even thought I was high or getting high again.

"No, I'm good Monty, but thanks," I half smiled. He took my hand into his, and then led me out to the room.

"Let Em Die" by Problem dropped, and Monty sat down, pulling me into his lap to get started. I began to work my hips, and I could barely get into it as I thought about Kantwan and how pissed he would be. But shoot, he would never find out, so I needed to make my money.

I began swaying my hips, and popping my ass harder in Monty's lap. The guys began cheering for me, and since I was feeling myself, I stood up and began gyrating my body for them. I then started shaking my ass, and when I saw all the money being thrown, I really put in work.

"T.W.D.Y" by Iamsu came on, and since the beat was cool still, I was able to continue moving my body. One guy stood up and stuffed two fifties in my little suit. I began working on him, and as I was about to expose my breasts, the hotel door burst open, and some nigga wearing a mask was holding an AK. Everyone screamed and scrambled around as the masked man walked inside all calm like a serial killer.

POP!

He shot the chandelier down, making everyone holler loudly. I tried to run to the room behind Monty, but the masked man yanked me back. His alluring cologne was immediately recognizable, and he stared at me for a bit before yanking me towards the door. I pulled away from him and grabbed my bag from the closet, before putting my hand back into his. I knew it was Kantwan, so I didn't fight him. We booked it to the back of the hallway, and then hit the stairs until we made it down to the parking lot.

"Get in yo' fucking car and go straight home!" he growled, making me jump out of my damn skin almost.

I was scared as fuck, so I rushed to my car and did what I was told. I contemplated driving to another destination, but he was clearly in a killing mood, and I did not want to be a casualty. I couldn't believe his crazy ass walked in and shot the party up! This new Kantwan had me horny, yet scared. I didn't know whether to run to somewhere else, or go home and let him fuck me.

I heard police sirens as I followed Kantwan, hitting all kinds of back streets until we finally made it to Augustine Road where we lived. We pulled into our garage, and he climbed out with his AK still in hand like a maniac. He waited by the garage door, and I slowly exited the car because I was frightened. As soon as I neared him, he grabbed my bicep roughly, and pulled me into the house.

"What the fuck did I tell you!" he gritted and backed me into the wall of the laundry area.

I'd never been this afraid in my entire life. This nigga was not playing, and I just prayed he remembered how much he cared for me before he killed my ass right here.

"T-to n-not go do the pa-party," I stammered like a little kid in trouble. My eyes were bucked, and if I bucked them anymore they would roll onto the floor.

"So what about that didn't yo' muthafuckin' ass understand! I told you I didn't want you showing your fucking body to other niggas and you just completely went against what the fuck I said!" He hollered down into my face, while waving the AK like a lunatic. My eyes were locked on the gun moving wildly, so I couldn't respond. "Don't you start that crying bullshit! If I was a different type of nigga, I would knock the shit out of you, but instead, I'm gonna go stay the night at my old house," he grimaced. He hit the wall space next to me, making me jump and scream, and then stormed off.

"Kantwan, don't leave baby—"

"If I don't leave Cheyla, I'm gonna end up knocking fire from you. Just get out of my face right now!"

I'd never seen him this angry before. I should've just sat my ass down and listened to him, but my dumb ass just had to be independent in a dumb way. I got paid though. I smiled as I remembered the money I'd made. Money did buy happiness sometimes.

I rushed out to the garage, and went into my car to get my money. When I pulled it out, I saw Kantwan throwing his bag into his car to leave. He stormed over to me, and I tensed up waiting to be slapped, shot, or punched. He snatched the money from me, and then walked over to power on the paper shredder that he kept in the garage.

"Kantwan, no! I worked for that! That's my money!" I screamed and cried as I tried to stop him.

He was keeping me at bay with just one hand, which angered me. He smiled and laughed as he dropped every single bill into the shredder, making me sob hysterically. Once he was done disposing of my money, I fell to the floor and cried.

"Get yo' ass in the fucking house and quit crying. You did this to yourself," he hissed before getting into his car, pulling the garage up, and speeding out in reverse.

I watched the automatic garage door go down, and then stood to my feet slowly while sniffling. I grabbed my bag that now just had my clothes, and then walked into the house. I took a bubble bath to calm my nerves, before getting into the huge bed and sinking into the sheets.

Picking up my phone, I texted him.

Me: *I'm sorry Kant, I'm gonna listen next time.*

I stayed up as long as I could, waiting for a response, but never got anything. I drifted off to sleep around 3am, because I'd finally tired myself out from crying. This was the worst night ever.

TWENTY-THREE

Ivy

———

$\mathcal{P}$ortland had finally contacted me from some random number. He claimed he wanted to see Donovan, and since Raleigh agreed for us to use her place again, I said it was okay. I was so close to cutting him off from my son, but I didn't want my baby growing up hating me because of it. I would let him cut his dad off on his own.

Raleigh had a few things that she wanted to say to Portland, so she was actually more than happy to allow us to use her space. Jersey was over his ass, but Raleigh was still trying to salvage their relationship. I didn't blame Jersey one bit. Portland was a child, and if we kept forgiving him and letting him act foolishly, he would never grow the hell up.

Raleigh and I were both sitting on the couch as Donovan talked gibberish to us. I scooped him up and began kissing his little fat neck, making him giggle loudly as hell. Suddenly there was a knock, and Raleigh shot up off the couch and booked it to the door. She snatched it open wearing a scowl, and Portland just laughed at her as he walked in. This nigga thought everything was a damn joke. I rolled my eyes at the thought.

"Hey man," he smiled down at Donovan.

"Say hi to your daddy, Donovan," I told my baby as he just stared Portland down. I could tell he remembered the last encounter, and how he was yelling at me.

Portland plopped down next to me, and reached out for Donovan, so I nudged him to his father.

"Can you give us a minute, Raleigh?" he asked his sister.

"Hold up, before I go I wanna discuss some things with you. For one, where the fuck have you been? And two, why don't we have some kind of number for you? And lastly, who the fuck answered your phone? Because that bitch has an ass whooping coming, talking to me like that!" She placed her hand on her hip.

"Man, I've been busy getting my shit together," he scoffed. Same old fucking story, nigga please. This nigga has been 'getting his shit together' for years. He needed to have some shirts made with that line on it, because it was definitely his slogan.

"Too busy to attend Daddy's funeral? Too busy to even collect the money he and mom left us? Too busy to see mom? Too fucking busy to see how Donovan is doing?" Raleigh ran off and raised a brow.

"He left me some bread?" Portland smiled. Wow, that was the only thing he must've heard; or the only thing he wanted to hear.

"You're disgusting sometimes, Portland. Here is Daddy's lawyer's card. You have to call him and meet him about the millions dad left you."

"Millions? Fuck. Thanks sis. And look, I'm sorry about not being around to help or anything. How is mom?"

"Why don't you go see her?"

"Nah, I can't be up in them prisons while on parole ma, just tell me if she's good, Raleigh?"

"Yeah, she's good, Portland." Raleigh shook her head and then walked to the back room.

Once they were done with their sibling argument, I nudged my baby towards Portland again so he could hold him. He tried to run off, but Portland snatched him up before he could.

"Ivy, I have to know why you always wanna meet here, and not where you're staying," he huffed and kissed Donovan's forehead. My baby just stared at him, wondering who the hell he was and why the fuck he was kissing him.

"Because I'm in a relationship, Portland."

He stopped and stared as if I just told him I killed his mother or something. "Oh, you got a man?"

"Yes I do, and he's the one I live with. He also doesn't feel comfortable with us meeting alone, so that's why I have us meet here."

Portland nodded his head and then chuckled.

"Wow, so that's why you have all this newfound strength. You got another dick to sit on," he laughed.

"Call it what you will, but just know that you and I are only co-parenting."

"Ivy, you love me, and you know that nigga can't make you as happy as I can. He doesn't make you feel the way that I make you feel."

"Actually, you're right," I smiled.

"I know I am."

"You've never been able to make me as happy as he can, so you're right in the sense that you two are totally different. I have never felt this good in a long time. I never realized how toxic our relationship was until I met him. So the fact that he doesn't make me feel the way you used to is kind of the point."

"What, you love this nigga? We ain't even been broken up that long, ma!" he hollered, making Donovan jump and furrow his little brows again.

"Don't holler over him like that, please. And I don't know if I love him yet, but I have very strong feelings for him. I like where our relationship is headed, and I can tell we're in it for the long haul."

"Well as long as you don't love him, I still have a chance," he reached over and rubbed my leg, making my stomach turn.

It was crazy how I used to crave his touch, and now I couldn't stand for him to even breathe on me. The thought of him sticking his dick inside of me made me gag. Got damn how times have changed.

"But see the thing is, I don't love you at all, Portland. I barely care about you, and the only reason I have some sort of care is because of Donovan. If we didn't have a baby together you wouldn't be in my life at all, especially now that Jersey doesn't fuck with you."

"Oh word?"

"Word."

"So this nigga got you that gone in the head? I know he ain't stroking that pussy like I was." He licked his lips.

"No, he's doing it better. I don't have to fake orgasms anymore," I lied.

Portland could make me cum long and hard, but the sex with Elijah was way better. I think it was because he treated me better, and because he really knew what he was doing. Elijah cared about making me cum, and pleasuring *me* mainly, whereas Portland just wanted a nut. Elijah would eat my pussy for hours if that's what I wanted, and I loved that about him. It made me treat him the same. I've never wanted to please a man as much as I wanted to please Elijah. And because we were both so hell-bent on making one another cum, our sex was off the chain. I've learned that selfless sex was the best sex.

Portland stared at me angrily, and I knew he wanted to swing on me. This nigga thought I would be sprung on him forever, and never knew this day would come. I didn't even know this day would come, but boy was I enjoying it.

"Look, I think I will go," I stood up.

"I can't believe you let another nigga get my shit!" He roared and dropped Donovan onto the floor, making him cry.

"What the fuck is wrong with you!" I screamed and scooped my baby up.

"What is going on?" Raleigh came out from her bedroom.

"Man, tell this hoe ass bitch to get up out of here and take that little nigga with her!" Portland yelled as veins popped from his neck.

"Portland, don't you act like that towards them, especially your baby," Raleigh stated calmly but angrily.

"Fuck the both of them. I ain't that little nigga's daddy no more since his mama wants to be a hoe!"

"That's how you want it, Portland? That's perfectly fine with me!" I shouted and walked to the door holding Donovan.

I couldn't believe the words coming out of Portland's mouth. I knew he was an asshole, but this took the fucking cake. I was starting to see that he only wanted Donovan if it meant having me. He felt like being Donovan's father was his way of keeping me locked down. Well his ass learned today!

"Yep! From this day forward, you're a single mother!" He glared at me as his chest rose and fell rapidly. I knew if Raleigh weren't here he would've pummeled me to the floor by now.

"No I won't, because he thinks my new nigga is his daddy anyway!" I hollered before pulling the door open.

Portland charged me, so I ran out of the house and to my car, holding Donovan tightly. Portland came out and tried to catch me, but Raleigh hopped on his back and tried to take him down. He nudged her back and she fell to the ground, just as I finished buckling Donovan in. He started towards me as everyone watched closely, and Raleigh called him all types of bitches. By the time he got close, I was peeling down the street and headed home.

I couldn't believe he was willing to give up his rights as a father, all because I'd been with someone else. Portland wasn't shit and as the days went by, I was more and more embarrassed that I had chased his ass for so long.

I pulled over once I'd gotten a little ways away from Raleigh's, so that I could calm down. Once I'd gotten myself together, I drove to Burger King and got Donovan a kid's meal since all he wanted to eat was chicken fingers these days. And he only wanted the ones from Burger King with his little picky self. After we got his food, I headed home.

"Guess who's home?" Elijah called out as he walked into the kitchen and hugged me from behind. I'd just finished setting Donovan up in his high chair with his food.

"Dad." Donovan smiled and then bit the chicken finger.

Elijah and I looked at one another, before we burst into laughter. I guess I just spoke that shit into existence. Portland would murder me if he were here to witness this shit. I found it funny that I'd referred to Portland as Donovan's dad hundreds of times, but he never said it, yet he just called Elijah dad. God works in mysterious ways I guess.

TWENTY-FOUR

Raleigh Warren

I stepped out of the shower, and began rubbing body butter into my wet skin. Once I was finished, I slipped on some panties and the matching bra, before brushing my teeth. Walking out of the bathroom, I cut the bathroom light off and scooted one of the boxes in the hallway to the side. I had boxes everywhere since I'd finally purchased a house and was moving. I couldn't wait to get up out of Browntown.

I entered my room, and cut Pandora on using my phone, before going into my closet to pick out my clothes. I chose to go with a cute and casual burgundy dress, and then paired it with some burgundy Nike Roshe sneakers. I wanted to look cute but still be comfortable for the day.

As soon as I pulled my dress down over my body, I heard the front door and rolled my eyes. Sonny's no good ass was walking into the house, and bumping boxes that I'd packed on the way. I acted as if I didn't hear him, and sat down in the chair in my room to slip on my socks and shoes. This nigga was getting on my last nerve, and I was two seconds from cutting his whack ass off.

"Good morning, baby," Sonny smiled and neared me. It's one in the afternoon nigga. He tried to lean down and kiss me but I pushed his head away. "Here we go," he sighed.

"No, it's all good," I said as I stood up to look into my closet mirror.

"Baby, I know I said I was gonna be back last night, but Portland and I were working on some things pretty late into the night."

"Oh, you're talking to Portland again? Because when Jersey and I were looking for his ass, you were acting like you couldn't find him either."

I grabbed my brush from my vanity, and began combing down my fresh weave. I usually wore my hair in it's short natural curly state, but I wanted to try something new, so I got it straightened with some tracks added. I really liked the long length, and I was enjoying not having to detangle and shit every damn day.

"And that was the truth, Raleigh. I couldn't find his ass. He just hit me up recently, and we got together about some work. Shit was going so well that I didn't recognize how late it was."

"I see."

I knew Sonny's ass was lying, because my home girl Diamond had already told me that she saw him going into his baby mama Marley's house last night around seven. I wasn't in the mood to fight with his ass, because this shit was getting hella fucking old. I was on my shit, and I deserved way better and much more than he had to offer.

I met Sonny when I was just 14 and he was 16 years old. I had no business having a boyfriend or even being interested one, especially my older brother's best friend. Sonny was sexy though with his smooth brown skin, short curly hair, and trimmed facial hair. I should've known his fine ass would bring me problems.

Anyway, over time we became cool because I was like his little sister, but soon I began to grow up and fill out, making him want to be more. I knew he had a girlfriend named Marley, but I wasn't really caring about her because I was young, in love, and most importantly dumb. I really thought Sonny would leave her, like he said, but the shit never happened.

So why didn't I leave? Well to be honest, I became okay with the fact that Sonny wasn't up under me all of the time. I enjoyed him smothering me when I was in my teens, but once I got to the ages where I could drive and shit, I wanted time to myself. Marley was kind of like a help to me, because she took some of his time. That was then, though. Now I wanted a man who could give all of his time to me with no bullshit. I'm over this fake ass shit I have with Sonny, and although I love him, I'm not in love anymore. I'm only here still for companionship really. Things were about to change though. Just thinking about it had me smiling in the mirror.

I smoothed down my edges, and then made a deep part on the side to perfect my Aaliyah swoop. Once my hair was how I liked it, I began putting on my jewelry, and my new beautiful new watch. Sonny's ass watched me the whole damn time, waiting for me to blow up on him. It wasn't happening today. Every time he did some fuck shit it made me care less and less.

"Where did you get that watch?" *From another nigga,* I wanted to say, but I just ignored him instead. "You look so pretty, ma," he said in a low tone. Once I turned my back to him, I rolled my eyes up into my head.

"Umm, I'm about to leave." I placed my hand on my hip after grabbing my purse.

"Where you going?" he asked surprised, as if he didn't just watch me get dressed.

"I signed up for a shift today, so I'm gonna go to work for a couple of hours. I don't want you staying here while I'm gone. Go stay with Marley's ass."

"Fuck you bringing up Marley for? I wasn't even over there yesterday."

"Diamond lives by her stupid, and she told me she saw you go in her house around seven, and you didn't come back out."

"Okay, I went over there to see Sonaya. I do have a daughter with her, you know."

"I do know that, so go over there now and chill with them." I pulled on his bicep and he snatched it away from me before standing up.

"I ain't fuck her, Raleigh. Let me know when you get off and I will come over and take you to dinner."

"Yep," was all I said as I switched past him out of my bedroom.

I locked up once Sonny came out, and then got into my new whip to head to my destination. I felt bad buying shit with my Dad's will money, but I needed things and that's what the hell it was for. Shit, it's not like I killed him or wanted him to die. But like my little sister, for some reason I didn't hate my mom like I probably should have. She was hurt, and yeah she overreacted like a muthafucka, but this was all my dad's fault.

I pulled up onto Eleventh Street, and parked in front of Plexus Fitness. I climbed out and placed some coins into the meter, then jogged across the street to go inside of Tonic Bar and Grille. I reached into my purse for my iPhone, and then went to send a text. I was so damn nervous that my hands shook with every letter that I pressed on.

Me: *Here.*

+1 (302) 555 - 4621: *I see you beautiful, look to your left.*

I slowly and nervously turned to my left, and then smiled when I saw my lunch date. I got closer, and before I even made it to him, his cologne hit me in the face like a ton of sexy bricks. He rose from his seat, and he was so tall that it made my panties wet. His hair was in two French braids, his facial hair was lined perfectly, and his jewelry was sparkling. The best part about him though, was his super full lips, which he licked upon seeing me. He was rocking some black jeans, a black polo, and some all black Nike Roshe sneakers. This nigga couldn't have possibly just gotten out of jail. He'd sent me plenty of pictures, but damn did he clean up well.

He towered over me and then pulled me into a hug, and when I pulled away, he surprised me by placing his soft full lips onto mine. I didn't care for light-skinned guys, but this nigga right here was life. If I had a diamond ring, shit even a candy ring pop, I would propose to his ass right now.

"How are you, shorty?" he asked as he walked around and pulled my chair out.

"I'm good, you?"

"I'm perfect now that I'm here with you."

I couldn't help but blush as I sat down. I crossed my legs because I was sure that my nectar would be dripping onto the floor of the restaurant in a minute.

"You don't even look like you've just gotten out of jail, Shea."

"I know, and that wasn't really the look I was going for anyway. My brother Kill that I told you about, really had shit set out for me nicely. I'm in the process of moving out of his crib." He sat across from me.

Okay yes, I knew that the nigga I'd been corresponding with from jail was my little sister's man's brother. I didn't wanna say anything, because I didn't know Ka'Shea and I would get so close. Plus, I needed to come clean to my people about Sonny and I first, I felt.

Ka'Shea had no idea that Jersey was my sister. I only gave him small details about me, because I felt it was selfish to talk about myself since he was the one caged up. The point of us writing, in my opinion, was for him to have someone to talk to, not the other way around.

This all started because my job handed out flyers for a pen pal program. I wasn't gonna do it at first, but my co-worker Shelby convinced me to. She sold me this sob story about how her brother killed himself because he was so lonely in the pen. I went ahead and signed up, and Ka'Shea Camren was assigned to me. When I saw his picture, I was super happy that I'd listened to Shelby. Over time we wrote back and forth, and we got real close to the point where we agreed to spend time and eventually be together once he was released. Surprisingly, he was released earlier than expected, and I can't say I'm complaining.

"Did you meet his girlfriend?" I asked, referring to Kill.

"Yeah, I did. Shorty is beautiful and can cook her ass off. I told her to hook me up with her sister; I was kidding though," he grinned and showed me his perfect choppers.

"That's funny that you would say that, Shea."

"Why?" he cocked his head just as a waitress neared.

"Sorry to interrupt, but are you guys ready to order some food, drinks, or appetizers?" she smiled and clasped her hands together.

"I will have the grilled salmon, a cosmo, and water," I responded.

"I'll have the NY Strip, and the House Tonic," Ka'Shea half smiled and she nodded to say okay.

Once she walked away I said, "Shea, I have two siblings, a sister and a brother. Kill's girlfriend, Jersey, is my little sister."

"Jersey and Raleigh, makes sense," he chuckled. "So why didn't you tell me that, baby?"

"We never really talked about my family that much."

"You're right. So tell me something about your family shorty, you know all about mine."

"Well," I exhaled. "Other than Jersey, I have an older brother named Portland—" he burst into laughter, cutting me off. *This nigga is fine af.* "What is so funny?"

"Your brother's name, shorty. Fuck, are your parents obsessed with states or some shit?"

"Yeah, they liked to travel a lot, and their favorite cities were in Oregon, North Carolina, and New Jersey."

"That's dope, I'm sorry, finish please," he said just as the waiter set down our cocktails.

"Well yes, it's us three. My mother and father split up when my dad decided to leave us for some younger woman named Trixie. And even worse is that we recently found out she's a man."

He swallowed hard and said, "Yo' daddy is a banana slammer?"

We chuckled in unison before I nodded. "Yeah, but my mom killed him so let's not speak ill of the dead."

"Damn, I'm sorry to hear that ma, even though I kind of already knew that. Kill told me Jersey's mom murked her dad." *Thank God he didn't mention me.*

"I see. So do you still feel the same about me? Are you really trying to live up to what you said? Or has your freedom changed your mind?"

"Nah shorty, I want you. But I need you to stop fucking with old boy."

"I need you to leave old girl alone," I giggled and he grinned.

"Shorty ain't nothing to me and you know that. I already told you what it was and you know I'm an honest ass nigga."

"Yeah, you are. It's deep with me and him though, so I have to ease out of that situation, Shea. I can't just up and leave."

"You do what I told you to?"

"Yes. I haven't let him touch me since you've been out."

"He's not suspicious?" He sipped his drink.

"No, he's too busy doing his own dirt. He get's frustrated when I deny him, but he gets over it quickly."

"So if he's doing his own shit, then why can't you let his ass go? What's his name?" he furrowed his eyebrows, making him look even sexier.

"I'm not telling you his name, Shea," I snickered. "But it's because he... well, I don—"

"You think I'm not serious about you," he cut me off and shook his head. "Shorty, I know my history with women isn't the best, but I promise you I ain't trying to do you dirty."

"How do I know that, Shea? I don't wanna get rid of one foul nigga just to hop to another one."

"I will just show you, aight?"

"Aight," I nodded and smiled.

We ate and talked some more, then Ka'Shea paid the bill. Sonny hadn't paid the bill for our meals since about four months before he went to jail. Come to think of it, he'd only paid for our meals a couple times since we'd been dating, and we'd been dating a pretty long while. I shook my head at my thoughts.

Instead of letting me go home, Ka'Shea booked a room at the Homewood Suites on Rocky Run Parkway. I was gonna decline at first, but honestly I wanted to spend some more time with his fine ass. If we had sex we had sex, I wasn't tripping too much. It sounds bad, but if you saw his ass you'd agree with me.

"I forgot to thank you," I said as soon as we walked into the room.

"For what, ma?"

"For sending me money even though you were in jail."

His homeboy Blow used to meet me at Dunkin' Donuts every

Saturday and break me off, courtesy of Ka'Shea. He offered to have his brothers do it, but I convinced him not to. I don't remember exactly how I did, but it worked. Now that my secret of being related to Jersey was out in the open though, I didn't care to remember my excuse.

What he sent was just spending money until my mother was arrested. When that happened, I had to put it towards the bills. I knew Jersey was wondering how I was able to stay afloat without mom, but I think because of all the drama, it slipped her mind.

"It's cool shorty, come here."

He fell back onto the bed, and cut the lamp off. The sun was still shining brightly through the window, so it wasn't quite dark. I walked to the bed, and then kicked my shoes off before crawling up next to him. Once I laid down on his chest, my hand ran up under his polo and caressed his six pack. His strong arms encased my body, making me feel so good that I closed my eyes to enjoy it.

"How long before this will be our normal?" I whispered.

"That's up to you, Raleigh."

"Will you wait for me?"

"Not long, but I will try. You better not fuck him though. I'm dead serious."

"You claiming it and you haven't even touched me yet," I giggled.

"That's right."

He reached across his body, and roughly spread my thighs with his hand, while his other arm stayed wrapped around me. He moved his hand down between my legs, and then pressed his lips against mine. As we kissed, I felt his finger enter me and began plunging in and out. I kissed him harder as he fingered me like crazily.

"Fuck," I whimpered before accepting his tongue back into my mouth.

"Your shit is gripping my finger, so I know it's tight," he grumbled before kissing me passionately. "I can't wait to be inside you."

"Uuhh, uuuh, Shea, I'm gonna cum," I cried lowly in between kisses. He stayed silent and continued working just his one finger in and out of me. "Aahh, uuh!" I screeched damn near as I exploded.

My legs trembled and my body quivered as I regained my composure. He licked my juices off his finger, and then I cupped his face to kiss him hungrily. Sonny was halfway in the door and halfway out, and I just needed to completely push him outside and to Marley's ass.

TWENTY-FIVE

Kilexis

—————

I was coming out of the liquor store on Broom Street, and when I looked towards my Maserati Quattroporte, I saw Margo's hoe ass leaning up against it. I didn't know if I was angrier at the fact that she was leaning on my expensive ass whip, or that she had somehow found me. For some reason this woman felt we still had shit to talk about, three damn years later. She was boosting my self-esteem, yet annoying the fuck out of me at the same damn time.

I walked as slowly as possible, until I finally reached my car.

"Get up off my shit, man, you're leaving fingerprints and smudges," I sighed and grabbed her arm lightly. She snatched it from me, but still got up off of my car.

"I see now that you don' got some money and shit, you don't fuck with me," she grimaced.

"I never fucked with you. I've been sending you money though, so what are you tripping for?"

"You ain't been sending me money, nigga! You've been sending one of your flunkies to get a list of what I need and then going to buy it! And it's only shit for Gregory, not even me!"

"Same shit to me," I shrugged.

"No! It's not, now that you got fatter pockets you don't feel the need to come and drop money off yourself!"

"Fuck do you want, ma?" If I knew how to roll my eyes I would.

"Kill, who the fuck is Jersey?"

I laughed and then stroked my beard as I stared down at her. She was really upset, and that shit was hilarious because she had absolutely no right to be. The bitch hadn't been my girl for the longest, and in my opinion, I led her on in no way. I wasn't smashing, and I wasn't being all lovey dovey, so for her to think we were in something was downright ridiculous. The only thing I did was provide for Gregory here and there, and put food in her fridge. I didn't pay her rent, get her nails and shit done, or anything else that would have her thinking I cared about her. I could only imagine how she would act if I was still hittin'.

"Where you hear that name?" I asked nonchalantly.

"From the bitches at my fucking job! They were talking about how you're about to have a baby and shit! Them bitches were laughing at me because I've been bragging about how you were my man!" She whacked my arm.

I chewed my gum slowly, and then adjusted my baseball cap while looking out into the street before speaking.

"Keep your fucking hands to yourself, you know better. Secondly, how is it my fault that you took your delusional ass up to work, bragging about some shit that you knew deep down wasn't true?" I squinted my eyes.

She shook her head repeatedly, and wiped the tears that flowed down her cheeks. Her tears did nothing to move me. Margo was a drama queen, and this was another one of her acts.

"Pregnant, Kill? You got this hoe pregnant?" she sniffled and stared up at me. "It's probably not even your baby," she smirked like that was gonna make me feel some type of way.

Margo was beautiful with her smooth brown skin, short black hair, and banging ass body. She was a rat though, and that overshadowed her beautiful looks. The way her work dress hugged her thick hips didn't turn me on at all, because inside she was pure trash. On top of being a conniving hoe, she refused to get a damn clue.

"She ain't no hoe, Margo, that's my girl. I'm one hundred million percent sure that it's my baby," I responded. I felt like I was on Maury or some shit, and it made me chuckle.

She gasped at my words, as if someone had stabbed her. I hadn't made a woman my girlfriend since Margo and I broke up, and maybe because of that she thought she had a chance still.

"Your girl? Really? I heard she was working at Starzz when you met her, so the baby could be anybody's. You know how them stripper hoes get down."

"I really don't care about her occupation. What I do know is that you have one more time to call her a hoe, before I knock fire from yo' ass."

She paused for a few moments in disbelief, and then said, "So you're stooping that low now, Kilexis? You're dating strippers?"

"It's an upgrade in my book."

"What's up, Kill!" Some random walked by, and I nodded my head up and then turned my attention back to Margo.

"An upgrade? You went from a working woman to a stripper, I don't think so."

"I went from a scheming ass hoe, to a beautiful, intelligent, faithful, and ambitious woman. A woman I love and that is having my baby."

"I fucking hate you! I hate you! You stupid muthafucka! I swear to God I hate you!" Margo screamed and cried as she swung on me repeatedly. We were on the sidewalk looking like some damn fools as I tried to grab ahold of her wrists and block her little punches. "You can't do this, Kill!" she hollered and continued swinging.

Finally, I'd gotten her wrists in my hands and shook the shit out of her. I pulled her into a bear hug, pressing her arms at her side, and then leaned down to whisper in her ear as she sobbed.

"Keep yo' muthafuckin' hands to yourself, Margo. Move the fuck on. If it wasn't clear that I have before, it should be very clear now. I don't want to see you again, or hear about you in any bullshit regarding me and my girl. I love her and there is nothing you can do to change that. If you fuck up again, I'm cutting off what I do for Gregory. If you fuck up a second time after that, I'm cutting off your head King Henry style." I pulled away from our embrace, and she just stared up at me with her wet face. "Have a good weekend, ma." I patted her shoulder and then jogged off the sidewalk to get into my car.

I didn't play them ex-girlfriend gone wild games. If she thought she was about to nut up and be meddling in my relationship, she had another thing coming. I just hoped Margo knew better, because I would hate to make Gregory an orphan.

TWENTY-SIX

Kantwan

———————————

I hadn't seen my shorty in a cool couple of days. She'd pissed me off by doing that damn party, and I needed to remove myself from the situation before I did something I would regret forever.

My dad told me to always subtract myself if I felt like I was gonna hit a woman. He said no matter how much I apologized, she would always have a loss of respect for me, and I would always have less respect for myself.

I refused to be that nigga that had hit his woman before; I don't care if it was just once. I was better than that, and I wasn't gonna allow Cheyla's stupid ass actions to turn me into something I wasn't. If I felt like she was gonna have me wanting to whoop her ass on a daily, then this shit wasn't gonna work. I knew it was possible for her to do, because I swear I was inches away from backhanding the shit out of her that night.

I pulled into my driveway, and just admired my house for a bit. Not that long ago I was living in my parents' old beat up ass house, barely making the house payments. And now I was in a cool little mini mansion in a quiet ass neighborhood. There were no loud ass niggas selling dope at the end of the street, or muthafuckas getting shot in the alley behind the house. I enjoyed the shit a lot. I still kept my parents' home paid up, because it had sentimental value.

My house wasn't on no Master P shit, but it was a nice size and had two floors. It was a perfect family home, and had way more space than I would ever need. I just hoped Cheyla could continue to share it with me and not be on no bullshit. If she was gonna continue to go behind my back and do sneaky shit, she could get the fuck out. I would get her an apartment, and pay the rent until she found a job, but our relationship would be done.

I got out of the car and then put my key into the door. When I walked in, I smelled pancakes, so I headed to the kitchen. When I entered, I saw Cheyla in a casual dress that stopped a couple inches past her nice round ass. Her smooth caramel complexion looked like butter, and her shoulder length hair was up in a ponytail. I hated how sexy she was, because it sometimes clouded my judgment. I would sometimes be lusting after her when I should've been gettin' in her ass about her behavior.

"Some for me?" I asked and leaned in the doorway.

She snapped her neck to look back at me, and then she cut the stove off and ran in my direction. Draping her arms over my shoulders, she pressed her lips against mine before I could talk any more.

"I missed you Kant, I'm sorry," she pleaded, before cupping my face and kissing me repeatedly. Because I was so tall, she was hurting my neck, so I picked her little ass up. "You forgive me?" she inquired.

"I don't know if I should," I squinted my eyes and licked my lips.

"Please baby, I love you and you're too fine to leave," she grinned, making me chuckle lightly.

"You love me?" I quizzed and she paused for a second before nodding.

"I've wanted to tell you since before we made things official, but I wasn't sure if I really was in love yet, so I wanted to wait and see."

"How do you know that you're in love right now?"

"Because I was physically sick these last couple of days that you were gone from the house. I tried calling and texting but you never responded. I couldn't even sleep, and when I did I would wake up in the middle of the night and cry. Finally, I googled it, and the Internet said I was in love."

"You googled it?" I laughed and then sat her on the counter, before standing between her legs.

"Yes, I googled it and it confirmed it for me," she smiled.

"Cheyla," I said before intertwining our fingers. "I love you too, baby, but this isn't gonna work if you keep pulling the shit that you did this past weekend."

"I know, and I promise I won't do anything like that again. I was just scared. Going to Mr. Warren's funeral just made me feel some type of way. You know how he left Jersey's mother, and I don't wanna be depending on you and then when you leave, I have nothing."

"I get you and I understand where you're coming from. Cheyla, if you wanna work I have no problem with that, I just don't want you at the club, ma. And I want it to be something where it won't interfere with school. You need to make something of yourself so that me or any other nigga can't leave you with nothing." I slipped my arms around her small waist, and pulled her to the edge of the counter. I leaned my head back some, and she kissed my lips.

"I was just paranoid for a second. But if I find something that fits my schedule I've created for the upcoming school year, I will take it. But for now I'm just gonna focus on classes."

"Good. And six classes is a job in itself."

"I know. I wanna finish as quickly as possible though." She pecked me again and caressed my fade, as I stood between her legs still. I ran my hands up her smooth thighs, lifting her dress up and off as I did it. "Kantwan, the food," she giggled as she lifted her hands up so I could pull the dress over her head. I was craving my shorty.

I ignored her and unhooked her bra to release her beautiful breasts. As I flicked my tongue over her nipples, she unbuckled my pants. I pulled away to remove my hoodie and shirt, and then stepped out of my sneakers, jeans, and boxers, before tugging her panties off.

"Look at him already," she said referring to my dick.

"I know; I need you to handle that."

She dropped down to the floor, and then began going to work on my rod. I threw my head back, and played with her ponytail as she gave me the best top in the world. I listened to her saliva gush in and out of her mouth, and that shit sent chills down my spine. Gripping her ponytail, I began pumping her face in a circular motion. She took every bit of me, and I knew I would be nutting any minute if she kept going. I pulled my pelvis away from her mouth, then stood her up and turned her around. I kissed all over her neck, and groped her breasts using one hand, as I positioned my dick at her opening with the other. Sliding into her was like the best homecoming in the world.

"Slow Kantwan," she whimpered as I began pushing the rest of my dick into her.

Her pussy was gripping the fuck out of my dick, and made me quiver a bit. I made her lie face down on the island in the kitchen, before I gripped her waist and began sliding in and out of her smoothly. I watched her close her eyes and bite down on her lip as she enjoyed the feeling of me invading her walls. I wound my hips into her, making her scrunch her face, and then soon after she was exploding on my dick.

"That was too easy," I chuckled and she gave me a lazy smile, looking over her shoulder.

I kissed and licked up her small sexy back, and then reached around to play with her clit, before I began beating it up.

"Aaah, uuuh, aaah baby, fuck," she cried and gripped the edge of the island.

I grabbed her arms and pinned them behind her back as I slammed into her. I didn't wanna cum yet, but I couldn't stop it. She stood on her tip toes and clenched her teeth together, before we both hollered and came together. I pulled her body up to hug her from behind, and then sucked on her neck.

"I love you, Kantwan."

"Say that shit again," I grumbled.

"I love you, Kantwan. I love you so much," she repeated before I turned her around to tongue her down.

Cheyla was gon' make a nigga crazy, but it was all worth it... I hope.

TWENTY-SEVEN

Elijah

———————

I was in my office checking some emails that Kill had sent over to me. We were discussing opening some businesses to clean our money, so I was just reading the little bit of information he'd emailed. We'd be going over it together in more detail during the next meeting with my other cousins, Ka'Shea and Kantwan. I couldn't wait because I was anxious to do some legit shit ASAP.

Also, I knew once I mentioned something legit to Ivy, she would be happy as fuck. I didn't like her worrying much, and even though she claimed she didn't because she believed me when I said I was on my shit, I still knew she was a little stressed about my lifestyle. That nigga Portland had really done a number on her, but I planned to clean all that shit up.

As I was reading an email, my pusher phone buzzed. I was slowly phasing that shit out, because I was no longer working that type of position. I didn't have the time because of my new position, and frankly the money wasn't needed.

I picked it up anyway just to see who it was, because if it was one of the niggas I was cool with, I may have one of the little homies meet them somewhere and give them what they'd text me for. I saw it was from a number I didn't recognize, so that caught me off guard.

Me: *Who is this?*

(302) 555-5311: *Portland, new number. I was wondering if I could cop from you and if you had any info for me to get down with your team.*

I locked the phone, and then abruptly left my office and jogged upstairs. I checked on Donovan and saw he was napping, then I went into the room where Ivy was. She was watching TV and painting her nails, looking all innocent and shit.

"Ivy, I thought you told this nigga Portland about us."

"I did." She looked up from her feet and frowned.

"So why the fuck is he still hitting me up as if everything is cool and shit?" I hissed.

She stuck the top into the nail polish bottle, and then set it on the nightstand all slowly. I knew right then her ass was on some bullshit.

"Well I told him I was involved, but I didn't say with whom."

"And why is that?" I furrowed my brows.

"Because I knew that he knew you, and I didn't think it was necessary for him to—"

"You didn't think it was necessary for him to know who the fuck your nigga was? I'm sorry, I don't comprehend, Ivy."

"No I didn't, because I knew it would cause problems!"

"So what! You should've thought about that before you agreed to be my girl!"

"I know Eli, I just didn't want him trying to fight and end up dead or something." She stood to her feet and walked to me carefully. "Baby, I don't need you wasting your time on him. Plus, I told you he said he wanted nothing to do with Donovan and me anymore. So it's not like I'll be seeing him again, which means it doesn't matter."

"It doesn't matter, huh?" I nodded my head and laughed. I sat down on the little couch in our bedroom and shook my head. I was getting real tired of this Portland shit.

"What, Eli?" She sat in my lap but I moved her off.

"Don't move me," she spat and then got her little ass right back into my lap.

"Ivy, if you're gonna continue to act like I'm some side nigga and Portland is your man, then you should just take your ass back to him. I'm not with these games and bullshit. I'm an adult and I expect to be in a relationship with an adult. If you think you wanna still be with him even a little, please leave me alone."

"Elijah, I don't want him, I told you that! I just didn't want to start some shit between you two!"

"That is inevitable, Ivy! You're his baby mama and I'm dating you! The nigga is gonna hate me no matter what! It's not your job to worry about that, it's mine! All you need to do is be upfront with this nigga and let him know what the fuck it is! I'm your nigga and either you gon' make that shit known or it's a wrap!"

"Okay! Okay! I don't have a problem with that, Elijah." She caressed my face and then kissed the corner of my mouth. She then began chuckling, and I looked over into her pretty face while still scowling.

"Fuck is so funny?"

"How mad you are. You must really care," she giggled. I just sucked my teeth and shook my head at her annoying ass. "I'm glad you care so much, Eli. And baby trust me, you're not something I wanna keep a secret and you should know that. I love being your woman, and I'm so happy that you didn't give up on pursuing me. I swear from the bottom of my heart, I thought not mentioning your name was keeping the peace. Otherwise I would've told him. I love being able to claim you as mine and you know that," she whispered the last part and kissed my ear with her sneaky ass. She got up from sitting sideways in my lap, then straddled me and said, "You're my little Mufasa."

"Ain't nothing little about me."

"Oh, I know, daddy," she smiled and then pressed her pussy down onto my hard dick. "I'm gonna tell him if we ever speak in person or anything again. And with the way you just acted, everyone better know who I am to you," she cocked her head.

"They already do with the way you be showing your ass on my Instagram."

Ivy stayed stalking my shit, and wouldn't hesitate to hit a bitch up that was flirting too much. She'd even taken it upon herself to unfollow bitches from my account behind my back. I didn't give a fuck though because I wasn't doing anything suspicious, and had no interest in the bitches I was following. Shit, the only reason I was following their asses was because they followed me. I was never the thirsty type, so posting half naked pictures on the Internet wouldn't get my attention.

Ivy laughed at my comment, and then stuck her small hands into my dreads, before planting her lips on mine.

"I'm sorry," she said in a low tone as we kissed gently, sensually, and slowly.

"You gon' make me kill you and that nigga," I responded in between kisses, as I squeezed her ass and pressed her further into my erection.

She said nothing as we began to kiss hungrily and undress.

TWENTY-EIGHT

Jersey

*A*lthough pregnant, I still wanted to stay healthy. My doctor said that if I stayed in shape while pregnant, that it wouldn't be too hard to drop the baby weight once I had my daughter. I was not trying to be out of shape and shit for a long period of time, because it would be too much to worry about while in school, and having to take care of my daughter. I wanted a head start so that I wouldn't have as much on my plate. Not only that, Kill had only been my man for a short while, so I didn't want him looking the other way because his bitch was looking sloppy. I knew he knew what my body could look like, but I never wanted him to forget, or be secretly wishing I'd lost weight.

"Gym time?" Kill walked out of the bathroom with a towel wrapped around his waist.

His six-pack was so perfectly etched into his abdomen, and his biceps had just the right amount of muscle. His beautiful chocolate skin glistened under the water drops from the shower he'd just had, giving him a bit of a glow. Kilexis was gorgeous from head to fucking toe, and I mean that literally, because his feet weren't bad at all for a guy.

"Yes, remember what my doctor said?" I raised a brow at him as I pulled my jacket on.

"Yeah I do, but just make sure you take it easy."

"I am, I'm just gonna walk on the treadmill and nothing else. She said no weights, only cardio."

"After that, would you like to go to the movies and eat tonight?" He flashed his beautiful smile, and sat down on the bed wearing only his towel still.

"Of course. You've been so busy that we haven't been out much," I said as I neared him.

I could smell his body wash in the air still, and it was like a magnet as I kept coming closer to him. Once I got right in his face, he rubbed my belly and then kissed it. I looked down to watch him as I caressed his neck tattoo that read *Hilltop*. He was so rugged yet calm and intelligent; I loved it.

"I know; I'm just trying to keep everything in order. But today I made it so I didn't have anything to do but you." He nibbled on his lip and groped my thighs.

"Good, but can we make it lunch because I'm gonna be hungry when I get back."

"When aren't you hungry, shorty?"

"Shut up, Kill." I pushed him and he chuckled loudly like he was so damn funny.

Before I got a way, he grabbed on my arm and stood up. I stared up into his sexy face, and he leaned down to press his lips against mine.

"I love you, Jersey."

"I love you too, Kilexis."

We kissed a couple more times, and then I left to go to the gym with a tingling clit. That nigga could always get me in the mood, and sometimes I hated it because I be having shit to do! But every time he touched or kissed me in a certain way, I was always ready to say fuck my plans and get on my back.

When I walked into the gym, I smiled because it wasn't crowded, and there were plenty of treadmills left for me to walk on. I hated when I had to wait for a muthafucka to get off, and then when I did get on, I had to stop after thirty minutes due to the machine being in high demand.

I placed my Victoria Secret bottle filled with ice water on the treadmill, and then climbed on to begin my workout. I made sure to keep a steady pace since my doctor said that was important, and even after forty minutes, I wasn't too tired and felt great still. By the time an hour came, my stomach grumbled so I stopped the machine, and then stuffed two Ritz Crackers into my mouth to tie me over until I got home. I would just make me a sandwich before Kill took me to lunch.

As I was walking towards the exit, I could see through the window that some woman was leaning up against my car. She looked pretty comfortable, and that low-key pissed me off. I hated for my friends to lean on my car, so why the fuck would she think she could when I didn't even know her?

I picked up my pace a little, and once I got closer, I shaded my eyes from the sun with my hand and asked, "Excuse me, can you get off of my car?"

She stared at me for a couple seconds and then got up. She had on a pencil skirt, what appeared to be a chiffon blouse, and kitten heels. She had short dark hair, brown skin, and her body was very voluptuous.

This better not be one of my brother Portland's hidden mistresses, I thought. A couple of times his little side hoes had approached me trying to get his whereabouts because he'd hit and quit. I wasn't in the mood for that shit today, and might haul off and slap a bitch.

"Are you Jersey?" she asked.

"Why?" I frowned as I placed my wristlet into my gym jacket pocket.

"I just wanted to meet the woman that my man left me for," she shrugged and then began to circle me as she checked me out. *Okay, here we go.*

I turned around to face her once she was behind me and said, "Look, I don't know what the fuck you're talking about, but if you're who I think you are, you need to move on."

Her smug expression changed swiftly, and she now looked surprised yet sad as she stared into my eyes.

"Who do you think I am?" she quizzed in a calmer tone, with much less attitude than before.

"You're probably Margo, Kill's ex, and the one who can't seem to comprehend that he no longer wants to be with you. Honestly, it's been three years, you shouldn't even be going to these lengths at this point. I mean how can you still even be attached to him when he hasn't touched you or told you he cares for you in years?"

"You don't fucking know me, okay! And you don't know what he tells me!" she shouted.

"Oh, please believe, I know everything Kilexis tells your deluded ass. And by the way, I don't want to know you, boo. But this is something I want *you* to know; keep your distance from me and from Kill. I don't know what type of bitches you may have scared off in the past, but I'm not the one home girl. Kill has moved on as you can see." I pointed to my belly. "So you need to go ahead and find some way to get over it, maybe a support group or two. But if you keep sniffing around either of us, it's gonna get you a well whooped ass. Now take that and do what you will with it Margo, I don't make threats I make promises. Now if you'll excuse me, I must go home and shower to get ready for my date with my man."

I hit my alarm and opened the door to my Porsche truck. She stood there with tears cascading down her cheeks, so I grabbed a tissue from my glove compartment and threw it to her. It just hit her collarbone and fell to the ground, since she acted as if she didn't see it coming.

"You could've at least caught it, wasting my fucking tissues." I rolled my eyes and closed my door before pulling out and going home.

That bitch had the game twisted, fucked up, and crooked if she thought she was about to play the fatal attraction role over this way. I'm not sure what punk bitches Kill dated before, but it was a new sheriff in town, and this one would whoop her ass like she stole something if she kept up her antics.

"Baby, that was good, thank you," I giggled as Kill removed my coat to hang up in the closet. I was able to convince him to take me to lunch, the movies, and then dinner.

"I'm sure it was. You love spending my money, huh?" He hugged my body from behind and rubbed my belly.

"I do like spending your money, but I don't mind treating you too."

"I know shorty, that's why I blow racks on you. I know you ain't around for the cash."

"You better know." I placed my hands on top of his as he continued to rub my belly. "That feels good Kill."

"What about this?" He pressed his hard dick against my ass.

"That too," I giggled as we walked towards the stairs together. "Can you carry my purse up the stairs, it's too heavy."

"Only because I love yo' little ass and we're behind closed doors. Otherwise, yo' ass would be shit out of luck, shorty."

"I'm sure."

As he started up the stairs, my iPhone fell out of the back pocket of the purse, but luckily I caught it. When I caught it, my thumb hit the home button, so my screen lit up to show a text message.

+1 (302) 555 - 3955: *I need an update Jersey, the reporters are blowing up my line.*

I rolled my eyes because I knew exactly who the fuck it was. I tapped the message box to respond, as I slowly ascended the stairs.

Me: *Trixie, what is all this for? Why would you want to harm me and siblings any further than you have?*

+1 (302) 555 - 3955: *Did I mention Dr. Phil's producer offered me as much as $50,000, just for me to go on TV and explain the story of your father and I in detail. They're offering that much and they don't even know the dirtiest part.*

Me: *Give me some time.*

I fucking hated this bitch.

I locked my phone and sighed heavily as I entered the bedroom.

I spotted Kill in the bathroom, running me a bubble bath, which made me smile.

"You okay, ma?" he frowned as he walked to the drawer to remove the candle lighter.

"Yes, I'm fine. Are you getting in with me?"

"Of course. You see this?" he pointed to his dick, which was damn near sticking straight up. It made both my top and lower lips salivate.

As I neared the bathroom, my phone chimed, letting me know Trixie had texted me back.

"Who is that?" Kill asked.

"Cheyla." If I said Trixie he'd be trying to kill her ass. I knew he wanted to badly as hell.

We removed our clothes, and then he helped me get into the huge Jacuzzi tub, before he lit the candles. I watched him with a smile, until he finally got into the water. It had the perfect temperature, and soothed my aching back.

Before Kill even sat down good, he reached and pulled me gently into his lap. We stared one another in the eyes, as he pushed me down on to his long and thick rod, smoothly.

"Damn shorty," he grumbled before taking my nipple into his mouth.

I placed my hands on his shoulders, and threw my head back, as my pussy throbbed around his member. Once he'd gotten his fix, he began guiding my body slowly up and down, causing us to both release soft moans. The candlelight seemed to only heighten our sense of touch, as we made love in the bathtub.

"Kill," I whimpered, as he leaned his head back for a kiss.

I hugged his neck tightly, and dipped my tongue in his mouth as he continued to move me up and down. My clit began to tingle letting me know I was on the verge of hitting my peak.

"Keep doing it like that," I whispered into his mouth before we resumed kissing.

"Cum on it, baby," he responded while sucking my lips.

I bit down on his lip hard as fuck, as I felt myself explode on him. *I see why Margo is buggin'*, I thought. My body trembled, and I let out a shaky moan as my fingernails dug into his shoulders. He used one hand to began thumbing my clit, while the other guided me up and down on his rod.

"Shit, Kill," I cried damn near as he sucked on my neck like a fucking vampire.

He was doing so many things to my body at once, that I couldn't control my moans or anything. He licked my face once I began sweating, and continued toying with my button, while hitting my spot. Moving me faster up and down, he latched his mouth onto my nipple and sucked with so much passion it was crazy.

"Fuck," he groaned and I knew he was near, just like me.

"Arrggghh!" we both growled loudly as we released together and in sync.

That's what I loved about my man. For that time period, I had completely forgotten about Trixie and his or her threats.

TWENTY-NINE

Cheyla

I was leaving the bank, because I had to get some cash out for the day. I didn't like swiping my card and shit, because muthafuckas were getting cleverer by the minute with stealing. I remember one girl that I used to work with at Starzz telling me someone stole her magnetic strip when she used it at a gas station. So to prevent any of that bullshit from happening to me, I stayed pulling out cash. In addition to that, Ivy, Jersey, and I were gonna go out to eat this evening, and I preferred to have cash when it was a group thing. It just made shit easier in my opinion.

As I was walking to my car, someone yelled "Cheyla!"

I looked over to my right and saw Monty... again. I let out a deep sigh, before turning to him as he jogged over to me. I was starting to think this nigga was following me. Why was he always everywhere that I was? That shit was starting to worry me, but I didn't wanna mention it to Kantwan because he would go over-board. His ass was trigger-happy and wouldn't hesitate to light Monty up. I wasn't trying to get anyone murdered, especially not a nigga who had saved me from getting raped.

"Hi Monty."

"Hey, I've been texting and calling you. You know after what happened at the party, someone said they saw the guy snatch you out."

"And all you did was call and text me, after someone told you I had possibly been kidnapped?" I raised a brow and he chuckled.

From his past actions you would assume that he would take things a little further in attempt to rescue me. I guess now since I had a man, he'd turned in his captain save a hoe cape.

"I mean, I didn't know what else to do."

"Um, call the police maybe, and tell them what happened? You know that's always an option."

I was glad he didn't make a big deal out of the situation since it was Kantwan behind it all, but damn, what if someone had really kidnapped me? All this nigga would have done was call my damn phone? Thank God it was just my nutty ass man.

"Niggas like myself don't call the police, Cheyla." *Nigga please*, I thought.

"That's obvious, Monty."

"But I'm glad you're okay, I was really worried for a second."

"Great way of showing it. But yeah, after the guy snatched me out, I kicked him in the nuts and was able to get away."

"Oh damn, you're lucky because that nigga had an AK. I wonder what his angle was, because he didn't even rob us and there was money on the floor."

"Who knows? Look Monty, I have somewhere to be, but it was nice seeing you."

"Cheyla wait, I was wondering if maybe we could go out sometime."

I told his ass when we were in CVS that I had a man. Didn't I? Yes, I did.

"Don't you have a girlfriend, Monty? And didn't I say I had a man?" I folded my arms and frowned.

"Man, Tahvi knows what's good, and if your man saw us together he would see the chemistry as well."

That was funny.

"No, he wouldn't. We don't have any chemistry, Monty. You were a cool ass customer and nothing else. I'm not interested in anything like that with you, I'm involved."

"Cheyla, come on. You know it's more than that shit. I can see it in your eyes."

"Really? Because I promise you I'm not interested. I have a man whom I love Monty, and it's not like that with you, aight?" I tapped his shoulder, and then he grabbed my hand to hold it and caress.

"Just one night please? I will pay."

"I'm not going on a date with you, Monty," I scoffed and pulled my hand away.

"I don't want a date, I wanna fuck, and I'm paying top dollar. I have two grand with your name on it. All you have to do is come to bed with Tahvi and I. Just lay there, and she and I will do all the work." His eyes scanned my body from neck to ankle.

"Are you fucking serious, Monty? You're disgusting."

I turned to walk to my car and he yelled, "So is that a no?"

I couldn't believe he'd just asked me to have sex with him and his fucking girlfriend like I'm some prostitute. When would niggas learn that strippers and hookers were not synonymous at all! One fucked for cash, and another danced for it! Two totally different things in my book!

I sped to Eclipse Bistro on Union so that I could meet my friends for food. This nigga almost made me late with his propositions. I was so damn mad I didn't know what to do. Monty had just disrespected me in the worse way. If I was a nigga I would beat his ass. Shit, if I was a petty bitch I would have Kantwan fuck him up and kill him. All I had to do was say the word and Kantwan would whoop his ass good.

I parked my car at the restaurant, and was happy to see my friends were already inside. I rushed past the hostess, and then sat down at the table with them. I had to tell them what the hell had just happened to me.

"Hey boo," Jersey smiled and sipped her water.

"Hey, why did that Monty guy offer me money for sex?" I

panted and set my purse next to me. I didn't feel like beating around the bush or giving unnecessary details.

"What? What did you say?" Ivy quizzed with a turned up lip.

"I said hell no. He was trying to pay me $2000 to fuck him and his ugly ass girlfriend."

"Niggas are bold these days," Jersey shook her head. "That nigga is lucky that you didn't call up Kantwan on his ass."

"Girl, ain't he?" Ivy shook her head.

"Oh, did you know earlier this week, Kill's ex approached me on some bullshit. I shut her ass down though, and it seems as though she got the hint. She's lucky I didn't tell because Kill would probably stop helping her with her son," Jersey chuckled.

"You're okay with him helping her with her son?" I asked.

"Yeah, I know he's not fucking her or anything so it's cool. The little boy has nothing to do with how trifling his mama is. I'm not gonna stop him from getting fed or clothed because of jealousy that doesn't even need to exist. I know Kilexis."

"I agree; Kill is the honest type. I can't see him fucking on her behind your back. I couldn't see any of them doing that to any of us actually," Ivy chimed in, and after I processed it I nodded in agreement.

Kantwan loved me and I knew he wouldn't play me or even think about doing so. That's what I loved about him. He proved that niggas could have looks, money, and women throwing themselves at him, but still be faithful and honest. I thank God everyday that I came to my senses about being with him before it was too late.

"On top of bitter exes, I'm starting to see new bitches are getting real bold. Now that Elijah is becoming a little bit more known, chicks have no problem coming at him," Ivy said.

"Yes, I know. One chick left her number in Kill's comments! I've seen chicks leave thirsty shit on his pictures before, but damn, your number?" Jersey frowned. "I couldn't even get mad because Kilexis would never go for someone so dehydrated."

"That's why I don't go on Kantwan's Instagram, because I would end up killing a bitch. I stay off it so I can have some sanity," I replied and the three of us laughed in unison.

Just because I trusted my nigga, didn't mean I wouldn't break my foot off in a couple bitches' asses. I wished I could break it off in Monty's ass though. Best believe if I saw his weird ass again, I would for sure be telling Kantwan.

THIRTY

Sondre "Sonny" Austin

One Week Later...

J was sitting on the porch sipping on a forty ounce of beer with my nigga Portland. We were watching people converse and chill, just like us. Sitting on the porch was my favorite pastime, and it was one thing I loved about my hood. Sitting up on a porch in them good neighborhoods just wasn't the same.

"So what did that Elijah cat say?" I asked Portland as I took a swig of my beer.

"Man, he never responded. I think he's a hater low-key, and don't want me to be making money like his ass."

"But why would he feel that way?"

"Nigga, I have no idea. I've never conversed or had any dealings with him ever, so I really don't know what the problem is."

"Aye, maybe them rumors are true."

"That shit ain't true my nigga, so quit saying that shit, aight?" he looked at me with a scowl. I just shrugged and chuckled.

A few homies that we had around the hood were telling us that Ivy was messing with that Elijah Camren cat. Portland refused to believe the shit, but everyday it seemed more and more true. I mean Ivy was completely off this nigga, plenty of people had told us, and now that Elijah nigga wouldn't sell to him or give him information on how to get put on. Come on now, how much more evidence did he need? I wasn't gon' keep harping on it though; shit, Ivy wasn't my bitch.

"Sonny, come here." My baby mama Marley peeked her head out of her crib, and looked down at me sitting on the porch.

"Aight, I'll be in there," I replied over my shoulder. When she went back inside, I looked at Portland knowingly.

"Nigga, I'm gon' front you the money for a crib, chill."

He'd just inherited a cool eight million from his father's will, and had promised to purchase me a crib like he'd done for himself. I wasn't sure what was taking so long, but I knew my boy wouldn't let me down.

I stood up, took another sip of my beer, and then set it on the porch step next to Portland. I entered the house, and saw Marley standing by the counter with her arms folded. Her face was knotted the fuck up, so I knew it was about to be a damn argument. I sighed and ran my hand over my face as soon as she started talking.

"Sonny, you're fucking with Raleigh Warren?" she asked and waited. My eyes darted to my phone, which was sitting on the counter, and I instantly got heated.

"Fuck you in my phone for?" I barked and snatched it from the counter, before slipping it into my baggy jeans.

"I didn't go through your phone, nigga! My home girl Diamond told me she knew you was fucking with her, and now you just proved it, nigga!" she screamed and chucked the cordless phone my way.

"Aye, what the fuck is yo' problem! After you had another nigga up in my shit, you got the fuckin' nerve to come at me about my shit?"

"You forgave me, nigga! And plus, I just started fucking with him after you got locked up! You've been fuckin' with Raleigh for years, you bitch ass nigga!" she screamed and cried.

I looked around her and into my daughter's bedroom, to make sure she was still asleep in her crib before speaking.

"Look Marley, I was… aye, where the fuck is you going?" I asked as she stormed past me out the door. "Marley!" I tried to grab her arm, but she moved out of my way quickly.

"You know your so called best friend has been fucking your sister!" she shouted down into Portland's face.

He was looking over his shoulder, and his eyes went back and forth between us before he stood up.

"What are you talking about, shorty?" he frowned in confusion.

"Man, she ain't talking about shit!"

"Yeah, Sonny has been fucking Raleigh for about as long as he's been fucking with me! Did you know that?" she rolled her neck and folded her arms as she talked, and then stared up into his face awaiting his reaction.

Portland looked up from her to me almost instantaneously, and I swore I saw flames of fire burning in his eyes. He slowly moved Marley out of the way, and she stumbled a little down the porch steps.

"You've been fucking my little sister?" he glared at me as he neared me, backing me into the house.

"Man it's... she ain't—"

WHAM! WHAM! WHAM!

He went in on me, punching me every damn where. Each time he swung, he landed a hit. My body began to ache as he continuously fucked me up, while Marley's hoe ass cheered him on. Portland pulled me into a headlock, and we began spinning around until we were outside again, and fighting on the sidewalk. I finally began swinging back, and punched him dead in the nose, causing blood to spew onto my knuckles.

"You bitch ass nigga!" he screamed as we continued to pummel one another.

"Aye y'all, someone don' called the fucking police!" one of the bystanders yelled.

Next thing I knew we were being pulled away from another. We were both bleeding crazily, and scowling at each other.

"I'm off you!" he spat as he jogged backwards.

I just stood there, panting heavily, and still in disbelief about what the fuck had just transpired. Once I gained some composure, I walked back towards Marley's house to handle her ass. Running up the little steps, I yanked on the screen door, and then twisted the knob to walk in. I realized the shit was locked, and then patted my pockets before remembering I'd left my house keys inside, and only had the ones to my whip.

"Open the fucking door, Marley!"

"Fuck you, nigga! Go find Raleigh!"

"Bitch, you better open this fucking door right now!"

"Make me, you bitch ass nigga!"

I've never wanted to put my hands on anybody as bad as I wanted to right now. Marley had pissed me off like no fucking other, and now I had no fucking place to sleep at the moment.

I pulled my phone out, and tapped Raleigh's name to see if I could go over there and spend the night. Hopefully, Portland wasn't over there acting a fool on her, because I would whoop his ass if he was in her face.

"Hello?" she answered.

"Baby, you home? If so, I wanna come by."

She sighed and paused for a few seconds before saying, "Come on, Sondre."

I hung up and then stood to my feet before taking a deep breath. My face was a damn mess, and I couldn't wait to shower in Raleigh's new crib. Matter fact, fuck living in the hood with Marley's ass, I was moving in with Raleigh. I would miss porch sitting, but it was worth the sacrifice right now.

As I walked down the few steps, I saw Diamond's messy ass coming out of her house. She looked at me as if she wanted to laugh, and then stuck her key into her door to lock it up.

"Stupid ass bitch!" I hollered to her before getting into my car and speeding off to Raleigh's.

Shit, hopefully Raleigh would quit tripping and let me fuck tonight. For some reason her ass hadn't been letting me touch her, and I was tired of it.

THIRTY-ONE

Ivy

Three Days Later...

$\mathcal{R}$aleigh said she wanted to see Donovan, so since I was off today, I decided to bring him over. Plus, I was anxious to see the inside of her new house.

Having the weekends off were a luxury, and even though people said I would start to hate it, I hadn't yet. I loved waking up early and cooking breakfast for my man and son. That was something I would never get tired of. Nor would I get tired of being dicked down for hours on Friday nights, and not having to worry about waking up early for work the next day.

I parked my car on the street, and then got out so I could get Donovan from his car seat.

"We're going to see Auntie Raleigh," I cooed and kissed his face.

He spoke back to me in gibberish, as I came up onto the sidewalk. I knocked on Raleigh's door, and she answered pretty quickly. Stepping into the house, I saw Portland sitting on the couch grinning.

"What the fuck Raleigh?" I turned to her frowning. I'd expressed to her that Portland no longer had the right to see Donovan.

"He wanted to see him and you weren't responding to his calls and texts," she sighed and sat down on the couch. I stared down at her astonished, as she pulled out her phone and began typing.

"Do you not remember that he dropped him and said he wasn't his father the last time I saw him!"

"I know, Ivy, he was just—"

"I was just angry baby, it was hard for me to hear you'd been sleeping with someone else and I reacted badly. I miss my son and I just wanna see him."

I scoffed and walked over to the couch adjacent to the one they were sitting on, and sat down before scanning her big beautiful living room. My phone buzzed right after, and I saw it was a text from Raleigh. I looked up at her and she was staring at me intensely, so I opened the text.

Ral: *He found something out, and I'm just doing this as a favor to get back on his good side.*

Me: *What did he find out?*

Ral: *Tell you later.*

I locked my phone up, and adjusted Donovan in my lap so I could put it away.

I noticed Portland was dressed way flashier than before, so he must've gotten his money that his dad had left him. I wondered if that was his Wraith parked outside. If so, his ass was really doing the most with his dad's money. He couldn't make it to the funeral, but he sure found the time to hit up Mr. Warren's lawyer for that check. *Weak ass nigga,* I said to myself.

"Can I hold him?" he asked.

"No, you can just look at him from over there. You dropped him last time."

"Ivy, are you ever gonna get over that?" he frowned.

"Portland, just take what you can get. I'm gonna go to my room upstairs. Ivy, when you're done, I will show you around." Raleigh stood up and left the living room, as Portland glared at her.

She looked a bit stressed and I could tell something was bothering her. I knew it wasn't my situation with her brother, because she was used to us being toxic. I would get at her later though, because I wanted to find out what was wrong and what the hell Portland could have found out about her that would have her doing favors for him.

There was silence between the three of us as we sat in the living room looking at one another.

"Mom." Donovan pointed to my phone that was sticking out of my purse, and I nodded to say he could play with it.

"What is that, Donovan?" I smiled and kissed the side of his face.

"Phone?" he looked back at me.

"Yes!" I chuckled and pecked his fat cheek.

Portland watched us interact, and a warm smile covered his face before he said, "Ivy, I said a lot of things that I didn't mean that day. Mainly that I didn't wanna be his father, and that I didn't wanna be with you. I love the both of y'all with all of my heart, and if you just give me a chance to do right, I promise I will. Look, my father and mother left me eight million dollars, and I'm in the process of buying a four bedroom right now."

"I'm happy for you," I stated dryly.

"You're happy for me," he repeated and scoffed. "Ivy, I got the house for us. I got it to show you that I still care and that I'm trying. I know all you wanted from me was to get my shit together and I am. I have a home, car, and I can buy you anything you want."

"That's not all I used to want from you, Portland. I wanted you to have your shit together, but I also wanted you to be a one-woman man. That was clearly something you just couldn't do for me, and now I have moved on."

"But I'm doing it now! I ain't fucking with no bitches!" he hollered.

"Yes you are! The streets don't only talk to you, Portland Warren! I've been known you had a crib, and that you got that bitch from Lynford living in it with you! How dare you ask to move me and your son in when you have another woman staying there?" I furrowed my brows. This muthafucka would never learn.

"Say the word and she's gone, Ivy."

"No, if you meant what you were saying she would've never

been there. But regardless, I have moved on and I am happy, Portland. I just wanna be a good mom to my baby. I don't want the drama that comes with being in a relationship with you. In addition to that, I'm just not feeling us anymore. So even if that bitch wasn't living with you, I still wouldn't be interested."

"Who is this nigga, man?" he yelled and his voice cracked as if he was gonna cry.

"His name is Elijah," I responded and waited.

"Elijah? Elijah Camren?" He cocked his head and I nodded. "Yo, wow," he chuckled and ran both of his hands over his face. His deep caramel complexion darkened, and I could tell he was angry. "So that's the nigga you opening your legs for?"

"That's the man that I'm with and that I love."

"Oh, now you love him?"

"Yes, I do."

"That was quick. Last month you didn't know."

"Well when you spend every day with someone that you're falling for more and more everyday, it happens."

"You can't do this shit, Ivy, you know how this makes me look?" he frowned.

"Have you spoken to Jersey?" I questioned.

"Nah, she won't answer my calls or anything, why?"

"You know her baby is by Kill," I informed him. He stared at me for a couple seconds and shook his head.

"That nigga Sonny told me Cheyla was with that Kantwan nigga, but I just knew he was mistaken."

"Nope."

"Niggas also told me you were fucking with that Elijah cat, but I didn't think you would stoop that low." I shrugged and kissed Donovan on his temple, while keeping my eyes on Portland. "Ivy, if you want Elijah to live, you will come home to me. Otherwise, I'm gonna murk his ass and have you alone again."

"I'd like to see you try," I said before standing up with Donovan. He'd passed out, so I laid his head on my shoulder.

"I'm serious."

"And so am I."

THIRTY-TWO

Portland

$\mathscr{A}$fter that little meeting with Ivy, a nigga was pissed as hell. I usually would call my nigga Sonny to vent, but he'd betrayed me and I wasn't feeling his ass at the moment. As I drove home, I kept pondering, trying to see whom I could call. My little sister Jersey came to mind.

Jersey was off me for not showing up to my dad's funeral. Matter fact, I didn't show my face for any of the shit that was happening with my parents. It wasn't that I didn't care because damn, I did, I just didn't know how to fucking deal. The only thing I wanted to do was get high and drink, so that I couldn't feel the pain of losing my parents. I wasn't that damn selfish; I just needed time. Jersey wouldn't even give me the chance to explain though.

I made it to my new home, and then pulled out my second phone to dial Jersey. She'd somehow figured out my other number and wouldn't answer, so I thought I'd try the one I planned to use for work; that was if I got any. Now that the only connect I had to the game was fuckin' my baby mama, I wasn't too sure about how to get on.

Anyhow, I needed Jersey's advice because she always gave me the real, and the best shit to do to get Ivy back. I knew she hated to help me out because she felt Ivy deserved better, but she loved me enough to assist anyway. Also, now that I knew she was having Kill's baby, I was hoping I could get in good with him once she and I made up.

"Hello?" she picked up and I swallowed the lump in my throat.

"Hey baby girl, I was trying to—"

Click.

She immediately recognized my voice and hung up. I tried dialing her back a couple times, but by the third time I'd realized she had blocked the number.

"Fuck!" I hollered and then went into my glove compartment to retrieve my blow. I hit a line, and then climbed out of the car to go inside my house. Weed hadn't been strong enough for the past month, so I'd graduated to stronger shit.

When I walked in my crib, I saw there was a table set up with candles and dinnerware and shit. Soft music was playing, and there were rose petals surrounding the table. I exhaled heavily, and then closed the front door behind me.

"Hey daddy," Breesha emerged and smiled widely.

"What's up, shorty?"

She neared me and I saw she was wearing a little negligée. I leaned down to kiss her lips, and then she tugged me to the table to sit down. I obliged and then watched her skip off towards the kitchen. She returned with a glass bowl of shrimp pasta, and then set it in the middle of the table before sitting down.

"I made your favorite, baby," she cooed.

"I see that shorty, thank you. What's the occasion though?"

She stood up without responding, and began scooping some of the pasta onto my plate. I watched her and then put my hand up to tell her that was enough. She took her seat, and then once she filled her plate up, we held hands to say grace. I could barely concentrate on the prayer, because Jersey, Ivy, and Sonny had me in my fuckin' feelings.

We began eating and made small talk throughout. Once we were finished, she collected the plates, and then returned with some blueberry pie. I ate two pieces of that, and by the time I was finished, I was ready to smoke a blunt and knock out.

"Baby, I love you," Breesha said once she returned from cleaning the plates. She slid into my lap, and draped her arm around my neck.

"I love you too." I squeezed her ass.

"For real?"

"Yes, for real. Don't ever doubt my love for you, shorty."

"Portland, I'm pregnant," she said and I pushed her out of my lap. "What the fuck!" she shouted and used the edge of the table to help herself up.

"Yo, I don't know what kind of sick game you're playing ma, but I ain't fucking with this!"

"Game? Game, Portland? Nigga, you've been fucking me with no protection and now that I'm pregnant you wanna pretend you've been careful?" she grimaced.

"Man, fuck this," I mumbled before snatching up my keys and phone, then rushing out of the door.

All of this shit was too fuckin' much, and I had no one in my corner it seemed. I'd lost my sisters, my girl, my damn son, *and* my fuckin' parents. A nigga felt like blowing his brains out right now.

I sped all the way to E-Way's crib, and when I parked, I scoffed upon seeing him and Sonny sitting out on the porch. I got out anyway, and then walked slowly up the porch and sat down next to E-Way. The three of us sat there quietly, staring out into the street as some random little kids played freeze tag. You could tell we all had shit on our minds.

Suddenly, a beer came into view, and I saw it was Sonny holding it out to me. I stared off to my right, and then looked back at him before taking it.

"We good my nigga? I'm sorry." He shook his head, and then held out his fist for a pound.

"Come on Portland, he ain't mean no harm. He loves your sister. Who else would you want her with? Some random hustler?" E-Way put in his two cents.

He was right, I didn't want niggas fucking with my sisters at all, but if I had to let them be with anybody, I would prefer it be niggas I knew. I honestly hated the idea of Jersey being pregnant by Kill Camren, but I had no say in the shit. I might as well enjoy what say I still somewhat had in Raleigh's life.

"We good, homie," I smirked up at him, and he smirked back before we dapped one another up.

For the rest of the day we just chilled, drank beers, and got high. I made sure to cut my phone off once Breesha started calling, because she and I were gonna be a wrap if she didn't get rid of that baby. And I had a feeling that she wouldn't. Fuck!

THIRTY-THREE

Kilexis

My older brother Ka'Shea and I were in my backyard smoking on some backwoods and just chilling. We'd been working hard and nonstop, so it felt good just to kick back. I needed to stop and smell the roses, and enjoy what my hard work had brought to me as Jersey said. I chuckled at the thought of my shorty and her know it all ass. She was right though. What's the point in working my ass of if I'm not gonna bask in the ambience here and there?

"I was thinking about switching out the traps," I said as I passed the blunt to Ka'Shea.

I smiled at Jersey as I watched her in the pool. She was lying on this little blow up lawn chair, just floating around in her two-piece bathing suit with her eyes closed. She made being pregnant look so sexy. Then again, everything about her was sexy to me, even the way that she ate.

"Why?" Ka'Shea finally asked.

"Because I feel like Axel's sons are up to some bullshit."

"What you think they gon' do?"

"I don't know. I'm feeling like they may try and rob them or something. This was their father's shit, and although I've switched some shit up, I feel the need to switch up more. I don't want them having any knowledge about how shit runs. That will only bring problems."

"Makes sense. But why would they even come at you like that?"

"Because they're jealous," I nodded as I continued to watch Jersey.

"Of what though? I mean I thought Axel said they were cool with him giving it to you."

"They probably were, until I told them I didn't have a position for their asses."

Ever since that little mishap with Dante and Ahmad, I hadn't heard from their asses. I wasn't sure if they were actually gonna try something, simply because I had no proof, but my gut was telling me they were on some fuck shit. I'd rather prevent the shit from happening, than have to do damage control because they sneaked me.

"Oh damn, were you being honest?" He looked over at me, referring to me denying them a position within the operation.

"Somewhat. I mean, I didn't have shit for them to do really, because I would rather it be my family in high positions. Or at least people I trust, and right now that's only people with my same blood running through their veins."

"Good old nepotism," Ka'Shea chuckled before taking a pull on the blunt.

"I guess, but it's not like y'all niggas don't know the game. The only one who is being favored without much experience is Kant."

"True, but it's in his blood like it's in ours. And he ain't acting like an amateur."

"That's because I worked with his ass. But umm, Ahmad and Dante don't know the game at all. I mean they didn't even work for their father when he was boss."

"I wonder why."

"Because he wouldn't let them. He knew they didn't know shit, and just like me, he wasn't about to let them fuck up a good thing."

I knew Axel refused to let his own sons get down because he felt they were ignorant to the drug game, which was true. So I'm not sure why they thought my ass was dumb enough to agree to let them get on. And they didn't just wanna work for me, they actually wanted to obtain a high position. Granted, Kantwan didn't know as much about the game as Ka'Shea, Elijah, and I, but my brother was smart.

The first thing you needed to have before anything in this shit was intelligence. A nigga who could cook up the dope, but was dumb wasn't worth shit. Just like a nigga who could pull a trigger and pop five niggas from afar but was dumb wasn't worth shit. Kantwan was clever, and that would get you far in any business, not just a drug operation.

"So I wouldn't worry too much about them then, if they're as green as you say they are," Ka'Shea handed me the blunt.

"I feel what you're saying, but dumb niggas do dumb shit. I wanna make moves before I have to do any major surgery."

"We should probably start weeding out niggas who we think may have some sort of relationship with them, because moving ain't gon' do shit if we take the snitches too."

"You're right, I'm gon' figure some shit out and find out if we have any niggas with loyalty to Dante and Ahmad," I replied and he nodded.

"So my little brother is about to have a baby." He looked over at me.

"Yeah, just a couple more weeks and she'll be here."

"I don't know if I can have a daughter, I'd be killing niggas left and right."

"Who are you telling, man? I'm already making sure my guns stay loaded," I said and we chuckled.

"So you love shorty?"

"Yeah, I do. That shit came out of no fucking where. I swear I was good by myself and then she just swooped in and fucked me all up, in a good way."

"I can't believe that bitch ass nigga Tommy was going cuckoo over her and hadn't touched her."

"I can believe it. That nigga always had a couple screws loose."

"True, he was high key obsessed with yo' ass. Shorty is beautiful though. She loves yo' ass too. I don't know why, but she does."

"Fuck you. So what's up with you and Mercedes?"

"Man, the same bullshit as before. I'm working on something else right now."

"Who? And when can we meet her nigga?"

"Soon, I promise. I need to wait until she's ready though."

"Alright, nigga. In a minute I'm gon' think you on your Jan Brady."

"Jan Brady?" he frowned.

"Yeah, remember that fake ass boyfriend she made up to compete with Marsha?" I smiled.

"You're probably the only fucking kingpin that watches *The Brady Bunch* my nigga," he grinned as I chuckled.

"I don't mind. I like being different."

THIRTY-FOUR

Ka'Shea

A Few Nights Later...

was chilling up in my bedroom smoking a blunt. I'd just settled into my new home, and was happy about how life was currently going for me. I had a flourishing career, money, a home, and most importantly freedom. I wished I had the shorty of my preference here to share it with me, but she was still dealing with her bullshit.

I bobbed my head to the Sade that I had playing from my portable speaker, when I heard my alarm system beep. I picked my phone up to look into the security system app, and I saw Raleigh's sexy ass at my door. I ashed that fucking blunt and hopped out my bed with the quickness. I grabbed some gum and shoved it into my mouth, before rushing down the stairs, cutting my music off on the way. Yeah, shorty had me that on it, and trust me I wasn't that type of nigga.

"What you doing here? I thought you couldn't come? Had me feeling like some weak ass nigga for sending my address to you," I opened the door for Raleigh.

"I know, I wasn't gonna come but I missed you."

"Oh, now you miss me?"

"Nigga, I tell you I miss your ass all the time, aight?" she smacked her lips and barged into my house like she owned the place.

As usual, she wore a dress that looked like a long wife beater in navy blue, with the matching Nikes. Her hair was in a ponytail that swept her lower back, and made my eyes dart to her nice round ass. Her caramel skin looked lickable, and I planned to do just that tonight. I smiled when I saw she was wearing the watch that I'd gotten her again.

I watched her walk slowly through the foyer, looking around and nodding in approval. I chuckled and just waited until she was done. She turned on her heels, and then turned to look at me.

"Would you like something to drink?" I asked once I got closer.

She looked up into my face, and shook her head no before setting her purse down on the last step of my staircase. We stared at one another for a few moments, before I dipped my tongue into her mouth and then picked her up. We kissed hungrily as I carried her upstairs and into my bedroom to give her ass the business. Finally!!!

Dropping her on the bed, I squatted down and began removing her shoes. I then took off her ankles socks, before I silently thanked God for giving her pretty ass feet. I planted kisses up her calves and to her thighs, while pushing her dress up. Once it got to be around her waist, I stood up to completely remove it. I smirked because I was happy that she wore no bra.

"You are so bad, Raleigh," I whispered as I stepped out of my clothes.

She smiled shyly, as I began to yank her panties down her thighs. My mouth began to salivate at the thought of tasting between her legs, so once I threw her panties to the floor, I dove in.

"Shea," she purred and rubbed her hands through my curly hair. I'd just taken my braids down earlier, because Jersey promised to do it over tomorrow.

I spread her legs wider, and then pushed one leg up towards her stomach as I continued to suck on her button. She whimpered and damn near cried as I gave her a tongue lashing like no other. I hadn't eaten pussy in years, and frankly I missed it. Mercedes couldn't get head from me even if she put a knife to my neck.

"I'm cumming Shea, shit," Raleigh panted and then gripped my hair roughly.

I pushed my face into her center even more, and went ham until her juices were soaking my beard. Standing up, I backed away and then dimmed the lights, before going back over to her.

"Get in the middle of the bed."

"I wanna give you head," she said and gave me a blank yet innocent expression. That shit was hella sexy.

"We can do that for round two, but right now I'm dying to be inside you, baby."

I padded to get a condom, and rolled it down as she scooted to the middle of the bed as I'd instructed. I climbed on it, and then positioned myself between her legs. Our lips met, and we instantly opened our mouths to introduce our tongues. Placing her legs in the nooks of my arms, I pressed my rock hard dick at her opening. She inhaled sharply as I began to force my way inside her tight wet walls.

"I knew this shit was tight, shorty," I grunted as I slowly moved in and out of her, getting her body adjusted to my girth and length.

"Mmm, uuuh, uuuh," she sniveled, as I wound my hips into her.

This was probably the best pussy I'd ever experienced, and I knew right then she had to be mine. Just the thought of another nigga gettin' in this angered me already.

I pressed her legs down towards the bed by the knees, and then began slamming into her. Watching her face twist, and listening to her soft moans was the shit. I took her nipple into my mouth, and sucked hungrily, making sure not to lose my pace. I knew I was about to cum soon, because she gushed on my pole, making the feeling of her walls even better. I slipped out, and then flipped her onto her stomach, before sliding in from behind.

"Grab onto the headboard, ma," I demanded. She wrapped her small hands around the stems in the headboard.

I gripped the top part of the headboard, and began fucking the shit out of her. Listening to her call out, and watching her ass bounce made my dick get even harder. I began to moan uncontrollably, as I beat her pussy up. Her shit began gripping my dick even more, and my body couldn't hold on anymore, so I filled the condom up with my nut.

"Shit, Shea," she panted.

Flipping her onto her back, I collapsed between her legs and tongued her down. She locked her arms around my neck, and then her legs around my waist, as we enjoyed one another's mouths. Once our breathing had calmed down, I rolled off of her, and carefully removed the condom from my dick, before placing it in the trashcan in front of my nightstand.

Cuddling up to me she said, "That was the best dick down I've ever had."

"Out of how many?" I chuckled.

"Including you, two." She glanced up at me and then laid her head back on my chest.

"So what's that mean for us?"

"I wanna be with you, and I am gonna be with you. I just have to break things off with Sonny, okay?" She sat up and stared into my face, while caressing my cheek. *Sonny*, I repeated his name in my head.

"I'm getting tired of waiting and hiding, Raleigh. My brothers and cousin already think I'm lying about having a shorty that I fuck with."

"I know baby, I get it. I promise, I'm just gonna break the shit off with him and we can shout it from the rooftops."

"You got one fucking week Raleigh, and you better not fuck him," I gritted.

"I haven't been fucking him this whole time Shea, and one week is enough for me. Just promise me you won't go hunting for other chicks."

I stared past her for a few seconds, and then our eyes met again. "I don't even want nobody else, Raleigh," I sighed. "But if you keep bullshitting it's a wrap."

"I won't." She shook her head and then tossed the covers off of my bottom half.

Crawling down my body, she stopped to tie her hair up in a bun, before dropping down and beginning to suck me off.

If she didn't stop with the games, I would be quittin' her ass. I didn't care how good the pussy was, or how fire the head was either.

THIRTY-FIVE

Kantwan

"You almost ready?" Cheyla yelled from the bathroom within our room.

Today she wanted me to come and meet her fucking brother. I really wasn't in the mood to, because I had heard some shit about him through the grapevine. However, I had to remember that it was through the grapevine and not some shit I had proof of. Plus, he was my shorty's brother and I needed to be in good with what little family she had. I would do just about anything to make her little crazy ass happy, so meeting her trash brother was small potatoes in my book.

"Yeah, I'm ready. We can't stay long though," I said to her.

"It won't be long Kantwan, I just want you to do this one thing for me damn," she sighed.

I pulled my cap down and then walked into the bathroom where she was putting on some lip gloss. I snaked my hands around her waist from behind, and hugged her sexy body tightly, while kissing her neck. She smelled so good.

"I don't mean to complain," I said in between kisses.

"I know; I just want you guys to get along because I love the both of you."

"I get it and that's why I'm going. You know I aim to make you happy, Cheyla," I looked into her eyes through the mirror, and she smiled shyly.

"Why?" she asked and twisted the cap back onto her gloss.

"Why what?"

"Why do you wanna make me so happy? Where did you come from? I swear you're too good to be true sometimes." She began putting some shit on her eyelashes.

"Sometimes God just places people in our pathways, and I love you. From the first day I met you I felt the need to protect you, baby." I rubbed up and down her flat stomach, and pressed my pelvis into her nice round ass.

"And you have. Remember that guy you beat up for me?" she chuckled.

"How could I forget. I followed your ass that night, because I knew you were into some reckless shit."

"I'm happy you did."

"Me too. I would've murdered that nigga if he had have done something to you," I stated more so to myself than her.

"Have you killed anyone before?" She began placing all of her makeup into its little bag.

"No, I've beat niggas up pretty badly; sent them to the E.R. But that's about it."

"My baby is lethal with them hands." She turned to look up into my face with her beautiful one.

"You know you don't need makeup."

"I don't wear it because I need it. I wear it because I like it."

"Fair enough."

She placed her small hands on the sides of my face, and then threw her head back a little for a kiss. I pecked her gently, and then she played with my chin hair for a bit, before we left the crib.

"This one is it," Cheyla said, looking at her phone.

We'd pulled up to a small little cozy townhome on Christina Landing. I was a little caught off guard, because I could've sworn he lived in Browntown.

"I thought you said he and his baby moms lived in Browntown on Read." I frowned as I continued to look the place over.

"They did, but he texted me saying he'd moved here," she shrugged.

I did the same and then parked my Mustang, before getting out and going around to open the door for my lady. I took her hand into mine, and then she led the way to the front. After she rang the door-bell, I kept scoping the area, and then made sure my heat was in place. You just never knew. The times where you thought you wouldn't need your heat were the days that you did. I never wanted to be caught slipping, especially not while I was with my girl.

"Sis," her brother Sonny pulled the door open.

Some chick was hanging all off of him, and I assumed it was his child's mother until Cheyla asked, "Who is this?"

We entered the house, and he closed the door behind us before saying, "Taren, this is my little sister Cheyla, and her boyfriend Kantwan."

"Nice to meet you Cheyla, and Kantwan." Taren licked her lips at me, and already I could tell she was a hoe.

I pulled Cheyla into me and kissed her temple, before we followed Sonny to the living room.

"So Sonny, umm, where is Marley?" Cheyla quizzed.

"She's at her crib, where else? I told you after that Wyatt shit it was a wrap."

The way he responded seemed like he was lying, but I didn't care enough to speak up on it.

"Oh okay, I thought you guys had made up. I never liked her ass anyway," Cheyla chuckled as Taren kept her eyes locked on me.

I pushed the beak of my hat up a little so I could see better. Taren was a cute light-skinned chick, but average as hell. There was nothing spectacular about her, but Sonny's demeanor showed that he wasn't serious about her.

"Sonny, who's home is this?" Cheyla asked that burning question.

"Oh, it's mine, little sis. Portland, umm, he hooked me up." He looked around the room, while nodding with a closed mouth smile. "So Kantwan, you and my sister, is this a serious thing or what?"

"Very serious," I nodded.

"Good, good. Umm, Kantwan I wanna holla at you for a minute, so can you come to the kitchen with me?" Sonny stood to his feet.

Cheyla gave me a smile, so I got up and followed him out begrudgingly. As soon as we got to his kitchen, I leaned against the counter and folded my arms. If he was trying to be on some, *don't hurt my sister or I'll hurt you* bullshit, I was gonna laugh in his face. This nigga didn't give two fucks about Cheyla. I even think he invited her over here with an ulterior motive, I just wasn't sure what it was yet.

"So Kantwan, I know you're Kill's brother," he smiled and I continued to stare at him. "So I was wondering if you could help me and Portland get on and make some bread." *And there's the ulterior motive.*

"I'd have to talk to him and see if he needs anybody. If he does, I will get your info from Cheyla."

"I mean umm, you can't just get me in the door?"

"No. Is this why you asked Cheyla to meet me?" I frowned.

"I mean yeah, and because I wanted to meet her man. She is my little sister, and I need to make sure she ain't with no fuck nigga."

"Well now that you know that she ain't, we're gonna be leaving," I got up from the counter.

"Aye man—" he grabbed my arm.

"Don't grab me my nigga," I snatched myself away from him. "You'll get a call from Kill if you're needed." I booked it back to the living room so I could get Cheyla. "Baby come on, I got some shit to take care of."

"Oh, you can just come back—"

"Nah, baby come on. I don't feel comfortable with you being here alone."

"Okay," she gave Taren a half smile and then grabbed her purse.

"Y'all leaving?" Sonny came into the living room with a beer like I didn't just tell his ass we were.

"Yeah, Kantwan has somewhere to be."

"Fuck that gotta do with you, Cheyla? You can stay."

"Nah, she can't stay." I looked towards him.

"I'm her big brother, I got her."

"And I'm her man, and I said we leaving." I neared him, clenching my fists.

"Kantwan, stop, I will see you later, Sonny." Cheyla took my hand into hers and then we left.

As soon as we got in the car her ass was pouting with her arms folded.

"This was pointless; it's only been fifteen minutes."

I had nothing to say, and I didn't feel like making any excuses. I leaned over and kissed her soft cheek, then rubbed her smooth thigh before pulling off. If I told her why her brother called us over here, that may break her heart, which I refused to do.

THIRTY-SIX

Sonny

The Next Day...

"So what happened?" Portland asked.

I was in the den of my crib, with him on speaker-phone. I told him that yesterday I was gonna meet with Kantwan Camren and get us on, and now I had to let him know that shit hadn't gone down as planned.

"Man, that shit went all the way fuckin' left. I pulled his bitch ass into the kitchen, and all that stupid muthafucka had to say was that he would see."

"Wow, and Cheyla is still gon' fuck with this nigga?"

"I mean she don't know that I'm trying to get on, so yeah."

"Maybe you should tell her and have her talk to him about it."

I smiled as this new little shorty I met named Erica walked into the den. She waved for me to come eat, and I nodded to let her know I'd be in the kitchen in a second.

"I don't know my nigga; it doesn't seem like she has much pull in that area with him. I don't really think she could do anything for us," I sighed and stood up off the couch to pace back and forth.

"Well, I had a feeling that they might not want to let us get down, especially now that I know Ivy is for sure fuckin' with that Elijah dude."

"How do you know for sure?" I frowned.

I'd told this nigga four hundred times that she was fuckin' with him, but he didn't believe me, just like he didn't believe me about Cheyla and Kantwan. I shook my head at my thoughts as he began to explain.

"She told me out of her own fuckin' mouth, so I know for sure. And to make matters worse, I think Raleigh is fuckin' with their older brother who just got out of jail."

My heart dropped into my stomach, and my brows furrowed at the sound of those words. I was so confused, that I had to sit down. Raleigh was my bitch and had never stepped out with or even looked at another nigga. She knew better than that.

"What? What the fuck would make you think that?"

"I was over her house trying to get her to help me make up with Jersey, and I saw the nigga text her phone. Remember that nigga they called Shea? He used to be Axel's top pusher before he got knocked."

I nodded my head as if Portland was in front of me before saying, "Yeah." I was silently praying to God it wasn't him. That would explain why she hadn't let me fuck in weeks. Please tell me she didn't let him hit.

"Well that's who I'm sure she's with now."

"Wow."

"Sonny, the food!" Erica called out through the house.

"Aight shorty! Give me like five more minutes!" I hollered back with my face balled up. I was angry as fuck right now, and I needed to know if this shit was true.

"Any way, bro, Axel's sons Dante and Ahmad are willing to help us out. They don't fuck with them Camren's either, mainly Kill, and they're willing to link up."

"Oh word?" I smiled, suddenly feeling a little better.

"Word, so we should be meeting with them next week and trying to get our shit going. We need to just take these niggas out and quit trying to be buddy buddy."

"I feel you. Well keep me updated then, bro."

"Fasho, one."

We disconnected and I slipped my Galaxy into my robe pocket before leaving the den. As I walked through the foyer, I heard the doorbell so I took a detour. I looked out through the window soundlessly, and saw it was Raleigh standing out there. She was looking good as hell in some jean shorts and a tube top.

"Look who it is." I yanked the door open and she walked in.

"Yeah, I had to get your address from E-Way nigga. Thanks for the invite with ya snake ass!" she spat and rolled her eyes.

My dick began to harden from just looking at her. Plus, the fact that I hadn't been inside her in a while had me a bit anxious too.

"Speaking of snakes—"

"Sonny, baby, you said—" Erica whined, but stopped upon seeing Raleigh. Fuck, I was so wrapped up in putting Raleigh on blast, I'd forgotten all about Erica.

"Really Sonny," Raleigh shook her head and scoffed. She didn't seem to be hurt though, and that angered me oddly.

"I will be in the kitchen." Erica sauntered away.

"Raleigh, it ain't even—"

She put her hand up to stop me and said, "Sonny it's over. I came to let you down easy, but seeing you've been occupied in your home that you didn't even tell me about makes me just want to lay it out there for you. I'm moving on and I don't ever wanna hear from you again."

"Is it because of Shea?" I raised a brow, waiting for her to lie.

"It is, now goodbye." She had the nerve to admit it like I'm some bitch ass nigga who wouldn't knock fire from her ass.

"Raleigh!" I tried grabbing her but she moved. "You fucked him? You ain't nothing but a hoe just like Marley!"

"Call me what you want, but this hoe is gone. I'm so done with you, your side hoes, and your lies. Bye nigga!" She threw her hand up in my face and switched out.

"You watch your fuckin' mouth talking to me like that!" I screamed as she switched her fine ass to her car.

I stood there in the doorway, panting angrily as she climbed into a silver Range Rover. Between Kantwan and Ka'Shea, them Camren niggas had my blood boiling hot. I couldn't wait to see what Ahmad and Dante were talking about. It was about to be World War IV up in this bitch.

THIRTY-SEVEN

Elijah

"**I**'m tired as fuck!" Kill shouted and ran his hands over his face.

"Nigga, so am I. What time is it?" Kantwan asked.

"Shit, 3am," Ka'Shea responded.

"I can't wait to go home and sleep," I sighed.

We'd just finished the count, and banded all the money up. The night had just ended, and we all had to be up and ready at 8am by the next morning, for a meeting with the team. I wanted to just get home, slide up inside Ivy, and then knock out. That was the plan and I was sticking to it.

What I loved about my girl is that no matter what time I got home, as soon as I told her my dick was hard, she was willing. That's exactly what a nigga needed; no fucking complaints just compliance.

As the four of us exited the warehouse, my pusher phone buzzed. I opened up the text and saw it was an un-stored number. When I scrolled up to read the previous conversation I'd had with them, I realized it was Portland. This nigga was fuckin' with me; I knew it. I stored his number so that I wouldn't be surprised by him anymore.

"Man, look at this shit," I shook my head and showed my cousins.

"That my shorty's brother?" Kill quizzed.

"Yeah man, still hitting me for a job. Ivy told me she let this nigga know we were together, and he knew exactly who I was. I'm not sure what the fuck he's trying to do, but I ain't with it."

"Go holla at that nigga," Kill suggested.

"Find out what the fuck he trying to do," Ka'Shea added.

"I might just do that."

"You want some company?" Kill raised his brow.

"Nah, I'm straight, this nigga ain't about shit."

The four of us dapped one another up, and then left the warehouse. I drove slowly, and then dialed Ivy through my car phone. I needed to make sure of some shit before I rolled up on homie.

"Hello?" she answered groggily.

"Aye what's up, did you let that nigga know for real, or are you still on some bullshit?"

"Eli, I told you that I gave him your name, and he knew exactly who I was talking about. Why?"

"No reason, goodnight." I hung up and then texted him back.

Me: *I got time to chat tonight. Where you?*

Portland: *On Conrad by Franklin.*

Me: *On my way.*

I drove over by my old crib, since that seemed to be his stomping grounds these days. I luckily found a park right in front of my old spot, and then texted this nigga to meet me outside. I went and sat on my old porch steps, and then suddenly I saw him jogging across the street in a wife beater. As soon as he got close, I stood to my feet.

"What's good?" he smiled and threw his hand out to dap me up.

I declined to do so, and then looked away for a few moments before looking back at him. "Fuck you trying to do homie?" I squinted my eyes.

"What? Man, I'm trying to work." His facial expression showed that he was offended.

"You're still trying to be down even though you know Ivy is

mine?" I raised a brow. He sucked his teeth and looked away for a few seconds.

"Yeah man, I ain't even tripping off of that."

"Oh word? Because from what she told me, you were 38 hot." I moved down my steps and got closer to him. *Please swing*, I said to myself.

"Nah, I ain't never tripped off no bitch—"

WHAM!

I punched his ass, and he stumbled and fell to the floor. I swear on everything I love it was a reflex and partially unintentional.

"Aye man, what the fuck is wrong with you!" he barked as people started coming out of their homes.

"Watch who the fuck you call a bitch, nigga. While she's mine she will not be disrespected," I stated as calmly as possible, although furious.

He wiped some of the blood leaking from his lip, before standing to his feet.

"Nigga, that's *my* muthafuckin' baby mama! Whatever y'all had ain't gon' last that fucking long!" he hollered at the top of his bitch ass lungs.

"Whatever you need to say to make yourself feel better my nigga. You know she's gon' and ain't never coming back. Now that she's gotten a taste of what it's like to fuck with a real nigga, she barely wants to give you the time of day, huh?" I grinned. He panted heavily and stared deeply into my eyes. "I can see why you're sprung though. Everything about her is addictive. Everything," I smiled and pulled my hood over my dreads, letting them hang out of the front.

"Man, fuck you!"

"Say whatever you'd like my nigga, but don't hit my line no more off of no bullshit. You ain't getting down with my people and that's that. You better use that money your daddy gave you. I heard it's just enough to get your broke jobless ass by for a couple years. By the way, this is the last time I let you live Portland, and it's only because of Donovan." I walked past him and bumped the shit out of him on the way to my whip.

"Watch yo' muthafuckin' back, you bitch ass nigga!!" he screamed.

And even though I wasn't looking his way, I knew spit was flying everywhere. I chuckled at how mad this nigga was.

I didn't worry about him trying to shoot me, because as much as he liked to play thug, he wasn't one. That nigga wasn't about to pull his hammer out on nobody; shit, he wouldn't even hit me back after I just decked him. Portland was a coward, and the type of nigga to have people kill for him because he was too scared; or the type to kill you in your sleep, hoping to avoid confrontation. I knew our little beef wasn't over, and I was gonna give him only one more chance to live for his son. If he kept playing with this fire though, his ass was for sure gonna get flamed the fuck up.

THIRTY-EIGHT

Jersey

August 4th...

"One more push, Ms. Warren!" my doctor hollered. I pushed with all my might, and then finally I felt her small body pass through completely.

I was in so much pain, and I couldn't understand how my mom was able to do this three fucking times. I breathed heavily as I watched the doctor lift my baby up, while wearing a smile that was wide as hell.

"Mr. Camren," she said and nodded him over so he could cut the umbilical chord.

He got to watch everything as Raleigh stayed by my side to calm me. I wanted him to hold my hand, but he just had to record and watch. I couldn't believe I had a baby, but I couldn't wait to take her home and raise her with Kill.

Once Kill cut the cord, they took my little baby out of the room, as a nurse began to clean up the mess. I didn't even want to know what it looked like down there, and I kind of felt bad for her. My stomach was way too weak for some shit like that, so there was no way I could work in that field. A bitch would've been gotten fired for throwing up all over the delivery room.

"How do you feel?" Kill asked me as he rubbed my curly hair.

"I don't even know. I'm in pain but I'm happy she's here," I half smiled.

"Me too." He leaned down and kissed me slowly.

I loved the way his lips felt against mine. My body reacted the same way no matter how many times he kissed me. Every time was like the first time, and I never got tired of it.

"Can y'all stop before y'all be back in here with baby number two," Raleigh chuckled and sat down.

"Nah, I have to give her a ring first," Kill chimed in, making me smile. He always knew what the fuck to say. He had me ready to let him fuck even though I was in no condition to.

"Alright, she's back," the nurse beamed as she entered the room with my daughter. "What is her name Ms. Warren?" she asked as she slipped her into my arms.

"Alexsia LaMyia Camren," I responded before kissing her small nose.

We couldn't name her Kilexis because it was too masculine, and we chose to save that in case we had a boy. He wanted a little Kill Jr., so we were gonna keep his namesake on the shelf for now.

"That's beautiful," the nurse replied as she wrote my daughter's first name on the whiteboard in the room.

Once she left, Kill pulled a chair up next to the bed, and I glanced over at his fine ass. I loved that small nose stud he rocked in his left nostril, how beautiful his chocolate skin was, how sexy his full lips were, which covered a set of beautiful white teeth, and that neat yet scruffy beard.

"Jersey, I told you I'm never one to make rash decisions, and I always think things through before I do them. I know that every-thing about us was so backwards, and probably the most untraditional shit I've ever seen or heard about, but I wouldn't change anything about it. Everything in my life is pretty complete, but there is just one part that's missing," he said and then reached into his pocket. Raleigh stood up slowly with her mouth open, as I began to slowly rock Alexsia. I waited anxiously as he opened the gray velvet box to expose a huge diamond ring. "Jersey, I want you to be my wife. I want this to be official, and I promise that things will only get better from here. I pondered over this for months, and I couldn't find one reason why I shouldn't make you my wife," he stated.

I blinked repeatedly as I stared down at the beautiful ring, damn near blinding me. Unbeknownst to me, tears began spilling from my eyes. Kill reached up to wipe them with his thumb, as I continued to stare at the ring. I never thought a man could make me as happy as Kill had, and it was just so surreal right now.

"Hello bitch!" Raleigh chimed in, snapping me from my trance.

"Oh yes, of course, Kill," I sniffled.

"And I don't want a long engagement, shorty," he added before slipping the ring onto my finger.

"Do we ever wait long to do anything?" I asked and we chuckled together. He stood up and then bent down to kiss me. I palmed the side of his face just how he liked, and let the tears flow as we kissed one another. He pecked Alexsia's head, and then kissed me again. "I love you, Kilexis," I said in a low tone.

"I love you more," he replied before crushing his lips against mine again.

"You know, usually this would make me throw the fuck up, but this is actually cute," Raleigh said as she walked to the foot of the bed and took a picture of the three of us.

"I wish my hair wasn't all over my head," I pouted and smoothed down my edges as if that would do anything.

"It's always like that, ma," Kill grinned down at me, making me smack my lips.

I turned my attention back down to my baby, and admired her beauty along with my big ass rock.

Life had gone from great, to horrific, and then to being phenomenal, and it was because Kill had just come into my life to bring the joy again. I'd finally found a man that you only saw on TV, and I don't just mean his looks. Kilexis Carson Camren was fine, smart, paid, and most importantly faithful and honest. I was gone in the head for this nigga, and there was absolutely nothing wrong with that.

About an hour later, Cheyla, Ivy, Kantwan, Elijah, and Ka'Shea showed up to visit me. They brought me flowers, and I was surprised that the boys bought me really nice pieces of jewelry. I was not gonna complain though, because diamonds really were a girl's best friend.

I did notice that Ka'Shea and Raleigh were acting awkwardly towards one another, so I made a mental note to find out what the hell was going on. But right now, I was just gonna enjoy my day with all the people I loved.

THIRTY-NINE

Raleigh

———————————

"*R*aleigh, would you tell us what the hell is going on now?" Jersey frowned as she covered Alexsia's carrier with a blanket.

I'd invited Cheyla, Jersey, and Ivy over because I had to come clean about all the illicit affairs I'd been having. I stood up as if I were about to make a speech, and then smiled shyly at the three of them. They all wore uninterested expressions, making it known they were tired of me beating around the bush.

"Okay, I am about to explain a few things, and I ask that you guys let me finish first before you ask any questions or yell at me," I exhaled.

"Get to the point." Ivy waved her hand in a circular motion.

"Okay, so, just recently I broke off my relationship with Sondre." Cheyla was about to speak, but Jersey placed her palm on her collarbone to stop her. "We started dating around the same time he got with Marley, and stayed together while he was in jail obviously."

"So that's who you were writing. I knew it wasn't some nigga from a foreign country!" Jersey shook her head.

"Didn't I say to let me finish first?" I frowned and she threw her hands up in mock surrender. "And actually I wasn't writing Sonny.

Well I was, but not as much because I was mainly writing Shea." They frowned up even more, and stared at me harder.

"Ka'Shea Camren?" Ivy interrupted, and I nodded before rolling my eyes at their refusal to follow my instructions.

"Yes, Ka'Shea Camren. So now, Sonny and I are no longer together, and I'm gonna be with Shea. Any questions or comments?"

"So when Shea said he had someone waiting on him, that was you?" Cheyla pointed to me and I nodded.

"And when mom said you were damn near knocking her down to get to the mailbox, that was to write Shea?" Jersey inquired, and again I nodded.

"Have you let him fuck yet?" Ivy grinned, making the others laugh.

"Yes I did, damn," I chuckled. "And it was just as bomb as I thought it would be in case you wanted to know that too."

"So that's the information that Portland had on you." Ivy shook her head and folded her arms across her chest.

"Yes. He whooped Sonny's ass when he found out," I sighed, and all three of their jaws had dropped.

"How did his stupid ass find out?" Jersey rolled her eyes.

She was really not fuckin' with Portland, and I hoped they made up soon. We'd lost enough family members.

"Marley's ass," I shook my head and Cheyla playfully gagged.

"What did my brother say about you dating Shea? I mean, does he even know?" Cheyla questioned.

"I just recently told him. He seemed angry, but he had another bitch in his home, so he couldn't really reprimand me too much, ya know."

"Does Shea treat you well?" Ivy questioned.

"He really does. Even though he is a little rough round the edges, he's so sweet and caring. I love it," I grinned as I thought about my boo.

"I'm starting to see that all of them Camren's are like that," Jersey chuckled and stared down at her engagement ring.

"So y'all aren't mad at me?"

"No, not mad. You just have to promise to always be honest from here on out, Raleigh. We love you and there is no reason to keep secrets, especially from me," Jersey replied, and Cheyla and Ivy nodded in agreement.

"Good, and I promise I won't be secretive like that anymore. Now I hate to cut this meeting short, but I need to go talk to Ka'Shea," I sighed after looking down at my phone.

He'd just text me saying he was gonna be home until the count later tonight. I already had my overnight bag packed, and I just hoped he wasn't mad that I'd taken longer than agreed to break it off with Sonny.

We hugged one another and said our goodbyes, before I grabbed my suitcase and hopped into my Range Rover.

I pulled up to Ka'Shea's house on Wynnewood Avenue in no time, and couldn't get out fast enough. I'd even scraped my leg with my suitcase from moving too fast. I couldn't walk in ashy, so I set my suitcase down to get my lotion out of my purse. Once I finished rubbing some into my calf, I stood to my feet to see Ka'Shea approaching me with a smile.

"I'm guessing this means something," he grinned and picked up my suitcase from the ground. Why was he so damn beautiful?

"Yeah," I nodded.

"What does it mean, Raleigh?"

He looked real good in a Nike jogger suit, with Nike socks and slide ins. His curly hair was up in a loose bun, and his facial hair was freshly lined up but still rugged. His smooth vanilla complexion was vibrant and seemed to have a bit of a tan to it, which was nice. Ka'Shea was a 6'3" god. I licked my lips as I admired his features before speaking.

"It means that I wanna be with you, *exclusively*."

"Why did you say exclusively like that?" he chuckled.

"Because that means cut off all of them little hoes you probably have, especially Mercedes."

"I've been cut off Mercedes and you know that. What have I been telling you for weeks?" he frowned down at me as I blushed. He looked so sexy when he frowned.

"That you're all about me."

"Aight then, you ain't gotta worry about who I have or haven't cut off. And if Mercedes starts looking like a problem, I'll get rid of her ass."

"Or I can," I chuckled and wrapped my arm around his as we walked into his house.

"Nah, the only thing I need you to do is feed me, fuck me, and keep a nigga happy, shorty."

"I guess I can do that, Mr. Camren. Just make sure you don't do anything that may land you back in jail," I said once we entered the house.

He closed the door behind us and said, "Well shit, I was planning on murdering that pussy." He neared me biting his lip.

"That is one crime you can commit. Ah!" I yelped as he picked me up. I wrapped my legs around his waist, as he carried me up the stairs to the bedroom.

It felt good to be with a nigga that wasn't broke, stupid, and hoeing for once.

FORTY

Cheyla

————————

Later That Night...

I'd just had dinner with Ivy and Jersey, to celebrate the birth of Alexsia, and Jersey's engagement. She'd been in the house for two weeks, and today she was finally able to come out and enjoy something small. Plus, I needed a drink after all that shit that Raleigh had dropped on us earlier.

"Bye, thanks again guys," Jersey hugged Ivy and then me.

"See you tomorrow, I wanna visit the baby again," I said as she slid into her car and nodded.

"Me too!" Ivy said before getting into her own vehicle.

She was pushing a Porsche Panamera, courtesy of Elijah, and it was a big step up from her old car. I knew Portland was sick about the shit, which made me chuckle out loud. Kantwan had bought me a new G-Wagon recently, and it had all the fixings! He would've gotten it sooner, but he wanted to pay his brother back for the house money and the other shit he'd loaned him when they first got started.

He said Kill refused the money for the longest, but finally took it back. Elijah also paid him back for everything. Kill then turned around and gave all the money loaned to him, right back to Axel. Like Kill, he tried to refuse it, but Kill wouldn't let him. Them Camren men had too much pride and hated to be helped. That could be a good thing, but it could be just as bad too. I just think none of them wanted to owe another man for anything, monetary wise.

As I was walking to my car, I felt a text come through. Assuming it was my baby, I stopped to pull it from my pocket and look.

"Ah!"

Suddenly I was sacked and grabbed from behind, before being dragged backward. I heard the doors of a truck open, and then I was pulled into it before it was closed back. The sack was pulled off of my head, and I saw Tahvi wearing lingerie, and Monty sitting next to her wearing all black. *Why me Lord? Why!*

"What the fuck are you guys doing!" I hollered and glanced back and forth between them, waiting for a response.

"I tried to give you a chance to comply, but you didn't want to," Monty smirked. "Now you're not even gonna get paid for your services, ma."

"Yeah, we've been plotting on you since you worked at Starzz, boo. You think my man was tipping like that for just those dance moves?" Tahvi cocked her head.

"Help!" I screamed hoping someone could hear me.

Why was I always being put into positions to be raped? This shit was not going down like this though. I had to get the fuck away from these weirdos ASAP! I was kicking myself because Kantwan had asked me to carry a tazer on countless occasions, but I always declined. I was so stupid sometimes.

Monty started towards me, and then yanked my ankle, pulling my body towards him and his girlfriend. I squirmed and kicked, but his little skinny ass was pretty strong. No wonder he was able to beat up that nigga in the parking lot of the strip club that night.

"Please, Monty!" I shouted as he sat on my back and pinned my arms down. Tahvi reached under my dress and began pulling my panties down slowly. I cried harder and yelled louder when I felt her kissing the back of my thighs. "Please! No!" I screamed and wiggled my body.

Monty was way too heavy as he smashed my body down with all of his weight. His big scrawny hands were pinning my wrists down pretty well, despite them appearing to not be able to. Tahvi's tongue ran between the slit of my pussy, and then she pulled my cheeks apart to begin sucking on my clit. I tried to scoot up and away from her nasty mouth, but Monty was too heavy. I was cringing at the feeling of her mouth.

"Damn," he whispered, and I assumed he was watching his freaky ass bitch lick between my legs.

BAM!

Suddenly the glass of the two doors were shattered, and the three of us jumped, allowing me to get loose. The door was snatched open, and I saw Kantwan standing there.

Monty shouted, "Aye nigga—"

POP! POP!

Kantwan immediately shot both Monty and Tahvi between the eyes, and then I climbed to my feet and ran out towards him, grabbing my underwear on the way. I jumped into his arms like a little child as I sobbed hysterically. He carried me without saying a word, and placed me into the passenger seat of his car.

After sending off a text he asked, "You okay shorty?" I nodded slowly while sniffling, and then he closed my door to jog around to the driver's side. "Did they hurt you?" he quizzed and I shook my head no. I saw his eyes divert to the panties in my hand, and his jaw tighten.

"She touched me with her mouth."

"Just her?"

"Yes, you came in before anything else happened," I sniveled. He stared at me, and when he saw me shaking, he pulled me into his arms.

"I'm sorry baby," he kissed the side of my face as I buried the front into his chest. I inhaled his cologne like I needed it to breathe, and hugged his torso as tightly as I could.

"I love you, Kantwan," I whispered while sobbing. I wasn't sure how my nigga found me, but I didn't even care in this moment.

"I love you too, and this shit will never happen again, aight?" he replied.

I just nodded as I continued to press my face into his chest. Once I calmed down a bit, I sat up and saw my car was gone from the lot.

"Where is my car, Kant?" I asked as we pulled onto the street.

"I had Kill come take it to the house." I just nodded and placed my head against the headrest.

The world of stripping was dangerous even after you quit. I was dumbfounded at the fact that Monty had gone that far, and now his stupid ass was dead. It just showed me that you really couldn't trust anybody; even niggas that you thought would never harm you. I couldn't believe he saved me from getting raped, then turned around and tried to do it himself.

Once Kantwan and I got home, we took a nice hot bath together, and drank three cups of hot chocolate before falling asleep in each other's arms. This made another night that he had to go out and save me, and I knew it was just a matter of time before he became fed up.

FORTY-ONE

Ivy

————

My old coworker Pound Cake, or Shamece, asked me to have lunch with her this afternoon. I didn't care for going out with girls who weren't Jersey, Raleigh, or Cheyla, but since she was always cool and had asked a whole bunch of times, I decided to oblige.

Shamece was beautiful and had ass for days, hence her name. She'd never had a man though and I always wondered why. Maybe it was because niggas didn't take strippers seriously. It was a blessing that I'd found Elijah, because all niggas wanted from strippers was some pussy.

We decided to meet up at Iron Hill Brewery, and I wasn't surprised because her ass loved some damn beer. For as long as I have known her, she had always loved beer and didn't care what brand it was.

"So how have you been, Ivy?" Shamece smiled as we sat across from one another at the table.

"I've been doing great, I guess you can say, you?"

"Girl, the same. All I do is make my bread and then keep it pushing."

"That doesn't sound too bad," I said as we chuckled in unison.

"You're right. So I know you're not working with me anymore, so where are you working?" She took a sip of her beer.

"I'm working at the call center for Wilton Roadside." I rolled my eyes at the thought of my nightmarish job. Everyday that I woke up, I asked myself if I really needed that damn job.

"Oh wow, what do you do there?" she cocked her head.

"Eat snacks, email my home girl, and take calls from mad ass people," I replied making her laugh.

"Damn, it was sounding good until the last part. That's the thing about Starzz, you rarely have an angry customer. You may have an aggressive or annoying one, but angry is rare."

"Yes, you have that right. That's the only thing I miss about it," I nodded.

"Yeah, but I hate that it's so hard to get a man when you strip. These niggas are so insccurc and want you to quit, knowing they couldn't pay your bills if you stopped." She rolled her eyes.

"Ain't that the truth! But I'm lucky to have somebody who could, if I did have to quit a job. He doesn't even want me working for the call center, because he wants me to focus on school."

"Damn, is this Portland?" She frowned as if she was surprised to hear me speak of him that way.

"Girl, no! That's done with, and I have someone new and so much better!" I waved her off.

Shit, she was right to be surprised. Everyone in Wilmington knew Portland Deante Warren wasn't shit.

"Oh girl, I was about to be surprised as hell. Because he's having a baby and I was gonna feel like shit thinking you thought you had a good man."

When baby rolled off of her tongue, my breath got caught in my chest.

"Baby?" I cocked my head.

"Oh, you didn't know? Girl, he's having a baby with some chick that he moved into his new house. I only know because Miami who works at the club is one of her best friends, and she said they had a threesome and shit. She was telling all of us in the back room of

Starzz how her friend is pregnant now. I think she's only like two months," Shamece nodded.

"Wow, I'm usually not surprised by what Portland does these days, but this one is still baffling." I sipped my beer.

Portland had done a lot of shit to me, but having a baby wasn't one of them. I didn't know why I was so angry, but for some reason I was. I felt betrayed, and I think it was because I knew he was messing with that chick while we were together. He swore she was just something to slide up in, but clearly that wasn't the case. She could have that headache though, because I was tired of carrying that burden. I was good right where I was.

"Yeah girl, but who is this new guy? And does he have a brother?" she grinned. I chuckled and then unlocked my phone to show her a picture of Elijah. "Ooh shit, girl. I wouldn't be able to function if I had a nigga like this. I'd be checking his whereabouts 24/7," she shook her head as we burst into laughter.

"It's hard to function when I'm away from him, but he's not that type. He's a good guy." I stared down at the picture with a smile.

"Damn, fine and faithful, where they do that at?"

"Same thing I thought before I met him!"

I finished eating and talking with Shamece, and then headed home. I wasn't feeling too good because of her news, and I just wanted to lie down. When I made it home, I heard Donovan and Elijah making a lot of noise in the den, so I just ascended the stairs and undressed for a shower. As I got out, I smiled at the sound of Donovan and Elijah still clamoring downstairs, before I turned on the central air, and slid under the covers.

My face wasn't in the pillow for two seconds, before the light flew on. I turned onto my back and sighed deeply.

"Why didn't you tell us you were home?" Elijah smiled as he bounced Donovan on his hip, making him laugh so loudly that my ears rang.

"Eli! What is that on his face?" I sat up and threw the covers off.

"Chocolate ice cream. Chill, the homie was relaxing and throwing them back. He got a little beside himself, but it's bath time," he responded and tickled my son. It made me smile watching them.

Elijah took Donovan into the bathroom, and then I stood in the doorway as he bathed him and made him laugh. I wished Portland loved Donovan as much as Elijah did, but I guess he just didn't want to.

"Dad, ducks!" Donovan picked up his rubber ducky and showed it to Elijah. I thought about stopping him from calling Elijah dad, but I knew it was too late.

"I know. Ducks are for babies though man, we have to get you something more manly to add to the tub." I chuckled at Elijah's response.

Once Donovan was all clean, Elijah put him to bed, and then returned to the bedroom. As soon as he sat down, I walked and stood between his legs. I just wanted to look at him and be near him for no reason at all.

"How was that lunch date with old girl?" he smiled.

"You mean your favorite stripper?"

"You were my favorite."

"Yeah right! And you know she said you were cute," I raised a brow and cheesed.

"What? Word? Let me get her number." I playfully punched him as we chuckled in unison. "I'm kidding, ma, you know I'm all about you." He stared up into my eyes and then kissed my collarbone gently. I kept my arm draped over his shoulders, as he adjusted himself, still sitting down.

"Kiss me," I whispered.

Our faces came closer, and then we began to suck one another's lips, before letting our tongues come in contact. We continued to kiss as his strong hands rubbed up and down my back, before he hugged my body closer and tighter. I refused to allow Portland to mess up what I had going.

FORTY-TWO

Kilexis

I leaned up against the wooden table in my warehouse, smoking a blunt. I was standing next to my older brother Ka'Shea, as we stared at the three niggas who thought since a new boss was here they could act up.

They were gettin' high off some of the product, and pocketing a few hundred bucks. Yeah, these niggas were about to die because of a few hundred bucks. They got paid more than what they stole, which made the shit even funnier. And I knew they thought that if they stole in small increments it would be unnoticeable, but unfortunately for them, I watched every damn penny. If the day's earnings were more than ten cents off, I would know. So unless a nigga stole by the nickel, they'd get caught.

"So y'all were having a funky good time, I see," I chuckled and handed the blunt to my brother.

They were tied up on some boards against the wall, with their limbs spread so that they looked like a couple of starfish. The three of them shook their heads wildly, since they couldn't talk. I'd already had one of my goons take their teeth out with some pliers, while I watched as if it was calming to me. Blood was still spilling down their chins and onto their shirts. Neither the blood nor their cries fazed me one bit though.

"I knew y'all were some fake ass niggas from the beginning, but I tried to give y'all a chance." I shook my head and took another pull on the blunt before passing it back to Ka'Shea again. "Twist it," I advised one of my goons.

They pulled the lever, and it yanked on my victim's limbs, almost pulling it out of its socket. The more the limb was pulled, the closer it came to snapping.

"Aahhhhh!!!" they all yelled in unison like some sort of choir, making Ka'Shea and I laugh loudly as fuck.

"I think I'm ready to go home. What about you Shea?" I asked my brother.

"I think one more twist and then I'll be satisfied," he responded.

The goons did as he'd asked, and we listened to them little bitches scream and cry. I picked my AK up from the table, and then aimed it at each one, blowing their heads open. All three of their heads exploded like some watermelons. Their brain matter slid down the board they were tied to, and it gave me a sense of relief.

Over time, I'd become immune to having remorse for killing niggas, especially disloyal ones. Now, murking a muthafucka was just the same as waking up and showering everyday. It was sadly my new normal. I'd killed plenty of niggas for Axel in the past, but not multiple times a week like I had to now. The bright side though, was that niggas were starting to shape up and get some act right, because they knew I wasn't playing around.

The clean up crew began scrubbing the area down, and then the criminal investigator who I had on payroll came and inspected the area for me. Once he confirmed that there were no remnants of my victims, nor anyone's fingerprints, we left the building.

"Damn bro, I didn't even recognize you in that room," Ka'Shea said as we headed towards Jersey's sister Raleigh's house.

I couldn't believe they were fucking with one another now, but anything was better than that Mercedes bitch. She was snake ass hoe, and nothing good could come from Shea being with her. It was odd that right after she caught him smashing someone else, he got knocked for possession with intent to distribute. He swore up and down she would never do that, but Kantwan and I begged to differ.

"I know. I've changed, I ain't gone lie. I'm a bit more callous wit' this shit. I feel like my heart is turning black."

"Just with this though right."

"Yeah, not with my shorty or my daughter. Or my brothers, but with these random niggas man, it's nothing for me to pull my heat out on their asses," I nodded as I pulled into the driveway of Raleigh's new home.

"I get it. I ain't never cared. You usually always had some sort of empathy for your victims back in the day."

"Not anymore," I shook my head.

"I know. Crazy ass. Well thanks, bruh," he put his fist up and we dapped one another.

"Aye, be careful, you know that nigga Sonny already don't like us, and now you got his bitch."

"Yeah, and I don't care. I think you need to be ready though, because I got a feeling we gon' have to kill your shorty's brother." I nodded slowly as he got out of the car to go inside Raleigh's home.

I knew that shit was coming, and for Jersey—I would try to prolong it as long as I could—but eventually, my baby would have to give up her brother. I just hoped that it didn't ruin our relationship. In order to keep that from happening though, I would have to make her understand that her brother was a threat. Hopefully he would come to his senses before we got that far.

When I got to my crib it was around 9pm, and this was the earliest I'd been home in a while. I'd be right back out the door at 1am to do the count with Elijah, Kantwan, and Ka'Shea, but these few hours were better than nothing. Anytime I could spend with my fiancée was a blessing.

I walked into the kitchen because I smelled food, and I saw Jersey in there cooking.

"Just in time," she smirked.

Her dark curly hair was in a low ponytail, and she had on some little ass shorts and a crop top. My shorty had bounced back like no other, and I didn't even know that was possible. I watched her closely as she moved around the kitchen like a professional, while getting visions of fucking her all over the place.

"I'm happy you're here so early. I only made pasta because I didn't know if you'd be here in time," she explained.

"That's fine. I love watching you."

"Oh yeah?" she grinned as she piled the food onto a plate for me.

"Yeah, I do. That's until I come to the realization that I can't even touch you."

"Just four more weeks, Kill." She set my plate in front of me, and then went into the fridge to get me something to drink.

"Shorty, that's a fucking month. But it's cool, I have plenty of discipline."

"You better!" she chuckled and filled my glass with juice. "Because I don't want to have to add you and some new bitch to my list of ass whoopings."

"Damn shorty, how many people are on the list now?"

"Just Margo," she shrugged and sat next to me with her food.

"Why Margo?"

"Because she stepped to me when I went to the gym." My jaw clenched as I stuffed some food into my mouth, trying to mask my anger. "Don't even sweat it, Kill, she's not worth it. I explained to her that you were my man, and that she needed to get over it on her own time, before I stomped a mud puddle in her ass," Jersey stated calmly.

"You know I don't want you fighting over me."

"I know, and I don't plan to but I will. I love you and I will kill a bitch."

We both laughed together.

"So I'm not the only crazy one. I don' already had to fight and kill over that pussy," I bit my lip and touched between her legs with my free hand, as I held a forkful of pasta with the other.

"I know, and that's why I let you do what you want to it."

"Jersey, is that you?" I joked.

"I guess I'm getting a potty mouth like you," she nudged me.

"I guess so. But once this month is over, I'm gonna be living in that shit." I looked down at her bottom half, and saw how little her pajama shorts were, making my dick brick up. I turned her to face me by swiveling her stool, and then dipped down to kiss between her legs a couple times.

"Kill!" she giggled and lightly pushed my head away, before turning back to her food.

I did the same but without laughing, because I was dead serious. We were gonna be attached at the pelvis' once these four weeks were over.

As we finished our meal, I kept glancing over at her every now and then, and she would blush. It was crazy that she said I still made her nervous. We knew each other very intimately, yet I still made her blush every now and again.

Once I finished, I stood up and grabbed my plate. As I walked it to the sink, I kissed on her neck a couple times. Placing the plate into the sink, I walked back by and grabbed her up from the stool.

"Kill, where are we going? My food!"

"We're about to dry hump or something shorty!"

▭

As I was leaving my work building, I looked up from my phone to see my car covered in some red shit. When I got closer, I saw it was spaghetti sauce along with some noodles thrown here and there. I stared at my car, and then began to circle it, taking in all of the damage that stupid bitch had done.

"She thought I was fuckin' around," I chuckled to myself angrily.

I took my phone out and dialed one of my goons named Rogue, because I needed him to get some shit done for me.

"What's up boss?" he answered after three rings like advised.

"Get Margo to my building. Tell her I want to talk about us in private, which is why I'm asking her to come here. Her son is probably at a babysitter like always, so that shouldn't be a problem."

"Got you. She'll be there soon."

"Make it no more than twenty minutes, and escort her through the back, making sure no witnesses are there. If she questions why you're being discreet, explain that we're hiding her from Jersey."

"Will do. See you in a bit."

I hung up the phone and looked my car over once more, before going back inside my building. Margo had me fucked up and she was about to find out just how much.

When I got to my office, I pulled a bottle of wine from the wine cooler, and set it out along with some glasses. I left the cork exposed, because I was gonna wait until she got here to open it. After waiting about fifteen minutes, I heard Rogue knock at the door, before bringing Margo in.

"Good afternoon baby girl," I smiled.

She fidgeted a little and then gave me a half smile. I stood up to walk over to her, and then embraced her tightly before walking her over to the couch to sit down.

"I-I'm sorry about your car, Kill," she looked up into my face.

"It's cool, I get it. Margo, I know I told you that I was done and that I loved Jersey, but I'm starting to feel things."

"Things like what?" she asked as I rose to my feet again.

"Things like, love."

I popped open the bottle of wine while my back was to her, so I couldn't see her reaction. I then filled the glasses, and turned around to bring them over along with the bottle.

"You feel like you love me again?" She took the glass.

"I do, yeah. I don't even know what the fuck to do though. I treated you real fucked up, and now I'm sure there is no chance for us." I sipped my wine.

She took a huge nervous gulp of hers before saying, "No Kilexis, it's not too late. I knew you were just confused and angry, but that's my fault. I went and had Gregory, knowing I shouldn't have. I had you at home but I was dumb."

"Speaking of Gregory, where is he?"

"I recently ran into his father, and he and his wife divorced so he wants to be in his life. I allowed him to take him for the day, I hope you're not angry about it, Kill. I still love you and don't want anything to do with him."

"Nah, I'm not angry. So what are you saying, Margo?"

"I'm saying that we can be back together if you want." She scooted closer to me and took another sip.

I sipped mine as well before saying, "But what about the baby I'm having with Jersey, that doesn't bother you."

"No, not at all."

She caressed the side of my face, which made me cringe on the inside. I set my glass down and then brought her into a tight hug. I could feel her breathing heavily, before she kissed my ear, making my stomach turn. She hadn't put her lips on me in years.

"Shit," she pulled away and clutched her stomach.

"What? You good?"

"Yeah I'm just- fuck!" she screamed and hugged herself while rocking back and forth.

"Baby, what's wrong? Are you good?" I rubbed her back as tears began to spill out of her eyes.

"Call 911, Kill, my stomach is hurting so badly. Oh, my gosh, fuck," she whimpered as I pulled my phone from my pocket.

"Damn shorty, hold on. What the fuck, shit was just about to get good for us!" I shouted angrily.

Suddenly, she began convulsing very lightly, as she laid across the couch grabbing at her stomach. A few moments later, she stopped and laid there. I touched her pulse, and it was no longer throbbing, so I stood up and knocked on the back of my office door.

"It's done?" Rogue walked in and I nodded before standing up.

"I made sure to use a lot of arsenic," I said and he chuckled.

He scooped her up and then took her out of my office so he could rid of her body in the basement. The clean up crew walked in and began wiping down and cleaning to make sure no remnants of Margo were there. Once my C.I. approved the area, we were all free to go.

The only reason I felt somewhat bad about killing Margo was because of Gregory. But now that I knew his dad is back in his life, shit didn't turn out too bad. Dumb bitch.

FORTY-THREE

Kantwan

____

One Week Later...

Cheyla and I were out at The Melting Pot, and it was the first time in a long time that she even wanted to leave the house. Ever since that nigga and his bitch tried to have their way with her, she'd been off the idea of coming out. I was happy, to say the least, that she was getting back to normal. I missed going places with my shorty.

"You okay?" I asked once we were seated.

"Yes, thank you for saving me."

"Shorty, stop saying that. I'm your man, the fuck am I supposed to do?"

"I know, but I just feel like I always have you in bad situations where you have to fight and shit."

"It's cool though, because you're worth that."

"I don't know about that," she stated in a low tone as she looked off.

"Well I'm telling you that you are. I do what the fuck I wanna do, and if I wanna spend my free time fighting muthafuckas for you, then that's my business. Look at me." She did as I asked, and then her beautiful smile finally appeared.

"I won't be causing any more trouble for you though, I promise."

"We shall see," I raised a brow and she cheesed.

The waitress neared the table and then took our orders. Once she walked away, Cheyla stretched her hands across the table and nodded for me to put my hands in them. I instead cupped hers in mine, and then rubbed the backs of them with my thumbs.

"I love when you hold my hands," she whispered. "You got some soft ass hands for a thug."

"I ain't no thug," I chuckled.

"Yes you are. You're just a chill thug, which is perfect. You're the perfect chemical balance baby."

"Your shit is a little off, but I like it."

"That's not nice!" she laughed.

"I know, but I'm being honest. Sometimes you ain't all there, but I like that shit. We balance one another out. You're off your rocker, and I'm sane, but it works."

"I guess," she giggled and shook her head. "What do you think our baby would be like?"

"Hopefully, it'll be a cool little mixture of us, not too much of you though."

"You are so mean, Kantwan."

"Baby, you know I'm kidding. If it was something wrong with you, you wouldn't be mine."

"True."

"I'm not the type to make bad decisions."

"I know. I like that. I was told you're supposed to let the man lead you, and I feel comfortable letting you lead me."

"Yeah, because if you lead, our house would be in flames." She tried to snatch her hands from mine but I gripped them tightly. "I'm fucking with you, ma. I love you, you add some spice."

"I love you too even though you're like those little sour patch commercials."

"Stab you and then kiss the wound?"

"Exactly," she laughed.

We continued to talk and take jabs at one another like we always did, until finally the food came. We both scarfed it down, and then my shorty ordered dessert. She usually claimed she was gonna get it, but would change her mind after eating. This time she went through with it.

"Big appetite?" I asked and she nodded with a half smile. After I watched her pretty ass eat the dessert she ordered, we went home.

Tonight was the night that I didn't have to attend the count, and I was happier than a muthafucka. Kill made it so each of us had two days off, where we didn't need to come help with the count. I liked that shit, because when the shit was seven days a week, on top of me monitoring the shipments, a nigga could barely function correctly. Also, after having a day off, I felt I worked better because my mind was clearer.

I pulled into the garage of our home, shut the engine off, and then caressed Cheyla's sexy thigh. Her head was resting on the headrest, so she looked over at me and smiled lazily.

"I'm so full, baby," she groaned and closed her eyes.

"Got a food baby in there," I touched her flat stomach. She looked down at my hand and chuckled.

"Or a real one," she responded and then our eyes met.

"A real one?" I furrowed my brows and she nodded. "You're pregnant right now?"

"Yes, Kantwan, is it that surprising? What did you think I was, a nigga?" She sucked her teeth.

"No, of course not. Get out the car," I said before climbing out.

She looked at me from inside the car, and then finally she exited slowly. I walked over to her, and she looked up at me with a blank expression, not knowing what to expect. I grabbed both sides of her face, and then kissed her soft lips a couple times.

"I guess this means you're happy?" she grinned.

"Of course I am."

I couldn't believe she and I were gonna have a baby. No wonder her ass was eating like she'd been in jail for ten years. We continued to kiss, and then I took her small hand into mine, to lead her into the house for some celebration sex.

FORTY-FOUR

Elijah

———————

Donovan and I were watching cartoons, and although a nigga was dozing off, I was determined to stay up. I had to be up out the house in about an hour, and taking a nap would just make my ass even more tired.

"Here, eat," Ivy walked in with a plate of waffles, cheesy eggs, bacon, grits, and a glass of juice. That shit woke my ass up real quick.

"Damn ma, thank you."

"Of course." She pecked my lips and then scooped Donovan off the couch to let me eat. I quickly changed the channel to watch some sports, so I could enjoy my food for real.

As I was eating, Ivy's iPad kept chiming. I looked down and saw there were some text messages, so I just ignored it. A few more chimes came through, so I looked down a little closer. I saw Portland's name, and I immediately became angry. I knew he was her baby's father and he had every right to contact her regarding their son, but when I saw the word love somewhere in there, it had my blood boiling.

I lifted the iPad and typed the code in to read the texts. I saw them talking, and he was apologizing for hurting her. It appeared he'd gotten some bitch pregnant, and Ivy seemed to care a little bit more than she should; at least it seemed that way.

I pushed my food to the side because my appetite was no longer, and then rushed up the stairs to our bedroom. I saw her lying in bed texting, and it made me chuckle angrily. Was she really laid up in my muthafuckin' crib texting this nigga?

"What are you doing?" I asked.

"Just relaxing, come join me," she smiled and set her phone on the dresser.

"Are you sure you want me to?"

"Of course. Why wouldn't I?" She peeled the covers off, and then got on top of them. She then removed her shirt to expose her perfectly round breasts and dime sized nipples.

"Oh, I don't know. From looking at your text messages it appeared that you would rather have your baby daddy come lay down with you."

She grabbed her shirt to cover herself, and stared into my eyes.

"Eli, it's not like that. Yes, I'm angry, but not for the reasons you think."

"Oh really? Please explain to me why you're so fucking up in arms about Portland having another child with someone else?"

"Because I knew it was the girl who answered his phone that time. I'm angry because it just reminded me of how much he didn't care about me!"

"Oh, okay. Well you can go figure something out with him and see if you guys can make it work," I said as I pulled some socks from my drawer.

She threw her shirt over her body, inside out, and then hopped down off the bed.

"What does that mean?"

"It means I don't wanna be with you anymore," I stated calmly.

"What? Elijah, are you serious?"

"As a muthafuckin' heart attack, ma." I looked up into her eyes as I pulled one of my Jordan's on.

"Elijah, I promise it's not what you think! I'm angry bec—"

"Because you still fucking care! I understand that what y'all had was deep, but I'm not about to do this shit with you, Ivy. I'm a good ass nigga and I'm not about to be dealing with you and your bullshit! You wanna be with that nigga, go right ahead because I ain't fucking with you no more." I stood up and grabbed a hoodie from the closet, before pulling it over my dreads.

"You can't just say that!"

She shoved the shit out of me, and I hit the closet door since it was unexpected. She began raining blows onto my chest, and they felt like punches of nothing because she was so small. I gripped her wrists into my hand, and pushed her lightly onto the bed.

"It's over, shorty, I gritted and then walked out of the bedroom so I could run my errands early.

▭

*I*t was around 3am, and I hadn't come back home since I'd left earlier at twelve noon. I couldn't look at Ivy, and I didn't want to. Entering the house, I hung my keys up in the little wall closet, and then went upstairs to my bedroom so I could shower. When I walked in I saw Ivy was asleep in the bed, which caught me off guard. I scoffed because I thought she would've been gone, but I guess I was wrong.

I showered, and when I came out into the room, I heard Ivy sniffling. I wasn't falling for that shit; I couldn't. She could cry a damn river and I still wouldn't give a fuck. I heard the covers rustling as I pulled some boxers from my drawer, but I didn't look.

"Elijah, I'm sorry. I swear it's not what you think. I don't want Portland; I was just angry that he'd lied about the girl in Lynford. I promise that is it, and I wanna be with you. I love you."

I just tied my dreads up, grabbed my phone off the dresser, and then left to sleep in one of the extra bedrooms after checking on Donovan.

As I was replying to a couple of hoes that had texted me hours before, Ivy came into the room. I exhaled heavily and then shook my head as her pitiful ass neared the bed. She was only in her bra and panties, looking good enough to eat. I was gonna miss fucking the shit out of her, but I'd get over it. She climbed into the bed next to me, and then slowly removed my phone from my hands.

"Yo, if you gon' sleep in here, I can go to other room," I stated in an irritated fashion. She ignored me and reached down to remove my dick from my boxers. I was mad because I was rock hard just from the scent of her body wash. "Move, Ivy." I tried to nudge her but her lips were already wrapped around the tip of my dick. "Ivy, fuck, move shorty," I moaned as she took more and more of me into her mouth. I watched her coat my dick with her saliva, as she moved up and down it with precision. "Shit," I grumbled. I palmed the back of her head and guided her up and down my shaft.

She took every stroke like a professional, and when I bumped her tonsils she gagged a bit, which had me ready to bust. She continued sucking me off, and a few minutes later, I was exploding into her mouth. She licked it all up, and then began massaging my balls, getting me hard as fuck again.

Standing up on her knees, she pushed her panties down, and then fell to the side to pull them all the way off. My dick was so hard it was ridiculous. I watched her closely as she positioned herself on top of me, and then slowly eased her tight wet hole down my dick. She began rocking her hips, and the whole time she did we kept eye contact.

Around, up, and then down; that was her motion, and the shit was off the chain. I lifted her off my dick, and then placed her on all fours. Sliding inside, I gripped her waist tightly, and began ramming into her center. I grabbed both of her arms, and held them tightly as I fucked the shit out of her. Seeing her face twist up, and her body begin to sweat was perfect.

"Mmm, uuuh, uuhh," she whimpered. I adjusted my grip on her arm and continued to fuck her silly from behind.

"This is my pussy, Ivy."

"Y-yes, it's your pussy, Eli," she cried out, stammering a little. I leaned down to suck on her earlobe, as I continued to pummel her shit.

"Uuggggh!" I called out once I nutted all in her.

Slowly sliding out, I fell to the side of her and breathed heavily. She cozied up to me, and kissed my neck.

"You forgive me? I promise it's just you and I, Elijah. I only want you."

"I forgive you Ivy, but I'm not fucking around with you or him. No more bullshit."

"I know, and there won't be." I could feel her shaking her head. "You didn't even kiss me, you just fucked me," she whispered.

I gripped her neck, and then rolled over to get in between her legs, before kissing her bratty ass nastily and passionately.

FORTY-FIVE

Jersey

———

Today I was gonna meet with Trixie, Tabari, or whomever the fuck the bitch was, and see if I could talk some sense into her stupid ass. My dad and mom had gone through enough, and her telling people that my father was into some other shit would bring all the chaos back.

It was still hard for me to believe that my father was gay or whatever, but if Trixie was a man then he definitely was... playing for the other team. Thank God for Kill's ass though, because my siblings and I had no idea that Trixie had a dick between her legs. Or maybe she got it removed. I don't know and I didn't wanna keep wondering about it. Regardless of whether Trixie was a man or a woman, what my dad did to us was fucked up.

Speaking of Kill, this nigga refused to let me drive myself to this little meeting. He wanted to take me in case anything popped off between Trixie and I. He just really didn't like Trixie's ass, and I couldn't blame him. She'd stolen our father, and after he abandoned his family for her, she turned her back on him for money. I hated her ass too.

Once Kill pulled into the parking lot, I grabbed my purse and then looked back at my daughter sleeping soundly. She was just the cutest little thing, and was the perfect mixture of Kill and I.

"Hit me if anything is seemingly going left," Kill grabbed my hand and kissed the back of it.

"I will, and it won't go left Kilexis."

He declined to respond so I climbed out of the car. He did as well, but after I'd gotten closer to the entrance, and a little ways from him.

When I walked in, I checked with the hostess and she confirmed for me that Trixie was inside and sitting down already. She grabbed a menu and then led me to the table. Upon seeing me, Trixie rolled her eyes and set her phone down. Now that all had been revealed, she looked so much like a man to me than before. Maybe it was because I knew she was a man.

"Hello," I nodded to her and sat down.

"What's up?"

"Nothing much, how are you?"

"I'm okay, but they're telling me I need to be out of the house in a week, so what are you gonna do about it?" she spat.

"Trixie, wasn't my father good to you?" I asked and cringed at my own question. She folded her arms and shrugged one shoulder. "Then why would you wanna do this to him? His reputation has been trashed enough because he left his family for you. Why do you need to go the extra mile?" I frowned.

"Because I want the house! I don't have money to afford a place, because his stupid ass left me nothing!"

"I get that Trixie, but honestly, do you think you deserve anything?"

"Yes I do! I spent years with your daddy, fulfilling all of his fantasies—"

"Trixie, please." I put my hand up and she smirked before sipping her water.

"Look, just give me some money, or let me keep the house, Jersey."

"Trixie, I thought you loved my father? Why would you do this to him?"

"He's dead, Jersey! What happens on this Earth is no longer his concern."

"So you don't care about his legacy? A man that sacrificed so much for you, you just don't care to preserve what's left of his reputation?" I raised a brow.

"He didn't care for me, because if he did he would've changed his will as soon as he left your pitiful mother."

"Look, watch your mouth about my mother!" I banged on the table making the silverware jump off onto the floor.

"Oh, I'm sorry, I didn't know you still had love for that murderer," she grinned.

I grabbed her glass of water and threw it into her face. She stood up, and out the corner of my eyes I saw Kill stand up from the table he was at as well.

"Sit down Trixie, you don't want any problems," I gritted while looking up at her.

She stared down at me with water dripping from her face, and then slid out of the booth.

"Have my money, or stop them from making me leave in the next three days, or I'm gonna start answering those calls to the house from the news stations and magazines. Your father's reputation will be nothing but ashes, and people will harass you and stare at you for the rest of your days if you don't do what I'm asking. Get it done, Jersey!" she grimaced and then shoved her big shades onto her face before switching off.

I watched her saunter out, and Kill walked over to the table holding Alexsia in the carrier. He nodded, so I stood up to follow him out. I was so angry I didn't know what the fuck to do.

As soon as we got into the car, he pulled off and asked, "You want me to handle Trixie?"

I paused for a second, took a deep breath, and then nodded my head yes. I tried to work with her, but she clearly didn't want that.

FORTY-SIX

Cheyla

———————

The last time my brother and Kantwan met, it was somewhat a disaster. However, Sonny was my only family and I needed them to get along. I also wanted to help my brother out because he said he needed money and wanted to possibly work with Kantwan. Kantwan said he would do anything to make me happy, so hopefully this was part of that.

We were meeting at a lounge by the name of Bobbi Rhians, and I was excited to see the two men I loved behave and become cool. I also would like to see them be able to get money together. Kantwan, his brothers, and Elijah were doing very well, and I wanted to see my brother enjoy those same fruits.

"Come on, baby," I whined as I looked into the mirror.

I wore some dark cigarette jeans, a white blouse, some red Louboutins that Kantwan just bought me for no reason, and a black leather jacket. My hair was hanging down, and freshly done as always, just like my hands and feet.

"Why are you wearing those shoes?" Kantwan frowned as he stuffed his iPhone into his jean pocket.

He looked so sexy and he wasn't even trying. All he had on were dark jeans, which weren't too skinny or too baggy, some Nike Air

230

Max 90, a quarter sleeve button up, and a baseball cap. His cologne permeated the air, drawing me to him like always. I played with his chin hairs, and then kissed his full lips once I got all in his space.

"What's wrong with these?" I asked referring to my shoes.

"Pregnant women aren't supposed to wear heels."

"Baby, that's when you're like eight months. My stomach is still flat," I chuckled.

"Whatever, come on so we can get this shit over with. I'm ready to have your legs over my shoulders," he squeezed my ass and kissed my neck. I nudged him off and then we left the house.

***

*W*e entered the lounge and followed the hostess to the seating area that Sonny had reserved. Once we got closer, I saw he had Marley with him this time. I shook my head because I didn't get my brother. Also because I was still in shock that he had been smashing Raleigh this whole time too. I wondered how he felt about her moving on to Ka'Shea. Anyway, the last time I talked to his ass he said he was done with Marley for good because she had betrayed him in the worst way. She'd already slept with someone else while he was locked up, so I wondered what the new betrayal had been.

"Heyyy!" I waved both of my hands as Kantwan helped me up the little steps.

This nigga was acting like I was about to have our baby now. I didn't say anything though; I just let him do his thing.

"Sup sis, Kantwan," my brother hugged me and nodded towards Kantwan. I pinched Kantwan's bicep and scowled at him.

"Oh, what's up Sonny," he threw up his hand lazily once we sat down.

I saw Marley eyeing him, and she nodded her head approvingly unbeknownst to Sonny. She was such a slut, but she had another thing coming if she thought she was gonna slut it up with my nigga. I hated for bitches to be attracted to Kantwan; he was mine and I didn't want anybody liking his ass but me. He was sexy as fuck though, so I needed to get used to it... I guess. I knew he would never play me either, so that partially helped keep me calm.

"So Marley, how is Sonaya? I haven't seen her in a long time, maybe she can come over to the house," I smiled trying to be nice to her ass. For some reason she kept my niece from me.

I didn't like her already, and then to find out she was fucking some nigga named Wyatt while my brother was in jail, just made me hate her ass even more. To make matters worse, she'd supposedly betrayed him again.

"Maybe," she fake smiled and sipped her cocktail. I hated her bourgeoisie ass.

I'd already discussed with Kantwan that we wouldn't tell anyone about the baby until month three, because I'd heard it was bad luck to tell anyone before. By saying that, I was trying to think of something to talk about to end the awkward silence. I knew Kantwan's ass wouldn't care if the four of us were silent the whole time, so I couldn't depend on him. I shook my head as I glanced over at him. He just cheesed at me.

"So Kantwan, how is business?" Sonny quizzed as Marley leaned on his shoulder.

"It's good."

"Oh, well you know I'm still interested in getting down." Sonny looked at me but was talking to Kantwan.

"I don't think that's a good idea. It's too many conflicts."

"What do you mean?" I asked Kantwan.

"I mean I don't wanna blow up anybody's spot, but Sonny knows he doesn't fuck with my brother Shea, and Elijah and Portland ain't cool," Kantwan explained.

"Isn't there a way to keep all enemies separate?" I questioned.

"Cheyla, stop it," Kantwan responded and waved a waiter over to the area. "Ain't no niggas any of us got beef with gettin' down."

"Aye man, I'm getting tired of you talking to my sister like she's stupid or something!" Sonny barked.

"Oh word? And what you gonna do about?" Kantwan asked calmly, not even looking Sonny's way.

Sonny waited until Kantwan finished ordering his drink, and then said, "We gon' have a fucking problem."

"Oooh scary," Kantwan sighed, and Marley chuckled until Sonny looked at her frowning.

"Sonny, calm down, Kantwan is good to me," I tried diffusing the situation.

"It sure and the fuck don't seem like it! He's talking to you like you're four years old and shit!"

"This is *my* girl! The way I talk to her isn't yo' muthafuckin' business, homie! She don't have a fucking problem with it, so you need to shut the fuck up!" Kantwan barked. I rubbed up and down the front of his chest, hoping to calm his ass down. He swore I was off-kilter, but so was his ass.

Sonny just sucked his teeth and looked off.

"I'm sorry, baby, if you feel like I talk down to you," Kantwan turned his attention towards me, and I cupped his sexy face for a couple of kisses.

"You don't and you know that already," I whispered and kissed him again.

CRASH!

Sonny slammed his drink into the table, making the glass shatter and people around us jump. He and Kantwan stood up simultaneously and neared one another so quickly, that I didn't have time to react. They began fighting wildly, and Kantwan slammed Sonny onto the table, bursting the bottles of liquor that sat there, as Marley and I screamed at the top of our lungs. Kantwan began wailing on Sonny so quickly his hands were damn near blurry.

"Kantwan stop!" I screamed as tears began to fill my eyes. "Stop!" I hollered again as I saw security nearing.

Kantwan looked over at me crying, and then he finally stopped fucking my brother up. He grabbed my hand and then pulled me down out of the VIP. Rushing through the crowd, we slipped out of the back exit and ran into the parking lot. We quickly got into the car and he sped the whole way home, passing some police cars who were obviously headed back to the lounge because of the altercation.

"Why did you hit him like that!" I sobbed hysterically as we drove home.

"Cheyla, baby, I'm sorry but he swung on me."

"I didn't see him swing!"

"Why would I lie? The nigga swung on me so I body slammed him and whooped his ass! I told you I didn't like that nigga and you don't get it! He's jealous and has no intentions on becoming cool with me without malicious reasoning! And on top of that, he's using you to get into business with us!"

I just shook my head and let the tears fall until we made it home. As soon as he got into the garage, I exited the car, slamming the shit out of the door. He followed me in and tried to grab my body from behind.

"Get off me!" I yelled and my voice echoed throughout the huge foyer.

"Cheyla, shorty, I'm sorry, aight? I didn't mean to fight him but he started the shit," he said as I wept loudly. He kissed my cheek and then my neck, as we gradually fell to the marble floors.

"He's the only family I have, Kantwan!"

"I know baby, I know, and that's why I tried. I'm sorry."

I just laid on the floor and cried so hard that my body jerked. He rubbed my back, and then scooped me up bridal style to carry me upstairs. I swear, why was it so hard for me to have more than one person at a time that I could call family?

1:30am the next morning...

I stared at the wall, because I just couldn't sleep. I shut my eyes abruptly when I heard Kantwan walk into the bedroom. After we'd gotten home from the lounge, he had to leave a couple hours later to go work with his brothers.

I listened as he went in and out of his drawers, preparing for a shower. Once I heard the bathroom door in our room close, I opened my eyes back up and continued staring at the wall. I just wanted my brother and boyfriend to get along, but clearly they couldn't. They couldn't put their pride aside for five fuckin' minutes to please me. I rubbed my flat stomach and took a deep breath, remembering that stress was bad in this stage of pregnancy.

Thirty minutes had passed, and Kantwan emerged from the shower. I shut my eyes to make him think I was asleep, and listened to him put on some boxers to sleep in. The huge bed moved slightly as he climbed in behind me, and I tensed up when he hugged my body.

"I know you're not asleep," he whispered before kissing my shoulder.

"So."

He turned me onto my back and looked into my eyes for a bit before saying, "Shorty, I know it's important for me to get along with Sonny since he's all you have, but you have to understand he has ill intentions."

"No he—"

"Yes he does. It's not quite obvious what he's trying to do, but he's up to something; him and Portland. I would love to be able to be cool with him, but there is too much bad blood already."

"You guys can't even put it aside for me?" I sniffled.

"I wish it were that easy baby, but the beef ain't just between he and I. You have to remember that he ain't fuckin' with Shea because of Raleigh, and Portland ain't fuckin' with Eli because of Ivy. The only reason they're still breathing is because of you, Jersey, Raleigh, and baby Donovan. You have to ask yourself, why would they still try to work with us, knowing that they don't like us?"

I began to think, and I knew he was right. Sonny and Portland were obviously up to something, because they would never try to work for some niggas who took their women. I knew Sonny and Portland well, and they wouldn't dare put something like that on the back burner, not even for money. They were gonna get revenge, I just wasn't sure how or when.

"I understand."

"You gon' rock with me?"

"You think it will get to that point?" I searched his eyes as if they had the answers.

"I'm not sure, but I need to know that you gon' be by my side if it does. I love you, shorty, and I need you over this way."

"You do?"

"Of course, you know that. I'm crazy about your crazy ass, especially now that this is coming." He rubbed my stomach making me half smile.

"Okay."

"Okay what?"

"I'm gonna have your back."

He looked at me, and then pushed his boxers down, before climbing between my legs. I didn't have on any panties, so I just spread my legs wider, welcoming him. We stared into one another's eyes as he pushed himself into me.

"Mmmm," we cooed in unison.

He slowly moved in and out of me, while pushing my gown up and then pulling it off. He took my nipple into his mouth, and began sucking hungrily while winding his hips into me.

"Fuck," he grumbled as I whimpered. "I love you, ma."

"I love you t—" He dipped his tongue into my mouth and began tonguing me down before I could finish.

I prayed that Sonny and Portland didn't make things worse than they were, because I would hate to go against my brother. But most importantly I would hate to see him perish. What would my little niece think of me knowing I was with a guy who killed her father? And how would I live with myself knowing the same thing?

FORTY-SEVEN

Kilexis

I stood in the pantry with the door cracked just a little, and watched Trixie walk into the kitchen wearing a night-gown. This was too easy, because since acquiring the house in the will, Jersey had a key made for herself. I told her little ass to have the locks changed, but she knew Trixie's thirsty ass would go ape shit and be all in the media if she did.

As Trixie made herself some tea, I gently silenced my gun, hoping not to make too much noise. I looked down and nodded to see that my blue shoe covers were in tact, and so were my leather gloves. Trixie pulled some bacon and eggs from the fridge, and then placed a pan on the stove. It was around 10am. I decided to kill her ass in the morning, because these days a little bloodshed was the best way to get my day started.

I slowly opened the door just wide enough for me to get out, and then walked slowly up behind her.

WHAM!

I whacked her across the head with my gun, and she fell to the floor as blood leaked from it. As I towered over her she screamed, but in her actual voice, which was damn near deeper than mine. I guess them hormones hadn't kicked in on her vocals yet.

"Who-who are you!" she cried out, now in a more feminine tone.

I said nothing and just let two off between her eyes. I walked to the back of the house, and then out the back door so that I could get to the alley. I spotted Stone driving by just in time, so I climbed in and had him take me to the warehouse to get my car. Once we'd made it to the warehouse, I burned my gloves, shoe covers, and mask, as well as my clothes, before putting on my Jordan jogger fit, and whipping out in my Lamborghini.

On the way home, I decided that I wanted some pineapple soda, so I stopped by my favorite liquor store on Broom Street.

"Kill!" the clerk Ernie grinned widely.

"What's up man? How you been, Ernie?"

"I'm breathing ain't I?"

"That's all that matters these days, ain't it?" I laughed. He clicked his tongue and pointed at me to say I was right.

"Get what you want, it's on the house!" he shouted to me as I walked to the back for my drink.

I always paid fifty dollars when I came here, even though the highest my purchase had been was only twenty. This was a black owned business, and I wanted to do a little something to keep it up, especially because it was my favorite.

"Now you know I never get anything on the house Ernie."

"Nah man, I refuse to take your cash!" he laughed as I grabbed some Hostess cupcakes for my shorty.

"And I'm refusing your handout," I replied and set my things on the counter so I could get my wallet.

The entrance dinged letting the store know someone was coming in, and when I looked towards it, I saw Sophie, Amelia's little home girl I fucked a while back.

"Hey Kill," she smiled and walked closer to me.

"What's good, ma?" I responded and took the bag from Ernie.

I put my hand up and he said, "See you later, son."

"I'm cool. How have you been?" she asked once I turned my attention back to her.

"Great. A nigga just had a baby," I cheesed as I thought about

Alexsia. "I see you did too." I pointed to the little baby she was holding.

"Yeah, her name is Kilenna."

"Cute," I nodded. "Well it was good seeing you," I added and walked to leave out of the store.

"Kill, she's yours!" She called after me, and I snapped my neck to look back her.

Shorty had to be fucking with me.

Become a VIP Reader!

*To join my mailing list text **SHVONNE** to **66866** and stay up to date! Also, join **Shvonne Latrice Reading Group** on Facebook!*